The Memory Taker

The soul journey runs deep.

Karen Weaver

Copyright © 2019 Karen McDermott.
Editor Teena Raffa-Mulligan

All rights reserved. No part of this book may be used or reproduced by any means, graphic, electronic, or mechanical, including photocopying, recording, taping or by any information storage retrieval system without the written permission of the publisher except in the case of brief quotations embodied in critical articles and reviews.

This is a work of fiction. All of the characters, names, incidents, organizations and dialogue in this novel are either the products of the author's imagination or are used fictitiously.

Making Magic Happen Academy books may be ordered through booksellers or by contacting:
Making Magic Happen Academy
www.makingmagichappenacademy.com

Because of the dynamic nature of the Internet, any web addresses or links contained in this book may have changed since publication and may no longer be valid. The views expressed in this work are solely those of the author and do not necessarily reflect the views of the publisher and the publisher hereby disclaims any responsibility for them.

The intent of the author is only to offer information of a general nature to help you in your quest for emotional and spiritual well-being. In the event you use any of the information in this book for yourself, which is your constitutional right, the author and the publisher assume no responsibility for your actions.

ISBN: 978-0-6485211-4-3 (sc)
ISBN: 978-0-6485211-3-6 (e)
Printed in Australia

Dedication

To my readers.
I write so that these words reach the hearts of those
who are ready to embrace new thoughts.

ACKNOWLEDGEMENTS

I would like to express my gratitude to all of my readers, without your unwavering support and belief I would not be living my writing dream of writing my mind musings.

To all of my children – Dylan, Eithen, Kiera, Saoirse, Eimear and Mary – you are my inspiration and passion. Thank you.x

To Kieran, I am grateful for you, thank you for all of the learning.

Mum and Dad, Thank you for your showing me what unconditional love truly is. You are very special people indeed. I am very blessed to have you guide me through my life.

To my brothers and sisters, thank you for your belief and your unwavering support.

My beautiful friends, both old and new, thank you for your support always, I am truly blessed.

To Bill and Bev, thank you for continuing to be such a positive in our lives. We were truly sent a gift the day we met you.x

To my muse, thanks for not giving up on me. X

CONTENTS

DEDICATION 3
ACKNOWLEDGEMENTS 5
CONTENTS 7
PROLOGUE 9
CHAPTER ONE *Mission Control* 1
CHAPTER TWO *Flashback* 8
CHAPTER THREE *Revelations* 14
CHAPTER FOUR *Assignments* 24
CHAPTER FIVE *Arrangements* 34
CHAPTER SIX *Dispatch* 41
CHAPTER SEVEN *Gilbert* 54
CHAPTER EIGHT *Delivered* 65
CHAPTER NINE *Rumination* 72
CHAPTER TEN *Frank* 76
CHAPTER ELEVEN *Carrie* 86
CHAPTER TWELVE *Joyce* 98
CHAPTER THIRTEEN *Henry* 107
CHAPTER FOURTEEN *The Visit* 116
CHAPTER FIFTEEN *Meeting Within* 126
CHAPTER SIXTEEN *Gathering* 133
CHAPTER SEVENTEEN *Connections* 142
CHAPTER EIGHTEEN *Detour* 152
CHAPTER NINETEEN *Ascending* 158
CHAPTER TWENTY *Necessitating Arianna* 176
CHAPTER TWENTY-ONE *Angela* 187
CHAPTER TWENTY-TWO *Déja Vu* 202

CHAPTER TWENTY-THREE *The Final Beam* 211
CHAPTER TWENTY-FOUR *The Crystal* 220
CHAPTER TWENTY-FIVE *When Harry Meets...* 230
CHAPTER TWENTY-SIX *Obsession* 239
CHAPTER TWENTY-SEVEN *En Masse* 246
CHAPTER TWENTY-EIGHT *Spellbound* 251
Epilogue 259
ABOUT THE AUTHOR 262

PROLOGUE

There is a place on the outer realm, between physical reality and eternal peace, where those who have left physicality before their time go to serve and wait until they are ready to advance. The Waiting Zone is a magical place from where the wisdom of life is distributed. Controlled by the Boss who is *'ever-knowing'*, he distributes the gift of wisdom to us messengers, providing us with the ability to assist needy souls with the necessary skills to advance towards heavenly Spirituality.

It is the responsibility of each messenger to ensure the safest and most enlightening passage for their assignments. While focusing on this advancement of souls, each messenger also encounters their own journey and progression along the enlightenment scale.

The journey is guaranteed to be a rough one, but in order to make their way heroically through the struggle they all must discover the warrior within. The strongest of spirits will then be rewarded with the breakthrough. This is the ultimate accomplishment for any soul because there is no way back from this level; the only way is forward towards an existence of peace and fulfilment.

It is now time for *The Memory Taker* to step forward. His job is not going to be easy. He must first save the shadowed minds and direct them towards the serenity of the light. His journey alone will be a turbulent one as he too has much to learn about life, love and happiness.

Will Gill be strong enough to help those in need and also help himself? *Join the Memory Taker* as he discovers the wisdom of life and why it is important that we accumulate as much inner wisdom as possible before transcending.

CHAPTER ONE
Mission Control

  The time has come when I must return. My role is important in the journey of enlightenment of some special spirits. Those who do not know the significance of the treasures I distribute may find my visit disturbing. However, for the greater good of these kindred spirits, I must intervene or the energy of obscurity will completely shadow the potential of the beauty that is. I visit from a realm of tranquillity, a home that was always meant for me, and where I have chosen to stay even though it may not be the norm.

  I am *The Memory Taker*, something to fear, I understand, but when you get to know why I exist you may choose to alter your views as I introduce you to *a spiritual understanding of obscurity*. Here in the Waiting Zone we work tirelessly for the good of humanity in preparation for the oneness that is greater than your actual physical being. It is a complex and demanding appointment, and I stand proudly in the knowing that I assist in the process of reaching a higher superior existence. Everything I need to know is revealed to me as and when I need it through the well of wisdom and so I am always confident in my ability to achieve the best results for all involved.

It never fails to amaze me that there are so many people who choose to not access their natural ability of awareness. By truly believing and experiencing the serenity that is being at one with your spirituality, divinity is never far away. Instead, many choose to fear the unknown rather than believing in the wondrous peaceful internal harmony that is this divinity. We are so much more than a physical form. We are eternal beings and our physicality is one step on the spectrum of being. The sad thing is that so many don't see it that way and give so much of their energies to what they can cram into their 'life'.

In some more disturbing cases, though, there are those who focus their energies on darkness, which in turn spreads dark waves across the world. It is through these energies that the undesirable manifests and multiplies. It is not sent from the almighty power, as only the sublime comes from the heavens. This is why I have such an important duty. I like to think I am an honourable warrior sent to save those who have been hijacked by the shadows on their road to true enlightenment.

My soul is like any others, except that I have evolved beyond my physicality. I have a job to do like any nurse or carer; my position is of equal importance to theirs because through love and guidance true healing can take place.

I sit here in Dave's place—our heavenly sanctuary—surrounded by an atmosphere of anticipation. This morning I discover who it is my energies are going to focus on for some time to come. No two cases are the same and that is why it is so important for me to reflect deeply and listen to my inner self for guidance before and during my dispatch.

I have gone within this morning already to seek the imperative guidance I need to successfully sail through this day of captivating magic. I sense I am going to be challenged on this mission. I will need all of my strength and love to complete the impending assignments successfully.

Sitting here on a white leather settee at the window of the most delicious bakery in all of creation, I contemplate the immeasurable task ahead of me. But my belief in the virtuous outcomes that result from my presence is strong. I confidently stand tall in the knowing that my intervention is fundamental in the enhancement of the pureness of the spirit. I know I can give my best without indecision.

Just as my thoughts have come together, I spot Arianna. Her beauty never fails to blow me away. She radiates purity in the highest degree of splendour. She enchants my soul, and I never fail to get caught up in the whirlwind that is her presence—we have a magical bond. She is unique to all existence, as she has not come here for the reasoning like the rest of us. She sees me and majestically gestures that she would like to join me. I nod, for her radiant energy—which forever beams—acts like a charger, re-energising my core back to its full capacity. She is pure perfection in its majestic form. I can't explain our connection completely, all I can say is that I believe she was created for me.

She graciously floats across the path and approaches me.

"Hi Gill, heavenly delights for breakfast, I see."

"Hey Arianna, you know me, I can never resist."

"You're just like my dad, you know," and she laughs the most sublime laugh I have ever heard and beams her perfect Hollywood smile.

"How are you this morning?" I ask.

"I am feeling wonderful this morning, Gill. Are you still on for catching up after the meeting? The meeting that you are supposed to be at right now." She raises her eyebrows at me.

"Are you all right, Arianna? Your eyebrows are doing something funny."

"Gill, the meeting!" she exclaims.

"Oh gee, is that the time…please excuse me, Arianna, but I must get moving or I will be late. Thank you, thank you."

I quickly gather my things, take one last bite from my heavenly delight, and dash across the path.

Luckily Arianna reminded me I was running late, or I would have sat on longer. I do have a problem with drifting off and losing hours at a time.

Suddenly the intercom announces, "Meeting in the grand boardroom is about to commence," confirming that I am indeed running late, and that is far from a good thing.

"Meet you here for lunch then," I call.

She giggles as I clumsily take my belongings and myself in the direction of the boardroom.

After a short elevator ride that seems to take forever I arrive at my destination. Outside the door I stop for a moment to pull myself together by tucking in my white-rimmed collar and my—quite formal for me—grey chino trousers, which I must admit do look good. I run the fingers of my free hand through my tousled, freshly-trimmed hair. Suddenly the door swings open and hits me on the nose. Oh boy, it hurts. I fall to the floor.

"Gilbert, what are you doing down there?" Boss asks abruptly. "You're late, and it is paramount to the smooth running of the mission that everyone makes the effort to be on time."

"Yes, I know, Boss, I'm sorry," I say in a higher pitched voice than usual. The pain is shooting upwards, stinging my eyes, and tears have welled. Of course the whole boardroom has had full view of the incident through the large glass panels that surround the office. I cannot see them from the outside, but I can feel everyone looking as they clearly have a ringside view. This will no doubt not be the last I hear of this incident.

I pull myself together, and Joyce—the kind receptionist—runs over and hands me some tissues, pointing to her nose. I realise immediately that there is blood streaming down my face. This is embarrassing but there is no time to change out of my shirt, so I dab at my nose, pull my shoulders back and head into the boardroom. Of course I get sarcastically applauded by everyone. I smirk and take a bow before quickly making my way to my seat as I do not want to hold the meeting up any longer with my clownish antics. Boss would definitely not be impressed, and it is always in my mind that he is Arianna's dad and I need to make a good impression... There I go again, drifting off!

My seat is at the far end of the long solid wood table with its unnatural shine, and I can clearly see my refection in it—not a good thing right at this moment, I can assure you. I finally reach my high-backed chair that was obviously chosen so we would not get too comfortable. Mind you, from what I have heard about past boardroom designs in this place, this is luxury.

Boss takes his position at the top of the room where he prepares us for the rundown of our next mission. All of our missions are important and approached professionally, ensuring that mistakes are few. I take my role as *the memory taker* seriously. It is I who visits the chosen few and guides them through their terrifying ordeal and towards a place of sublime tranquillity; beyond the realm of the common human consciousness that many people chose as their safe haven while occupying their physical form.

"Right, everyone, as you know we are now focusing on our missions with a new perspective. New, as in different from any mission perspectives previously encountered. Does everyone understand?"

A chorus of "Yes, Boss" echoes around the room.

Our Boss has a presence about him, not in his stature as he has a rugged scrawniness about him (of course, I would never say that to his face) but in his demeanour; he is abundant in wisdom and worldliness. However, these are my perceptions and by reorganising my thoughts I can accept the 'what is' rather than try to change it to 'what is not'.

"Here are your individual missions," Boss informs us as he walks around the massive table with a bundle of twenty-four gold files, each with our name sketched beautifully in calligraphy on the front cover. I am intrigued to discover the assignments within my mission that I will be guiding this time around. I have completed my training and this is going to be my first solo mission. My soul purpose for existence has begun, and I am not going to mess it up.

"Now before you open these files I want you to know that some changes are going to be introduced incrementally in order for us to keep up with supply and demand for entry into the Waiting Zone."

"What do you mean, Boss? I don't think I am comfortable starting this assignment with the thought of a transition in the middle of it." I bravely speak up and relief rushes through me when everyone else agrees.

"Valid point, Gill, but hold on a sec. There are not going to be any dramatic changes like you seem to be anticipating. I am talking about how times have changed, and we are now taking delivery of more and more magnificent 'rudiments of giving' that come from our exquisite presence here in the Waiting Zone. We are expanding and with this responsibility comes an increased workload as these rudiments need to be meticulously redistributed appropriately. Are you guys here with me on that?"

Again a chorus of "Yes Boss" echoes around the room. I have just realised how compliant we all are.

I shall certainly have to contemplate the implications of such a demanding transition later but right now it is time for me to focus my full attention on the job in hand—my assignments. These cases will consume my very being for however long it takes to complete the mission.

I look at the golden file with my name glowing in calligraphic writing on the front cover. Inside is the key to enlightenment for the lucky few who are in line to receive the gift I have to deliver. The *Beams of Wonder* that I will behold are a true gift from the Almighty, greater than anything imaginable. They will make a difference to those who receive them.

CHAPTER TWO
Flashback

Finally Boss gives the nod that we are all eagerly awaiting. I reach for my file, feeling the energy that is all powerful rushing to meet my outstretched hands. As I lift it a rush of love ripples through my core, and I know I am going to meet some beautiful souls as I connect instantly.

I open the file. I see the profile of my first assignment. Initial observation from his photo indicates that he is around his late sixties, and he is quite bald and stocky in build. He has a caring, round face but in his eyes there is some distance. I will read some of his notes. His name is Frank, he is sixty-eight and a father of four, two girls and two boys, now grown up. He and his wife live together in a house on a hill, getting on with life as they always have. He has started showing signs of memory loss for some time. Before these signs became evident he had started his spiritual journey and this has freed his soul to advance towards the light of eternity; a far more positive result than the alternative.

He has a family who loves him very much, but their healing love is overshadowed by their personal pain and sadness over his illness; so this healing love that is fundamental in conquering the obscurity is finding it hard to get through to him at a vital phase of the infirmity. This is interesting but also quite common in these cases. I shall assess further the advancement of his condition when I visit.

Looking at my next profile I am in shock. This lady does not fit the 'normal' stereotype for those who suffer this obscurity. She looks very youthful and angelic. She is blonde with a slim build, and she has a glow that surrounds her. I immediately get the feeling that she is special, and I am hooked to learn more. Scanning her details I see that her name is Carrie, and she is forty-eight years old. She is a devoted wife and mum to her two children, one of whom has been sent from here. There is a bright star beside her profile which indicates that I must meet with the Boss to be informed of the circumstances surrounding her case. What I do know is that she has evolved spiritually at a very young age and that gives me reason for the obscurity. I glance up at the Boss, and he is looking back as if he knows I have just observed the notification. He is very insightful and aware. He obviously has the ability to pick up on any relevant thought frequency. I often wonder if he has always had this ability; maybe someday I will have the tenacity to ask him.

Then suddenly, wow, what a flash! This is going to be an intense flashback, one that I cannot simply ignore. It has been a while since I last encountered a vision this strong. In fact, I believe it was sometime before I passed on an entity to this realm.

I close my eyes and my thoughts guide me to an unfolding occurrence. I envision a young woman, blonde, and sense that it is Carrie. She is quite distressed, in tears, and wailing uncontrollably as she drives a white 4x4. She is not alone. She seems to be in the company of some young adults, one of whom looks like a younger her, so I come to the conclusion they are her children. The car is going quite fast which is worrying as she is approaching a junction.

"I can't slow down," she shouts. "I can't remember how to stop the car."

Her passengers are now equally distressed as they observe the fast approaching red light. The car goes faster and faster as Carrie seems to keep pushing on the accelerator in a bid to stop the vehicle.

"Watch out!" shouts one of her children from the back seat, looking horrified.

The car dashes through the red light and Carrie's passenger grabs the steering wheel and steers around the oncoming traffic that is dramatically swerving to avoid collision. It is total mayhem with a mishmash of cars going in all directions. Phew! She has successfully manoeuvred through the potential crash zone, but wait, another potential disaster looms as now she is rapidly approaching a school zone. My heart is racing so I cannot imagine what those in this runaway car are experiencing. The person in the passenger seat suddenly grabs and pulls up the hand brake which noisily grounds the car into a spin and then to a sudden stop. Tears are flowing from Carrie's eyes as she seems to have just experienced a huge realisation. Everyone disembarks from the car which is now in the middle of the road and holding up traffic as the busy school pick-up has begun, and children are swarming around to see what happened. Angry witnesses are starting to assemble, vocally expressing their opinions without considering any possible justification. The police arrive on the scene and are planning to take Carrie to the station for *questioning. Potential disaster has been avoided on this occasion but, for Carrie, I reckon her distressing journey has just begun.*

"Gill, are you okay? You were shouting."

"Oh what, was I? I am sorry. Yes, I'm fine."

I seem to have been entertaining the boardroom again.

Boss gazes down at me and remarks, "A real entertainer you are this morning, Gill. Anything more you would like to add to your performance today?"

"No, Boss, sorry, Boss. It won't happen again."

"Ah, that's a real pity, Gill, as I would have been the first to invest in a ticket to your next performance."

Everyone laughs and so do I. Nice to have the opportunity to experience this light-heartedness in the boardroom as it can be somewhat serious and formal for the most part. Well, I speak from the perspective of my short experience as the Memory Taker and it is not as if it is a slave camp, it's just that Boss runs a tight ship.

I gather up my files and decide to wait until later for an introduction to my other assignments.

Jeepers, look at the time again. I am supposed to be meeting Arianna soon and again the anxious feelings that are now written all over my 'read like a book' face have not gone unnoticed by the Boss. To my relief he calls an end to the meeting, and we are now free to go. I wonder if he knows I plan to meet with his one and only angel. I can never seem to interpret how he perceives me, but maybe I am just slightly self-conscious about it all. Emotions, of course, that I have created within myself and therefore are mine to deal with.

I am making my way to the door when I hear Boss call.

"Gill, could I speak with you for a moment?"

A shiver shoots down my spine, and I pray he has not been hearing my thoughts. I make my way over to the desk.

"I need to meet with you before dispatch to fill you in on a few important details to enable you to carry out your mission successfully. Are you free now?"

I begin to believe he knows of my intended liaison with his precious daughter and does not approve. I may be being slightly over conscious, but I must not rock the boat so I reply.

"Right now, at this very moment?"

"Yes, Gilbert, right now this very moment; unless you have something equally or more important to achieve?"

"Erm, no Boss, sure thing. I will be right behind you."

"Sometimes I do hold concerns for you, Gilbert, I feel that you make things harder than they need be," he says, shaking his head in dismay.

With that, he turns around and heads in the direction of his office. I reach for my messenger to contact Arianna—it's not working. Why, oh why do these things happen to me? I have to think fast. So I pick up my notepad and scribble a note.

Have to meet with your dad, will be with you as soon as I can. Gill. x

Now who can I trust to deliver this message? There's Josie. I know she is Boss's receptionist but she is also Arianna's friend so I will ask her.

"Josie, would you do me a huge favour?"

"Sure, Gill, if I can help you in any way I would be happy to," she responds in a very pleased-to-see-me way.

"Oh, thank you so much, Josie. Will you bring this note to Arianna, she is in Dave's place waiting for me, but I have to meet with the Boss."

"My pleasure, Gill, it's my break now, and I could do with a fluffy pink creamer anyway."

She makes me feel as if I am doing her a favour. I have often wondered about Joyce and how she came to be here. Each journey to the Waiting Zone is personal to our experiences of being present in our physical form. Joyce's presentation is not a common group here in the zone. She is young—around my age—but she is demure. With her styled-to-perfection chocolate brown hair and flawless peachy skin she oozes quality, but there is something in her eyes that indicates something is missing. See there I go again, I must get moving or my position could be on the line. I have worked hard to get to where I am now, I can't afford to mess it up.

CHAPTER THREE
Revelations

    I speedily make my way to *The Den*, which is what we call Boss's office. Even though he isn't fierce, he does have a kingly presence that demands respect. I approach the office with its expansive glass frontage that seems transparent on the outside but it does not reflect what is going on inside.

    As I approach the doors, I take a moment to politely greet the receptionist. To my astonishment Josie is sitting there perched elegantly at the desk, a fluffy pink creamer to her left. How did she do that so fast? I am taken aback for a moment and I think she picked up on that as she smiles sweetly in my direction and says, "Boss will see you now, Gill, go ahead on in." I try to stop myself from thinking these thoughts as I am in no way comfortable with the prospect of them, but it is plain to see she is flirting with me.

    In my attempt to ignore her behaviour I send a confusing smile back at her, just as the doors open and I am drawn in by what feels like a magnetic energy flow. Inside is amazing, the walls don't seem like walls, this room gives the impression that it has no boundaries; it is amazing.

"Come on in, Gilbert, have a seat," Boss says, gesturing towards a big white fluffy chair that sits opposite his masculine sturdy one. I sit down and seem to be swallowed up and it feels like I am sitting on a marshmallow. Boss seems to be smirking at my discomfort.

"Are you okay?"

"Yes, I am fine, Boss, why do you ask?"

"Well the bloody and bruised nose has given me reason to enquire, Gill. Do you want to go get that sorted out before we continue?"

Oh yes, I had almost forgotten about that. "No, honestly Boss, it is fine. It looks worse than it actually is."

"Well if you don't mind I will ask Josie to clean it up a bit."

"There's no need really," I reply but it is too late as he presses his finder on the buzzer.

Josie efficiently responds. "Yes, Boss?"

"This young man has encountered an unfortunate incident earlier this morning and needs some treatment. Would you fetch the first aid kit and tidy it up a bit for him please?"

"Certainly, Boss, I will be right there."

I am feeling quite embarrassed and really awkward. To heighten this further, within an instant a knock comes to the door and Boss calls, "Come in."

In scurries Josie with a little nurse's hat on and carrying a big white box with a green cross embossed into it.

It is all strangely quiet while she encourages me to lean my head backwards on the big white fluffy chair that I am trying my best not to speckle with red blood.

She gently administers the necessary first aid, and I feel a little uncomfortable with the way she is looking at me. She is gazing deep into my eyes. I have always believed the eyes are the window to the soul and you can tell so much about someone simply by looking into their eyes. In Josie's eyes I see something that I can't quite make out. There is something there. I quickly look away as she just as intently looks into mine and it makes me uneasy to say the least.

I check to see if Boss is watching, and to my relief he is busy writing in his file.

Josie has finished cleaning me up the best that she can but she still is peering down at me in a peculiar way. Momentarily she looks over at the Boss, and I take advantage of the brief opportunity to scramble awkwardly out of the unconventional and totally impossible chair. I am also suspicious about the predicament I have been placed in at this moment. But as I have made a successful escape from the situation I shall move on. Something like that being misinterpreted could really hamper any chances I could possibly have with Arianna.

Boss gestures to Josie that she may now leave and she slowly catwalks her way out of the room.

"Take a seat, Gill," Boss instructs again.

I choose to avoid the chair of entrapment no matter how intriguing it is, and I opt for the most sensible yet uncomfortable of options. "Thanks, Boss," I say as I take a seat.

"Now Gill, feeling better and ready to get on with our discussion?"

"Yes, I sure am, Boss."

"Well if you are happy to commence with our meeting, I am also."

"More than happy, Boss."

"Right you are then. Well I suppose you are wondering why I have asked you here."

"Yes, I am curious to know, Boss."

I nod and he begins to enlighten me.

"Gill, this is your first solo assignment. How do you feel about that?"

"I am excited, Boss. I truly know that this is my calling. I have been created for this sole purpose and I feel fulfilled and focused on my forthcoming quest."

"That's good to hear, Gill; I trust that you are capable of completing your mission with optimum results. There are, however, a few things that I need to sort out with you before you dispatch."

Again, I nod compliantly.

"Firstly, one of your assignments, Carrie, has been visited by us before. I encountered her when I was *The Visitor* over eighteen years ago. She is a very special lady and I am saddened to think that obscurity is trying to capture her beautiful mind. I needed to inform you of this fact as her daughter, who is now eighteen, is one of our gifts, her aura shines so bright that she is a magnet for all beauty. She is pure of thought and heart and this beauty needs to be protected. Carrie was the one who provided this protection thus far and now she is in need of protection from obscurity herself so we must be resilient. We will all encounter obscurity throughout our lives, Gill, and it has a high chance of affecting us physically if it can break through our natural protective defences. Carrie has always been about helping others and so her defences have been down at times. This coupled with the many years of negative energy absorbed from her husband, whom she holds so much love for, has taken its toll and her beautiful mind has made her go inward to complete her journey. Her soul has the potential to reach optimum enlightenment and it can and must be saved. She has experienced a spiritual growth that not too many experience in their lifetime. She is unique and we must ensure that she makes her way to heaven harnessing the magnificence of all that she has become."

"She sure does sound like a special lady, Boss. I will certainly ensure that I will guide her through the obscurity to the magnificence that awaits her."

"Oh yes, another thing, Gill. Her daughter is very aware of all energies and she may pick up on your presence. So please be careful not to parade yourself in her presence too much, it may be detrimental to your mission."

"I shall keep that in mind, Boss, I really appreciate you keeping me informed. I look forward to this mission. I stand tall in knowing that I can shine the light through the obscurity, which will give the gift of hope and enlightenment to these chosen few."

"There is, however, another complexity. I do hope that this will not become all too much for you to absorb."

"The more information I have the better I can prepare myself for situations that might subsequently arise, so I sincerely appreciate all of the information that you can provide me with in advance, Boss."

"The final piece of the puzzle of Carrie's dilemma is Frank, your first case. He is her father. He lives on the other side of the world from her. Their sadness is that they both want to reunite but as life and circumstance have it they are now powerless in their quest to give each other one last embracing hug. I would like to give permission on this occasion to allow the assignments to connect. Would you be comfortable with changing things slightly to enable this to happen, Gill?"

"Most certainly, Boss. This may result in being an imperative part of their journey of enlightenment as obviously they are very close but have been separated physically for such a long time that their connection has been weakening."

"I know you will do a wonderful job, Gill. Your training was immensely successful and you were definitely created for this position."

"Thanks, Boss, I appreciate you saying that, I feel the same. To have you affirm that further enhances my confidence."

"Gill, can you articulate to me your thoughts and feelings connected to your calling if you so wish?"

"Sure, Boss. For me this is my destiny, I will, for eternity, be fulfilling the duties of the Memory Taker. I will be beaming the light of enlightenment for those who are experiencing the unsettling shadows of obscurity. A quote I once heard comes to mind: *You can shine a light into the darkness delivering hope and relinquishing fear; but it is impossible to impose darkness into light.* This expression demonstrates to me that light is far superior to dark. The power is for those who have hope and belief in the lightness that visits, not the obscurity that imposes. Good will always overcome the bad, as good feeds on hope and love, whereas bad feeds on fear and pain. I am confident in the knowing that I am the man for this job, Boss. Just because this is my first unsupervised mission doesn't mean that I will make a mess of it. I promise you will not be disappointed with my performance."

"Gill, that is all very impressive and I do not for one moment doubt your ability to successfully complete the task ahead. I have faith in you as I have faith in the rest of the messengers here. I desired you to share your thoughts with me so that I could determine the strength of your character before I proposed what I am considering."

"Boss, you could trust me with your life."

"I admire and appreciate your magnificent confidence in your ability, Gill, and I have some further revelations that I must share with you before you go on your way."

"Okay, this isn't going to be a regular mission, is it?"

"No, Gill, it is not. You know my daughter, Arianna?"

My hearts skips a beat. "Yes, Boss, I do, we are very good friends."

"Friends, yes, that's good. Well she has expressed an increased curiosity lately about the realm of humanity and so after much soul searching, my wife and I have decided to allow her to accompany you on this mission. If you don't mind, of course?"

A smile beams from one side of my face to the other; an explosion of emotions engulfs my focused mind. How wonderful this is. "Mind, no, of course I don't mind. I can't think of anything more perfect."

"Gilbert, I cannot emphasise enough how important it is that she comes in contact with no obscurity. She must only observe. She will travel with you and until you release the beams she will reside with our trusted friend, Claire. She is Arianna's godmother and guardian angel. When she reunites with you during the mission, should she at any time cross any of the constraints that I have outlined here on this piece of paper, you must contact me immediately, do you understand?"

I take the sheet that Boss has prepared and promise I will take good care of his precious daughter. "Yes, I understand completely."

"Right, now that is sorted, I wish you the best of luck for a successful mission. You have the power to shine light through the obscurity, giving hope and happiness to those who bear the cross of the shadows. I know you will do your job well, and I look forward to evaluating with you on your return. You may go now, Gill, if you have no further questions."

"No, Boss, I have no questions." I stand and shake his hand. "Thanks, Boss, I won't let you down."

"I hope not, Gilbert, I really do."

I walk towards the doors that slide gently open to rebirth me to the zone. I again gesture goodbye and then depart the room.

Josie makes a beeline for me but I quickly make my way past her and to the open lift. I get there just before her and the doors close before she can enter. I don't mean to be so rude but with everything that now swooshes around in my mind I cannot possibly deal with another tricky situation.

Once safely in the elevator I think, "Wow, I didn't see any of that coming." I need to gather my thoughts, but I must also contact Arianna straight away. I wonder where she is. Does she know already what her father has just revealed to me? She is going to be so excited. I switch on my messenger to locate her.

She is still in Dave's place. I shall make my way there straight away.

As I approach I see Arianna and begin to excitedly wave at her. She quickly turns her head away. That is strange behaviour. She is usually thrilled to see me. She must not have seen me. I eagerly make my way over to her, only to discover she seems to be giving me the cold shoulder.

I cautiously ask her, "Hi, Arianna, is everything okay?"

"Everything is fine, Gill, I just don't like being stood up is all."

"What? Stood up? Did you not get the note I sent you? Josie said that she…"

"Don't start to blame someone else, Gill, you could have had the decency to let me know what was going on."

Her arms are folded in front of her defensively and her head is turned away. Wow, she is even more beautiful when she is all fired up. I have never witnessed this side of her before. I gently take her arms and guide her over to our favourite table, where I encourage her to sit. When I am sure she is not going anywhere, I sit opposite, so that I can explain."

"Arianna, I would never stand you up. After the meeting your dad..."

"My dad? So you are going to blame him now, are you?"

"No, not at all. Just hear me out for one moment please... Your dad wanted to tell me that he is letting you come on the mission with me so you can experience and absorb the essence of humanity that you so crave."

Her face says it all. Her glow is back, she beams in all directions.

"Really? You are not just saying that?" she says, jumping up and down in excitement.

"Yes, really. There are conditions though. I have the list right here."

She stands up and twirls around as free as a bird that has just taken flight. "I don't need to see any restrictions, Gill, my dreams are coming true. I never thought for one moment that this day would come. I must go pack."

"You are so sweet, Arianna, you don't need to pack. All that we need will be provided for us. We need only prepare ourselves emotionally for the sights we will behold when we dispatch. I am sorry to dampen your excitement, but we must remember the main reason we are visiting—to help some beautiful souls."

"Yes of course, Gill. I am going to recharge my enlightening energy right now. I will go and focus on my inner self, so that I can realign my thoughts towards a more giving nature. It is when we give that we receive the gift of giving. This is such a beautiful gift filled with sparkling treasures to be shared again and again."

"You do have beautiful thoughts, Arianna. May I join you in the enlightening room?"

"Yes, of course, that would be wonderful. Our energies combined will send powerful vibrations rippling through all domains. Miraculous healing can be achieved during these precious moments, don't you agree, Gill?"

"Arianna, I cannot express how much I agree. We are all energy, whether we are in our physical or spiritual form. Our energies, when harnessed and directed at goodness, create miracles. I believe that our combined energies on this mission are going to bring miraculous beauty and love back to humanity. Providing hope to those who are deserving and even those who are not, because forgiveness is the highest form of growth towards true personal enlightenment. I feel this will be a magical mission."

"But, oh what fun we are going to have on our trip, Gill. I cannot contain my excitement."

"I don't doubt that for one moment. It certainly will be magical. Oh yes, and one very important thought has just occurred to me."

"What is that, Gill?"

"We must definitely stock up on extra supplies from Dave's place."

"Oh yes, of course that goes without saying," she responds humorously.

I have a wonderful existence, I think as I absorb the sheer serenity that is my being.

CHAPTER FOUR
Assignments

Here in my cosy apartment I finally have the opportunity to study the rest of the people I have been assigned to facilitate on this mission. Under normal circumstances I would have already caught a glimpse of all inhabitants by now, thus providing me with an insight into each candidate who will be in receipt of a beam. Until this moment I have not had the opportunity. It has been a full on day and one I would not have anticipated in my wildest dreams to have evolved in the way it has. I must now suppress my distracted thoughts and focus on what is important for my mission to be completely successful.

As I did have an opportunity for a slight introduction to my first two files, I will look at the others.

Joyce

Pulling out file number three I discover my third encounter on this mission will be with Joyce. She is in her late seventies. Looking at her picture I instantly feel that she is very loving and her aura glows bright. She has dark hair and chocolate brown eyes. She is of petite build and she is dressed well, indicating that she has had a privileged life. From her profile I see that she has always been a giver. She has encountered many hurdles on her journey through life but she has always gotten up, dusted herself off and got back on the road to recovery. There is something though, something that led her to her spirituality. A thought-provoking quote comes to mind. *Religion is for those who fear hell, Spirituality is practised by those who have already experienced it.*

I feel that Joyce has experienced a deep challenge at some point. Her personal faith and oneness with God is strong. She understands that everything happens for a reason and therefore is open, aware and understands that things happen to make way for our desires to be fulfilled and for our righteous journey to be pursued. She has three children who adore her and other non-related close connections also. A lot of love surrounds this lady.

Interestingly, I read on to discover that she has a deep connection with a women's circle. She truly is blessed and enlightened in such a way that her loving energy is connected to other similar loving energies. Together this compilation of magnificence has the potential to create miraculous healing. Loving energy is the biggest healer of all and can far surpasses the expectations of medical intervention alone. Although when thought about rationally, medical treatment is created through love, which is a powerful healer in itself, and when both medicine and healing love combine, miraculous things can occur. Medicine is created out of a love of healing after all.

I am excited at the prospect of delving further into the depths of this loving energy, I can feel it already. I can only imagine the intensity that I will open myself up to experiencing when I encounter this beautiful lady. I shall look forward to gifting my time and energy in this direction.

Henry

Next is Henry. He is seventy-five years old and quite unique in appearance. He has greyed hair that reveals he was obviously dark-haired in his day, his eyebrows are shaggy and dark with no greying and they dominate his appearance as they magnetically draw my attention. He appears to have some sort of problem with the alignment of his eyes, but this all seems to add to his character. I read on and am shocked to discover that he is an actor, a very successful actor in fact with more than fifty years working in front of the screen without much of a break. I often find that those who enjoy acting are fulfilling their desire of escapism from their true self for whatever reason that may be; they are also tremendously gifted with the art of persuasion.

Suddenly I get a flashback, so I immediately refocus my line of thought to allow the intervening knowledge to channel its way directly to me. I often think of this process like a déjà vu. It is as if I have been sent a preview of an event that has happened or one that is going to happen; this is sent through the universal energy channels that we all have at our disposal but not many allow themselves to open. This is a connection I have come to appreciate immensely, although there was a time when I did not.

I seem to be inside the gates of a big house. It is white and has pillars all across the front of it with a balcony that dominates the front half way up the face of this grand home. Big gates close off the entrance to the property and a black road leads straight up to the stately mansion. The magnificently manicured gardens and groomed trees that border the perimeter of the estate are splendour of the highest degree. This indicates there is financial wealth in abundance here. However, I must stress that I personally do not deem a successful life to be one that has accumulated financial wealth. My definition of a successful life is someone who has accumulated the wealth of wisdom and spiritual growth we should all strive towards; and that is not by having a bulging wallet, in fact if you take time to observe the world, it is those who have less financially who are happier, or those who have accumulated peace and happiness before they were gifted with the financial wealth. They are happy with what they have, whereas many of those who have money often strive towards having more. Greed, one of the seven deadly sins, yet disturbingly, a natural instinct for so many.

The vision is clear. I see a van speedily race up the driveway and pull up outside. It is a bright neon orange colour with Buzzbox Bailiffs in big black writing on the side. Two men quickly jump out of the van. One is big, strong and dark skinned, the other is smaller, thinner, and of pale complexion; he has a nasty look on his face. They both confidently approach the front door and knock loudly. There is no answer, so the big guy walks over to the back of the van, opens the door and takes out a piece of equipment that looks like it will do damage to whatever it comes in contact with. This doesn't look good.

Returning to the door the big guy stands in position as the smaller guy shouts loudly, "Open up or we will let ourselves in."

The big guy takes a step back and gets ready to use the tool to charge at the door. He swings his big strong arms back and as he is swinging forward at full force, the door opens and he just misses a screaming lady who is standing in the doorway with a horrified look on her face.

"Take whatever you want but don't hurt me or my father, he is a sick man."

The men smile arrogantly and walk past her. Suddenly she catches a glimpse of their van and she shouts, "Hold it there just one minute, you are not burglars. You are bailiffs. What are you doing at my family home?"

The guys look at her in bemusement, then at each other. The smaller guy composes himself and approaches the newly poised lady.

"Sorry, Madame," *he says sarcastically as he gestures a bowed head while touching the tip of his quite worn flat cap.* "Is there a problem?"

He continues walking towards her, forcing her to take a few steps backwards towards the wall until she can no longer move. Now standing with her back firmly against the wall and behind the open door, she cannot escape. Fear is written all over her face but she seems to find strength from somewhere deep inside her demure frame that breaks right through the intimidating atmosphere.

"You must have the wrong house. Why are you here? Who sent you?"

"This is 256 Sunshine Parade?" *enquires the smaller guy.*

"Yes," *she answers, her voice trembling.* "But there must be some mistake."

"Lady, do you think that we would make a mistake? We are just here to take what is rightfully owed to our client."

"What? Who? Why?" *she says more desperately.*

"We don't have time for this. Hank, just go take enough to cover the costs."

"No!" *she shouts.* "This isn't right. Do you have permission from a court or anything to enter this property?"

"Yes we do, you let us in. Let me see, what were the exact words? Take whatever you want but don't hurt me or my father, he is a sick man," *he says mockingly.*

"Well I take it back, I don't let you in, now get out of my father's house."

"Lady, you are really starting to annoy me now, and I need you to know that you do not want to see me annoyed. Do you hear me? It is your father who has signed this document stating that he has donated items to the amount of $25000 to Mrs Helena Pringle. He has not answered any calls or replied to any correspondence and so it is our duty to collect what is owed. Now leave us be to do our job."

"Will I make a start, Joe?" says the big guy in a very deep voice.

"Yes, Hank, get to it," he arrogantly replies.

He goes as close as he can to her. His face is so close their noses touch. She closes her eyes tightly, dreading what his next move may be. He smiles, knowing how uncomfortable he has made her feel. He takes a step back and places the letter in her hand. She waits for him to move away but he holds out for a few more uncomfortable moments. When he finally does depart she quickly opens the letter. She stands staring at it in amazement. She knows her father has been unwell but she didn't know it had gone this far. To imagine that her vulnerable father has been taken advantage of in this way has left her speechless and heartbroken.

I return to the now. It is always so disturbing for the family of those who suffer the shadows of the mind. They are the ones who are often left to deal with the consequences that regularly arise due to the confusion associated with this disease. If only they knew that it is not all darkness; that although there is so much sadness connected to the situation, for the sufferer there is internal light shining brightly within the visible darkness.

Angela

I pick up my final file and open it. To my amazement a white glow beams out at me. *This is an angel* is my first thought. Her aura encapsulates me. This lady has done so many wonderful things during her time on earth that she is now considered a saintly presence. She has unselfishly sacrificed her own personal desires to help others. Her name is Angela; she has long grey locks gathered in a ponytail that drapes down her back. She is of a slight build but holds a very big heart in that tiny frame. I look forward to getting closer to this lady and experiencing what it is like to be close to energy so pure. She is ninety-two years old and still working to help those in need, even when she should stop and allow others to assist her. Maybe this is the key to a long, fulfilling life. I ponder momentarily about how she would possibly need my assistance. Surely her saintly existence during her lifetime has been filled with wisdom and spirituality, enabling her to reach her highest enlightening potential. All will be revealed in time, I expect.

So there it is. I have now been introduced to all of my assignments. They may only encounter my energy for a short while but it will hopefully serve its purpose. I do hope that by my coming they all receive the full potential of the beams I have the honour of distributing. When the shadows of the mind have an impact on the end of a life it is hardest for the family and loved ones. In time those afflicted come to experience inner beauty, whereas those watching the exterior impact are left to contemplate a harrowing display of uncharacteristic behaviour and vacancy of the mind that provokes deep sadness because the person that they have known and loved is no longer familiar to them. If only they understood that.

I suddenly realise that I am going to be very busy on this mission, especially with Arianna joining me at the beginning, for with that comes added responsibility. However, I am so looking forward to spending some one on one time with her. She will be staying with Claire, who is the earth-based *Wish Giver*, but it is a relief to think we will get to spend some time alone without feeling we are under constant surveillance. I am looking forward to it considerably.

I will make myself a warm drink and get some shut eye before my early start in the morning.

But what is that noise? There is a light tapping noise coming from somewhere. I listen more carefully and it seems to stop so I get back to making my drink. What! There it is again. It sounds like it is coming from my bedroom, very peculiar! On opening the door I jump back when I see a shadow at my window. It isn't until I take a proper look that I realise it is Arianna and she is looking to come in. Ordinarily I would have been very excited but under the current circumstances I am not totally comfortable with this, but I can't leave her out there so I run over to the window and open it enough to allow Arianna access.

"What are you doing, Arianna? You could get in so much strife!"

"I have just met with my parents, Gilbert," she explains, distressed.

"Come in, come in," I say.

She does so and sits on the edge of my bed. I begin to have disturbing visions of Boss walking in and seeing her there, so I suggest we move to the kitchen. She agrees but looks at me in a curious manner. My heartfelt wish would be to keep her in my bedroom, not guide her out of it. But out of fear and respect I choose to honour my sensible intentions and continue to navigate this radiant beauty to my kitchen, where she settles herself comfortably on my bench top. This is curious as there is a perfectly comfortable chair right beside her, but I choose not to make an issue of the fact.

"Gill, you are never going to guess what!" she says in a rushed voice.

"What, Arianna, please tell me."

"Mum and Dad have just told me that I am going to be babysat by my godmother when I join you on your mission."

"Really?" I try to look and sound shocked but as I have already been informed of this when I met with Boss earlier I do not do it convincingly.

"You knew and didn't tell me, didn't you?"

I hang my head in shame. I should have told her everything because it is only when we are armed with all truths that we can progress towards our goals without hindrance. By not telling Arianna everything I knew it has led her to heightened disappointment whereas it could have been accepted as a part of the deal when I told her about her dad's plans. I cannot change that now and I need to help heal the wound of disappointment.

"Gill, I finally get the opportunity to experience what it is like to be on earth and with my best friend, and my parents think that I cannot be trusted to take care of myself. It just makes me feel emotions I have never felt before. I think I am feeling anger."

"Arianna, try to think of it in a positive way. Now you will get the opportunity to experience what it is like to be in human form; you will be born into the world. I will come and spend as much time with you as I can and to be honest it will be a good thing to have your godmother as someone to turn to."

She thinks about it for a few moments and replies, "You're right as always, Gill. I will have to take time to fit in, won't I?"

Spontaneously she jumps off the counter and wraps her arms around me.

"Oh Gill, you are the best friend, you always make everything okay again. You are wonderful. Thank you."

My heart pulsates with desire encountering this show of affection. Then she kisses me right on the cheek, and oh how I wish this moment could last forever, but then she pulls away.

"I must go get ready. I will see you in the morning," she says as she quickly makes her way back towards my bedroom and out of the window.

In a few short moments she has come and turned everything on its head, just like a whirlwind. I watch as she departs, and oh my heart so wants her to stay. I have a slight ache in the knowing that she only thinks of us as friends when my heart feels so much more. I give myself a shake, I must pull myself together and refocus. I now fully realise that this mission is going to be more of a challenge than I anticipated. The added distraction of Arianna may be a struggle but one that I am prepared to endure because after the struggle always comes the opportunity of a breakthrough.

I have total faith in the process of the stages of the spiritual soul, of which there are five, and when given some consideration they can be associated with many spiritual advancements, including emotional. The stages I speak of are The Call, The Search, The Struggle, The Breakthrough, and The Return. My job is to assist those through the struggle and navigate them towards their breakthrough. This is when they can be truly enlightened. I know it is worth it in the end. Until you have encountered a breakthrough you will never know what it feels like to make your way successfully through a struggle. All too many choose to reside in the struggle for too long and it can be damaging to our mind, body and soul. Often the struggle is something we cannot avoid and is repeatedly considered to be beyond our control, but we will be guided through it successfully if we choose to listen to our inner spirit.

I am grateful for this reconnection to reasoning as I prepare myself for what is to come. I never did get that hot drink so I will do just that and then get some much needed sleep.

CHAPTER FIVE
Arrangements

I awaken to the enchanting glow of the morning. I do love this part of the day and the energy it creates as it recharges my core organically, which in turn prepares me in the best possible way for the day ahead. I used to often ponder about why the cockerel awoke so early, and I now realise his purpose is to alert everyone to the potential of their day. It has to be much more energising than lying in your bed but, hey, that's just my perspective.

I run through the expected protocol for this morning and what I need to do to best prepare myself for the day ahead. I have at least five minutes to spare before I have to leave and so I quickly dash to Dave's for a revitalising refreshment prior to the ever chaotic rush for departure commences.

On leaving my quarters I hear my messenger beep. I am supposed to have it with me at all times, but I know I won't be long so I ignore it, choosing to check it when I get back.

Taking up my regular seating position in Dave's, I take a moment to focus on calming my nervous excitement about the anticipation of what is ahead. This feeling is quite intense and something I have not experienced in such intensity before. I feel like I have just been gifted with the emotions connected to the responsibility of the mission I am about to embark on. This is my first solo mission and being nervous is to be expected, but I do hope that I shake this unsteady feeling quickly as it is distracting and the last thing I need right now is any more distraction.

To regain the grip I need I attempt to think worst case scenario. *What would that be? I suppose not having a successful mission and losing my position as Memory Taker.*

I have worked so hard since coming here to earn this role, it means everything to me to do a good job. There, that wasn't so hard, now I can focus on the task in hand as I know what my priorities are.

I quickly finish my drink and grab a last bite of my heavenly delight, then make my way back to my quarters with a more confident focus. Arianna is at my door waiting for me. She appears to be sad and her usual radiating glow is dim.

"Arianna, is everything okay?"

"Gill, Dad has changed his mind, he won't let me come."

"Why?" I ask, concerned for Arianna as I know she is so desperate to explore the unknown. Although I have to admit I was also a little concerned for myself, as I was looking forward to some one-on-one time with her, but I can't help but identify that this may be a blessing in disguise if I hope to have a fully successful mission.

"He knows I came here last night and now he won't let me go with you," she declares in devastation.

I know how much this means to her, for since we became friends she has always asked what life is like on earth. Strange for me to experience such interest and enthusiasm for a place I chose to leave, but on the other hand I can connect because just as I aspired to experience another dimension, so does she.

"Gill, are you listening to me?"

"Oh yes, sorry, you just took me by surprise," I reply.

"Can you do something, please? I will be forever grateful. You know how much this means to me."

"Yes, I do, but your dad isn't going to want to listen to me right now, is he?" I have suddenly realised that Boss will definitely not be happy with me, he thinks that Arianna and I…Oh my, this isn't good, it is certainly not a positive to get on the wrong side of the Boss.

My messenger begins beeping excessively. I open my door and go to invite Arianna in as she is in need of comfort but then I remember what got her into bother in the first place.

"I will just go get my messenger. Will you wait there for a minute?" I dash inside to collect it and see I have many missed messages from Boss. This is without doubt not a good scenario as no one ignores the Boss. He wants me to meet him in his office ASAP. And I have left him waiting so that I could go and have a snack at Dave's. Could this situation get any worse?

I hear a mumbling at the door and call to Arianna, "I won't be a minute."

But as I turn around I am taken aback at the sight of a very cross Boss.

"Boss, I am sorry I can explain."

"Explain!" he roars. "Not only did you have my daughter in your quarters last night, you have chosen to ignore me summoning you this morning."

"I can explain, Boss, really I can."

"Dad, give him a chance to explain, please," Arianna pleads.

I have never seen Boss in such a rage. He is usually totally in control of his emotions. I have no idea what I am going to say, but I cannot make matters any worse.

Boss takes a seat and I sit opposite.

"I will go get us all a drink."

Arianna leaves us and Boss stares at me awaiting my response.

"Sir," I humbly begin. "I don't know what you think happened here last night but nothing did, I promise you."

"You mean to say that Arianna did not come here last night?"

"Well, yes, she did, Sir, but only to talk."

"She broke a golden rule, Gilbert, and I cannot trust her with all of the temptations that there are on earth. They will damage the pure beauty of her spirit."

"With all due respect, Sir, I feel that if she doesn't go it may damage her spirit more. I know how much Arianna has always been curious about what human life has to offer. She continuously asks me about it."

"So you admit that you have increased her curiosity," he says, sitting forward.

"To be honest, Sir, I do not think that anything I have said could suppress her curiosity and goodness knows I have tried. When I think of Arianna and her desire to experience life on earth, I think of a story I once heard about a caterpillar that lived in Siberia. He had unwavering faith that one day he would become a butterfly. He munched each year and each year he froze, but when he thawed out he continued in a desperate bid to munch his way to becoming more than he was. Finally the year came when he had munched enough to move to the next stage of the cocoon where he had time to contemplate and prepare for his new coming. That year he became a butterfly and he never froze again. After the struggle comes the breakthrough. Arianna does not know what it is like to struggle as she has always been a butterfly. She has comfortably resided in peace and harmony and so it is really not surprising that she is curious about the process of evolution. The butterfly in the story knows what it is like to be a caterpillar and therefore appreciates the hardship the caterpillar endures to reach its tranquillity. If she doesn't experience being a caterpillar she will never appreciate being a butterfly."

I look at Boss and he stares at me without responding. To my relief his face is no longer as red as it was. He sits back in the seat and places himself in a more comfortable position. He is not a big man but he has such a presence that it dominates the energy of the room. Then he says, "But how can a butterfly become a caterpillar without cutting off its wings, Gilbert?"

At that moment Arianna returns with some drinks for us all, and she places them on the table in front of us. She kneels down on the ground beside the table. She looks at me and then at her dad.

"Okay, what has happened here?" she asks continuing to look from one to the other of us in search of an answer.

I don't reply. I sit unresponsive.

Suddenly Boss sits forward and takes a drink and then sets it back down.

"Arianna, I know how much you want to experience what it is like to be human. I as your father would like to protect you from that and had hoped you would realise you have been privileged to live in a harmonious place. I have always hoped that it would be enough for you." He pauses for a moment. "Gilbert has helped me realise that your spirit is curious and until you experience what it is to be a caterpillar you will never be grateful for being a butterfly. I have to encourage myself to let go, allow you space to grow, and trust that your mother and I have equipped you with enough knowledge and judgement to make the right decisions. I am going to let you go on this trip..."

Arianna jumps up and hugs her father. "Thank you, Dad, I promise I won't let you or Mum down."

They hug for a moment and then Boss continues, "What I was going to finish with was that, although I trust you, I know the temptations that will come your way will be challenging. I hope that with Claire and also Gilbert here that your best interests will be well taken care of."

"Yes, Dad, Gilbert is a very good friend," she says, beaming a radiant smile in my direction.

"Arianna, you must remember that you must not cut off your wings just to fit in, you may disguise them but do not cut them off as they will never grow back. You may pretend to be a caterpillar but you can never truly become one because, if you do, it will be difficult for you to return home. Do you understand what I mean?"

"Yes, I think so, Daddy," she says angelically.

I am relieved that the outcome of this situation is a positive one, and my relief must be written all over my face.

Boss gets up and gently places Arianna beside him. "If this dispatch is going to happen we had better get moving."

I look at my watch and think, *Holy crap, it is almost here; I am really paying the price of my complacency this morning.*

"Certainly Boss, please let me show you out."

"Thank you, Gilbert, we will see you soon down at dispatch, we have some important goodbyes to say." He indicates to Arianna that she will be leaving my quarters with him.

"Oh, yes, poor Mum, I must see her," Arianna exclaims. "Thank you, Gilbert." She hugs me on her way past.

"You're welcome. I will see you soon, huh!"

"So you will," she replies happily and then continues to follow her dad down the hall.

I close the door, lean with my back against it and slide right down to a crouched position on the floor. "Wow, what a morning," I say out loud.

With that, I hop up and finally get everything ready for dispatch.

CHAPTER SIX
Dispatch

Making my way towards dispatch I see Arianna's mum, Sydney, making her way towards me. She seems to be happy to see me, which is a relief.

"Hello, Gilbert. I know we don't have much time but I would like to thank you for being such a positive support to Arianna. She really needs someone like you right now." Tears come to her eyes and she blurts out, "Please take care of her for us."

Before I have the chance to respond she has dashed off in another direction.

All of a sudden I see an image. A flashback is coming through and it is not the perfect time. I must really need to see it.

The location is a picturesque cottage surrounded by blossoming flowers of all colours, so vibrant that I can almost smell them. Lush green fields are all around. There is some activity in the garden. Three children ranging from six to ten are playing there happily. A woman is at the window watching them, and I am drawn to go towards her. On entering the home I get a warm feeling that this is a loving home. I make my way towards a door that is open and I hear some voices coming from inside. To my surprise I see Arianna standing there. She is not the same glowing pure Arianna that I know and love. She is dressed in jeans and a black t-shirt and her hair is a little messy. Beside her there is a backpack and the energy in the room is downbeat. There is an older lady standing at a sink doing some washing up. I do not move and I soon come to realise that this is not a flashback, it is an insight.

"Aunty Claire, I have to go see him he needs me."

"Arianna, it is my duty to protect you during your stay here. Jake is not in a position to be a positive influence in your life right now, and I want you to stay away from him, if you don't things will just get worse instead of better."

"But I love him," Arianna says, crying into her hands.

Claire approaches and puts her hand, which is covered in washing up bubbles, on her shoulder. "Arianna, that is not love you are feeling. You know deep down that it isn't, if you would only listen to your spirit. You are letting your spirit be overshadowed and controlled by lust, desire, temptation, and ego. I have seen it happen to so many people; please don't let it happen to you."

Arianna looks at Claire and in that moment she has connected directly with her spirit.

Then the back door slams open and three children come running in.

"Mum, there is a man out the front and he is shouting for Auntie Arianna, he looks strange and we are scared."

Claire looks to Arianna.

"Jake!" Arianna shouts as she grabs her rucksack and makes a dash for the door.

Claire gets there first and closes it tight, blocking her exit.

"Move, he needs me."

"Arianna, stop and think, please don't do this," Claire pleads.

But Arianna has a strange look in her eye. "He came for me, he loves me" she says. "Jake, I am in here," she shouts. She looks at Claire. "Sorry, Aunty Claire, I have to go, my spirit is telling me to."

Then she dashes out through the door I am standing at. As she passes me she comes to a halt and looks around pausing, for a moment from her mad dash. Then in through the front door comes a guy who is rugged in appearance.

"Ari, come on, I am waiting for you," he calls aggressively.

Arianna gives herself a little shake and runs towards him and out the front door and all that can be heard is the slamming of car doors and a car speeding off with music blaring from every open window.

Claire is now standing at the door frame I am positioned at and she looks directly at me, her eyes filled with helplessness.

Her attention is then distracted towards three little frightened faces that are peering up at her with quivering lips. She quickly shakes herself into another mindset, with a little help from me, for I absorb some of her anxious energy to help her mentally adjust from worried aunty to caring mum mode. "Okay guys, who wants ice-cream?" she calls to her three children in an uplifting tone.

I hear voices calling me. I remember that this is not the reality of the now I am currently existing in, well, not yet anyway. I open my eyes to findthat I am surrounded by everyone who is in dispatch. I give myself a shake.

"Oh yes, yes, I am fine everyone, thank you," I say and as they all get back to what they were doing I sigh deeply. Boss is observing me with a knowing look in his eye. What am I to do? Should I stop Arianna from coming with me? If I do she will live an unsettled life here but if she comes with me she may end up in danger. I don't have much time to make any decisions and is it my decision to make? I look to Boss again and again he looks back the same way. Suddenly I realise that he has also had this insight and that is why he was so determined not to let Arianna go. It had nothing to do with coming to my room. He was in a desperate bid to save his daughter from being exposed to this and yet he chose to let her go. Why? Then into my thoughts pops a story, the story I told him about the butterfly. I have already influenced this whole situation and now I understand that this insight has been gifted to me by Boss. He is the gifter of wisdom and insight here. Sometimes we have to endure the struggle to emerge triumphant; if someone interferes during the process we may not experience the highest potential of the situation.

He is standing beside Arianna and Sydney. I walk towards him and he comes to meet me.

"You did provide me with that insight, didn't you, Boss?"

"Yes, you need to be prepared, Gilbert. I know you have feelings for Arianna and it was not easy to see her in that situation but she has much learning to do now that she has chosen to experience humanity. She will need you to support her and be there for her. It is not going to be easy juggling the assignments and now this, but it has been devised that things don't advance until after you have reached the point of enlightenment with each individual. I will try to assist you when I can, but it is best that I don't interfere too much or I may hinder Arianna's crucial spiritual development. Oh, and Sydney isn't fully aware of the circumstances, and I think it is best that she doesn't know all of the details."

"Yes, sir, I will do my best."

"I know you will, Gilbert, and I am grateful for your true intentions towards Arianna. Now we had better get you ready for your dispatch."

"Oh yes, dispatch, I had almost forgotten."

"Yes, dispatch, Gilbert! Are you sure you are prepared? Good job you have plenty of time to adjust your thinking before you transcend."

I agree, and we make our way over to where Arianna and her mum are locked in an embrace. It is then time to enter the dispatch entrance. Boss has kindly prepared all of my necessary accompaniments, had he not I do not think I would have made it on time to collect *the beams* and the very special *Crystal* that I am honoured to be in charge of distributing. I am not fully aware of the reasoning of the *Crystal* yet but I trust it will be required at some point. It encompasses miraculous potential.

It is important for me to align my awareness to the task in hand. Dispatch is always a busy area as messengers come and go, but today I could liken the experience to an airport terminal as Arianna and her family bid emotional farewells to each other. This is my first time encountering such an emotional departure from here as it is usually more like a business class departure lounge where those dispatching are leaving on business. I must intervene.

"I am sorry, but we really must get going," I say cautiously.

Three heads look my way with tears in their eyes.

"Yes, of course," Boss responds, trying to suppress the emotion of it all. He knows the Arianna who leaves him today will not be the Arianna who returns.

One last hug and Sydney says, "Please take care of our girl, Gilbert."

I nod and smile to reassure her that I will.

She then says to Arianna, "Please listen to your intuition, it will guide you, and give Claire a big hug from us."

She finally frees her from a protective embrace and Arianna takes position by my side.

"I will be fine, Mum, I promise," she says.

Boss and I look at each other, and he braves a smile.

"You kids best be on your way," he says.

Arianna takes my hand, and I lead us forward towards the doors that lead to the long Corridor of Contemplation.

As we go through the doors and arrive at the other side she exhales a sigh of relief.

"Oh boy, Gill, that was tough. I really thought they were not going to let me come."

"It is hard for them to let go, Arianna. Usually people come forward from human form to entity for the first time, not backwards from entity to human form for the first time."

"I never thought of it like that. So I am one of the special ones?"

"Yes, Arianna, you certainly are that."

There is a moment's pause and so I take the opportunity to explain the corridor.

"Do you see how long this corridor is?"

"Yes, it is quite strangely long, isn't it?"

"Well, it is like that for a reason. It is the Corridor of Contemplation where messengers have time to think clearly before they arrive at departure. It is an opportunity to ensure that you are making the right choice because once you leave you cannot return until it is time to. What I am trying to say is, please use this time to make sure you have thought through your decision to join me.

Things are going to change, Arianna, and you won't always be able to control the outcome."

"I have thought about it lots already, Gill."

"I know you have but have you thought about what if things take an unexpected turn?"

"What do you mean, Gill? You are scaring me here. Do you know something?"

"No, not at all." I stop and look her right in the eyes. "Arianna, you know how precious you are to me, I want you to be safe and I want you to maintain your pureness of heart. That innocent beauty you have is so precious, and I am afraid there will be people that will take advantage of you."

"Gill, you are precious to me too, you know that, but this is something I must do, something I have always wanted to experience, and if I don't follow through I will never know. I will never be content with only being here in the Waiting Zone, you are bound to understand that."

I drop my head in acceptance. I have just had affirmed what I have known and expressed to the Boss. I know how he has felt knowing that he has had to accept it too. Lifting my head and looking into those magical gateways that are looking back at me I reply, "What are we waiting for? We had better get a move on."

She beams a smile and grabs my hand. We run in unison down the rest of the Corridor of Contemplation. We have no more contemplating to do and so we speed up the process and feel free as birds in that moment, giggling and embracing the freedom of it all.

We reach the door where Harry is standing waiting for us, watching us. I never knew what to make of this man when I first came here but in getting to know him I have discovered that although he gives the perception of being laid back and slow, he runs a pretty tight and efficient ship here. He never seems to stress even if things are not working out, and I do believe that even though there have been a few close shaves I have been reliably informed that there has never been a late dispatch. I have often wondered how he came to be here but I have never been brave enough to ask. I catch a glimpse of a smile as we approach him. I can imagine we are a sight to behold; we are like fun-loving, carefree teenagers.

Harry always has a way of reconnecting the mind to the heart and very few missions have ever been abandoned because he has always had the ability to bond with everyone.

"Hello, you two, so we have been granted permission to travel together?" he enquires.

"Yes, we have, Harry." I hand him the permission note that Boss provided me with, although I do not doubt that Harry has been well and truly informed beforehand.

"That's grand, that is," he says, looking at us both.

I smile and look to Arianna, she is just standing there as if unable to respond or not wanting to in case her dispatch is denied.

"Well, welcome and it is time to get you both into the adjustment room, follow me," Harry instructs.

We are guided into the adjustment room, the purpose being that our eyes refocus from the dazzling white they have come to recognise as normal to the warm glow of life on earth. Arianna seems to be in awe of the differences that are occurring right now. The energy is beginning to become more raw and there are background noises that are not totally recognisable but can be picked up on a frequency beyond my conscious identification.

When we enter the room the warmth of its ambience instantly hugs us. Arianna is taken aback initially and stumbles backwards. But Harry is in position right there to save the day.

"Mind your step there, young lady," he says, dignified as ever.

"Wow, that's stunning."

I had a different reaction as I preferred the pureness of the brightness that I had come to enjoy, and I did not want to return to the glow so my eyes had trouble adjusting. However, with Harry's wise experienced coaching I came to unblock my unwillingness to return in the knowing that I was carrying out an important duty and that I would return soon after. Harry always has a way of making you accept and honour your thoughts without you realising that you have.

"I see we have an eager aficionado here," Harry observes.

Arianna radiates enthusiasm at him.

"Now, Gilbert, I will leave you to show this young lady how to manoeuvre your eyes to ensure maximum adjustment is achieved."

"Yes, certainly," I respond.

"Well, make yourselves comfortable, and I will be back to test your progress in a few moments."

"Yes, Harry," we both reply.

"What does he mean, manoeuvre your eyes?" Arianna asks.

"Yes, come here and watch me," I say, then start wiggling my eyes around, to the obvious amusement of Arianna who is laughing so much her eyes are watering and she is clutching her side.

"Oh Gill, you make me laugh so much," she gasps.

"Okay, you do it and then we can relax for a few minutes."

Then she starts to wiggle her eyes and I can't help but laugh as she adds silly face movements to create a whole performance.

I try to pull myself together by walking away and after a few moments I look around to see Arianna scanning the room. I am then bombarded with a sequence of questions.

"What's this? This is beautiful, what does it do?" All of which come flying at me at once as the excitement of these earthly artefacts totally consumes Arianna. This doesn't bode well for her trip as she may get consumed by the bedazzling array of materialistic possessions and suppress the peace and love that she can discover within, which is the true treasure of life.

I take a seat in the big cosy armchair and have to admit that it is so comfortable and a pleasure to experience.

'Maybe this is all part of Arianna's learning,' I tell myself.

She continues to skip around the room and then she suddenly stops and stands totally still, staring at a painting of a country scene. There is a cottage with smoke coming from the chimney and children playing ball in the garden. All around are fields of lush green grass with animals grazing there. The sky is blue and the clouds are fluffy. I take a moment to appreciate the beauty of it also.

Arianna then moves away from the painting and takes a seat on the coffee table in front of the chair I am sitting in.

"Gill, may I ask why you left this place of beauty?"

She catches me right off guard. I try to look away but she is so close and staring right into my eyes. Her eyes are no longer transparent, they are the bluest blue I have ever seen and I am mesmerised.

"Gill, did you hear me?" she sweetly calls.

Not wanting to answer, I pause. To my utter relief Harry enters the room, and I am saved.

"Now if you two young things would like to come over here I will be able to commence with dispatch."

We both go over to where Harry stands. He checks our eyes and we both pass the test.

"Well, haven't you both done well," he exclaims.

"Can we all take a seat out here in the hall?" He gestures to three seats—one placed facing the other two.

"Is everything okay?" I ask, knowing that this is not a regular part of the dispatch process.

"Now you both will be travelling together through the vortex. When you arrive on earth you will be different entities, you are both aware of that?" he enquires in a serious tone.

"Yes, but what does that mean?" I ask.

He looks to Arianna. "Young Arianna, you are going to experience humanity and therefore will gain a physical form for a time. You are not destined to stay there forever and so we are not entering you into another form of physicality other than your own as we do not deem that appropriate given the circumstances of your arrival to the Waiting Zone. This is a unique experience that you are embarking on and you must be aware of this fact."

"Sorry, so does that mean that I am going to be different than Gill?"

"Yes, it does, Gilbert is still going to remain as an entity. You will be able to fully connect with him so long as you allow your spirit to be consciously connected to his. You will feel his energy and maybe even see him but it is important to remember that you must at all times remain consciously aware of this connection. Is that clear?"

"Yes, I think so," she says, looking to me a little saddened.

Harry looks right into Arianna's eyes and says, "Arianna, you are there to learn and experience life in human form. You must not forget the place where you come from. The peace, love and tranquillity of your spirit is always there even when you think it has abandoned you. Be true to yourself."

He says it twice and with such intensity that it penetrates even my mind. I have not seen Harry work like this before, and Arianna is in a daze.

With a lot for us all to absorb there are a few moments of awkward silence before Harry guides us towards the vortex. He clicks his fingers and Arianna seems to quickly come round. It was as if she was in a trance or under a hypnotic spell. Who would have known that Harry was so multi-talented? He then turns to face us so I brace myself and hold Arianna's hand and she tightly grasps mine.

"It is time for us to move on now that your eyes have adjusted. Has the rest of you adjusted to the fact you are about to transcend?" he enquires, ensuring that we are also prepared mentally.

"I am ready," I respond and I look to Arianna.

"Yes, yes, I am ready," she quickly replies, giving herself a little shake.

We go through to the vortex room, which is quite big. The room is dominated by the big black vortex. It is right in the centre of the room and it is large, oval-shaped and rimmed in gold. It is about ten feet tall and six feet wide, and it has a washing-machine effect in the centre, as it swishes around and around—faster than you can imagine. Its sheer intensity takes me aback every time I see it. Each time I witness the magnificent phenomenon that is the Vortex, I feel part of something bigger than big. This is Arianna's first time to witness this superlative sight. Her eyes are glistening and her energy is electrifying.

"Oh my, isn't it just beautiful?" she exclaims.

"It certainly is a sight to behold," Harry responds.

We all stand for a moment, mesmerised by the swirling motion of the Vortex.

First to snap out of the trance is Harry. "Righteo, let's get you kids dispatched," he says, making his way over to a control panel.

"Now if you would like to position yourselves over there on the two parallel platforms, I will adjust the settings accordingly for your dispatch requirements which will allow you both to travel together," he instructs.

We make our way to our allocated positions. We are situated right in front of the porthole. The energetic vibrations are exhilarating in the extreme. I cannot liken it to any experience I have encountered in my earthly form.

Arianna is facing me. She takes both my hands in hers and says, "This is magic."

She is glowing in excitement and anticipation of her dreams of experiencing the earthly realm coming to fruition.

"Ready?" Harry calls.

"Ready," Arianna replies.

"Ready when you are, Harry," I say.

"May you have a successful voyage. We will leave in 5, 4, 3, 2, 1." Then we are off.

CHAPTER SEVEN
Gilbert

Travelling the vortex is quite daunting at first as you tend to get thrown about quite a bit and the sensation is unique. It is something that gets easier each time you do it.

In what can be perceived as not much time at all we arrive at the designated earthly destination.

Our location is quite open given the nature of our entrance. Our entrance point is situated on a hilltop overlooking a valley and a town. We are usually an entity when we arrive, and we don't disturb the goings on of the location, but on this occasion that is not the case. Luckily, as I scan around there is no one to be seen in the immediate vicinity. On this occasion I have arrived first, so it is my job to ensure the surrounding area is clear for Arianna's arrival. She will take a physical form, which is a complex process. I rush over to the large tree that shadows our entrance. Unrecognisable to a human eye, there is a hatch that harbours supplies that are required from time to time. On this occasion, Arianna will need some clothes that have been kindly left there by an earthly messenger along with identification documents, money, and other earthly requirements.

I once again check the surrounding area and as there is no one around I indicate that the way is clear. Almost immediately Arianna comes through the vortex.

She stands there in all of her physicality. The exquisite beauty of her physical form encapsulates every morsel of my being. She looks around in amazement, not realising she is naked – or possibly unconcerned due to not understanding the social laws that govern the earthly realm.

I snap myself out of the mental grasp that has momentarily taken over me.

"Arianna can you hear me?" I call in hope of connecting. She is unresponsive, and I am concerned. I try again.

"Arianna, please let me know if you can hear me." Still there is no response. "Arianna!" I shout.

Finally she responds. "Gill, is that you? I can't see you."

"You have to allow yourself to connect to my energy, Arianna, remember what Harry said." I nervously await a response.

She closes her eyes and then reopens them.

"I can see you, Gill." She sounds relieved, then realises she is not wearing any clothes and her cheeks flush.

"Oh sorry, Arianna, here are some clothes for you." I indicate the bag situated beside her. She hunkers down and quickly unloads the contents onto the green grass. I turn around for a few moments to allow her some privacy.

"I am ready, Gill," she informs me so I turn back around. She is wearing some earthly clothes which are not of her usual style, a pair of fitted jeans and a peach coloured blouse, however she still radiates beauty. She is one of those amazing creatures that could wear a bin liner and still look wonderful, certainly in my eyes.

"So what happens now?" she enquires.

"Yes, well now we will make our way to town and get the train to the Madison Valley station where Claire is awaiting your arrival."

She nods but then shakes her head. "To town?" she asks.

"Oh, you do have a lot to learn, don't you?"

"It seems so, Gill, however will I do it?"

This is the first time I hear fear in her voice.

"Don't worry, Arianna, you will know all you need to know in no time. Sure, isn't that why you are here – to learn?"

"You are right, Gill, as always," she says, relieved.

"So, because you are in a physical form we must use tangible transport. I could transcend my energy from location to location as my assignments are situated worldwide but on this occasion I will accompany you to your destination."

Her head drops again so I try to lift her spirits.

"It is going to be fun to experience, Arianna. Just wait until you see how people rush around and connect with each other."

She smiles, and so I explain to her about her identification card and what she will need money for. She picks it up, and I help her to quickly sort it all out.

After all of that I need to get some exercise and release some tension and emotion so Arianna and I decide to jog to the station.

We run for a while and then take a little rest on a bench beside a big lake. It is revitalising to watch the water in the big fountain as it gushes upwards before cascading back into the pond again, only to be recycled by the fountain all over again.

"Gill, why are you here? Why are you the Memory Taker?" she asks, taking me aback. I sit quietly and unresponsive for a moment. I have always been cautious about sharing my experience with Arianna as she doesn't have another earthly example of life to compare it to, but maybe it is time.

"Well, Arianna, I can honestly say that I am now part of the Waiting Zone realm because that was my destiny. I truly believe that I was created precisely for this position. The mind is such a powerful thing. If I can help ease the pain within someone's heart and mind that is the obscurity and guide these enlightened souls to their true destination, then I am fulfilling my gift that I have been so generously given."

"That's beautiful, Gill, but why are you here? Why did you choose to leave your physical form before your time? Was being here really that bad for you? I am sorry to keep asking, but I am just trying so hard to understand."

"Oh, right." I sense that Arianna sees my reluctance but yet she waits patiently for me to reply. "Well, it's a long story, Arianna, and you may think it is not a happy one, but it is my journey and important to me. Are you sure you still want to hear it? You may not see me in the same light again," I say, knowing that she is curious.

"Yes, I would love to hear about your journey, Gill, and I will not judge you, I promise."

"Okay then. This is my story," I reluctantly reply.

"When I was younger—like five or something—I always felt deep down that I didn't belong. Belonging...that's an emotion which can make you feel secure and loved. Even though I say this, please don't get me wrong. I was loved dearly by my mum and dad, but I never felt that I was where I should be. They were such good parents and deserved a son far better than me. I always felt that I was living a parallel life to the one I was destined for. It was really unsettling for me, and I never felt happy, I felt as if I was always searching. As time went on my parents got more and more concerned for me. They brought me to counsellors, they brought me on trips around the world, they brought me to every activity that they thought would be a fun experience for a child, all in a desperate bid to make me happy. Any other child would have been jumping for joy, but not me; all of their efforts and finances were wasted on me. I must have seemed like the most ungrateful kid ever.

"My school years were not a good experience at all. I was bullied all through school and I had no close friends—well, being realistic, who would want to be friends with someone as miserable as me?"

"Gill, I don't understand, you are not miserable at all."

"Not now maybe. Now I am fulfilled, and I am embracing my true vocation, my soul is revitalised and I am truly joyous; but back then I could never have felt this way no matter how hard I or my parents tried. How can I explain it so that you understand it better?"

I search my mind for an enlightened answer and I come up with...

"Well, often people feel that they have been born the wrong gender. This can be very unsettling and confusing for them. They don't feel like they belong in the gender they have been born with and often make the hard decision to change gender. I never felt like I belonged in my physical form, I just kept going through the motions of each day as it came to me without seeing any future ahead. I survived each day as best I could. My poor parents really pulled the short straw by having me as their only child. I was always perceived as 'different' and therefore, of course, being bullied was inevitable because many people don't accept anyone who does not do things the way that society expects them to. Non-conformity led to me being isolated and branded a nerd as I didn't go out of my way to make friends nor do the silly immature things that the other kids my age were doing. Of course all of my teachers were deeply concerned for me and gave me special attention, so I was perceived as a teacher's pet by the other kids, which of course I was not. There was one counselling teacher, Mrs Jane Hicks, who I bonded with closely. She helped me realise that others' thoughts were not within my control but that my own thoughts were and how I let their views affect me was in my control. When I realised how powerful this mindset was, life seemed a little more bearable. I kept reminding myself that I can only be responsible for my own thoughts and actions and this empowered me. I no longer had to bear the cross of other people's judgements. I just had to be responsible for my own thoughts and expectations of myself. She would always share with me her words of wisdom, *'Others' opinions of me are none of my business'*. With this realisation I thought it would be a turning point for me and I suppose it was.

"Jane and I started seeing each other more regularly. We would organise counselling sessions and she would help me by simply being receptive. It wasn't long before I began to feel a warm glow, something I had not experienced ever before. It was as if she could bring the best out in me. She never judged me or felt concern for me; I was just allowed to be me when I was with her.

"One day after a few months of counselling sessions we were in her classroom and I made a pass at her. Totally inappropriate, of course, but it was what my heart and mind were telling me to do for so long, and I reckoned that I had nothing to lose by giving it a shot. To my surprise she let me kiss her and she kissed me back, sparks flew, magic happened and from that moment on our bond grew deeper and deeper. I had never experienced such amazing freedom of the heart before. Of course what we were doing was not acceptable socially as I was a student and she was a counsellor. This was nothing new for me as I had never felt that I conformed to society but she did hold concerns from time to time. But we couldn't help ourselves. We never intended to feel the bond that we did, we certainly did not set out with the intention to fall in love, but it happened. Even though she was married to one of the other teachers—dull Mr Hicks—we still managed to squeeze in plenty of time to get together. It was like a whirlwind, and I felt so happy when I was with her, and she must have felt the same or she would not have taken the risk. My parents were so happy to see a positive change in me and so they scheduled more counselling after school hours so that I would get even more benefit from it, which of course made me feel even happier, but not in the way they would have hoped for.

"Then it happened, the day our secret was discovered. I had been stupid enough to keep my thoughts and feelings noted in a diary and my mum found it. She was totally outraged and horrified with her discovery. I tried to make her see reason as she had been so happy seeing me happy after many years of me feeling nothing at all, but she refused to listen; instead she got onto the school board. From then on my life took a nose dive, the one thing that made it worth living was taken from me in an instant.

"Jane refused to have anything more to do with me. I was being interrogated by all sorts of people. For my own sanity I went into a protective cocoon. I felt like I now had no one that I could trust in my life. I always moved on during life because of my mum's and dad's love and now I felt betrayed by them. I no longer felt loved at all…by anyone. I certainly did not love myself.

"The time came for the court case. They were putting Jane on trial and would you believe she could have gone to jail? She visited me during this time even though she wasn't supposed to come in contact with me. The look in her eyes tore my heart. She said that she regretted ever meeting me, that I had ruined her life and that she had no choice but to tell the court that none of it was true, that I had imagined it all and that it was a fantasy. I didn't respond. What could I have said to make it better? She wasn't going to change her mind, even though I know she didn't truly mean what she was saying.

"I sat there as she told them intimate details from our sessions and how I had made a pass at her but that she responded by re-establishing our boundaries and saying that if it happened again she would have to cancel our meetings. She said that everything in the diary was a figment of my imagination. Everyone believed her story and so she went back to work and I was expected to just get on with my life as if nothing had happened. The bullying got way worse afterwards. Every day something happened. I couldn't even sit and eat my lunch in the canteen with everyone else because someone would tamper with my food, throw something at me, or simply not leave me alone. I wished to be invisible during these moments.

"Home wasn't much better; I found it very hard to forgive my mother for her betrayal. Her intervention created a huge impact on my life just when I had begun to finally feel alive and happy. It was a vulnerable time for me and Mum was whizzing around unremorseful and as if nothing had happened, she had a way of dusting things under the carpet and ignoring them. But it had happened, it was real and nobody could change that.

"I decided to go within myself and start listening to me. I asked myself questions such as *Why have you never been able to feel happy with anything? What is this unsettling feeling inside that I have always had?* I asked myself many questions. The realisation came when I read a book that gave me reasons. I realised that I have always been on a journey of enlightenment and that I am connected completely to a higher source than my physical form and in that entity I am eternal. I always knew this deep down but to have it affirmed, well it was revolutionary for me. I was now in the knowing that there is more to life than there appears and I couldn't wait to experience my true enlightenment. I truly believed that there was a powerful energy influencing us and that what had happened to me happened for a reason. I chose to forgive and move on. This was an important step in my redemption as resentment can easily fester into obscurity, and I didn't want any more obscurity in my life. I believed I experienced obscurity for a reason and that that reason would reveal itself in time.

"I thought long and hard about every aspect of my life. In the faithful knowing that there was more to me than just my physical form and that my fulfilling destiny was not on earth, I decided to leave my physical being. It was one of the hardest things I have ever chosen to do. But do you know what?"

"What?" Arianna replies, hanging on every word I am saying.

"I never once felt scared; it just felt like the right thing to do. I knew there was a more tranquil existence for me.

"So one morning after my mum and dad had left for work I got up and got dressed, brushed my teeth, made my bed, did everything that I normally would have done. Then I went to the medicine cabinet and took two bottles of pills. I went and sat on the back patio that overlooked our beautiful garden. It made me think of Mum as she put so much effort into her garden and it responded in being so beautifully vibrant. For a moment I felt guilty because I knew what impact this would have on her; but she would only have the pain of watching me being miserable forever more anyway and this way she could move on and do all of those things that her and Dad had put off.

"I picked up the notepad and began to write.

Dear Mum and Dad,

I want you to know that I love you both very much. If I were to look for a reason to stay on this earth right now you would be that very reason. In that lies the problem as I have nothing else in my life. I have been on this earth eighteen years now and I still don't feel like I fit in or that I belong. I know that there is something better waiting for me and so I have made the decision to seek it earlier instead of waiting for my time to come.

Please know that I have gone to a place where I am going to be truly happy, and I will keep a watchful eye on you both like a guardian angel.

I will love you eternally,

Your son Gilbert.x

"I tore off the page, folded it up, and started to slowly take one tablet at a time with a sip of water. I didn't feel anything for some time so I sat and enjoyed my surroundings. I remember feeling total peace in those moments. As I drifted, I could feel it, the destination that I knew was always there waiting for me. I could feel utmost fulfilment and being drawn to the splendour of the sublime.

"Then all of a sudden I could feel myself being dragged back. I tried so hard to stop myself; I could hear my mother's voice in despair screeching for the paramedics to bring me back to her. I allowed myself to drift back. I knew I couldn't leave her like this. I opened my eyes and held my hand out to her and she rushed to my side, tears flooding down her cheeks. 'Mum, please let me go,' I said. 'It is so beautiful, and I belong there. I love you.'

"The next thing I remember was coming to the Waiting Zone. That was two years ago and I have never looked back. I am doing exactly what I am destined to do; I have even relinquished my access to the kingdom of heaven because this is my heaven, here with you, Arianna."

"Sorry, Gill, it is just so sad, your poor mum," she says emotionally as the tears stream down her face.

"I didn't get to tell you the end. When I got here I was chatting to your dad and when I gave up my passage to heaven I released my gift. So my gift was returned straight back to the exact place that I came from. So now my mum and dad have the opportunity to raise the son they always wanted because my little brother was born exactly a year ago. Although my mum misses me terribly she knows that little junior was a gift from me. That fills my heart with joy."

"Oh Gill, that is so lovely. Are you going to visit them when you are here? Where did you live?"

"Well, I don't know for certain but stranger things have happened for sure. Better get moving here if we are going for our jog."

"Right you are, Gill, race ya," and she speeds off for me to catch her.

CHAPTER EIGHT
Delivered

We run hand in hand as fast as we can down the steep hill like two deeply connected spirits. I did not expect Arianna to respond in this way to my story, I suppose I hadn't really expected to tell her it in the first place, but now I am glad I chose to share it with her; I no longer feel that I have anything hidden. I feel surprisingly emotionally lighter and free. *A journey shared and not hidden can be soul releasing.* We stop momentarily to catch our breaths and then proceed to make our way down the steep hill towards the valley. At first we walk but then we pick up speed and in no time at all the wind is rushing through Arianna's hair, and she looks so free as she holds her arms out wide and her head back, embracing every moment. I love to see her like this.

On our way to the station we see many things, all of which are new to her and she is enthused about everything, so much so that even I strain to be enthused at the things she is in awe of which many people take for granted. This goes on the whole journey. Arianna keeps talking to me and people keep looking at her strangely because, of course, they cannot see me the way she does. I choose not to highlight this fact, it may make her feel uncomfortable, and I wouldn't want to ruin the magic she is feeling. This is the first moment that I have ever felt the desire to embody a human presence. The feeling is alien to me, and I choose to distract myself from it.

When we reach the bottom of the hill and make our way to the train we just keep smiling at each other. Then as we stand on the platform waiting for our train to arrive, the remnants of the magic we shared earlier are still close to the surface of my heart and evident in my stature as I stand taller than before. Arianna and I playfully tease each other. Commuters walk past and cannot take their eyes off Arianna as she stands there glowing with magical energy, smiling the most radiant smile. I know she is feeling the magic between us too and this connection has a deep-rooted impact on me. Oh, how I desire her.

In my focus on Arianna I did not heed the impact our intense energy was having on the commuters in the vicinity. It must have taken them by surprise as they commence their mundane everyday groundhog existence, and because they cannot see me they condemn Arianna's behaviour as extremely odd. Arianna has also begun to notice the reactions of others and the shadow of their judgemental energy is starting to overcast her glow. In seeing this, a lady approaches Arianna. She is well dressed in a colourful stylish dress.

"My dear, you look so happy and radiant, don't ever lose your glow, it is beautiful," she says and then walks off.

Arianna stands tall again and shines from within. This can easily be seen glowing outwards.

"She is right, you know. There will be many people who will want to take that away from you because they are jealous and fear witnessing true happiness," I say, trying to enlighten her innocent mindset about the way of life for some people here on earth.

"There is beauty within everyone, Gill, you need only look deeper."

"That may be so but there are those who have buried that beauty so deep. I admire your innocence, Arianna, but you can't make someone realise their potential beauty if they do not want to reveal it."

"You are worried about me, aren't you, Gill?"

I pause for a moment before I respond. "Well yes, I am a little concerned, Arianna, but I also trust in the process of the spirit, especially when someone is overwhelmed with desire to experience something. That shows me they obviously have learning to experience."

"You are so wise, Gill."

"Ha ha, wise, me? No. Well, maybe slightly experienced and gifted by the wisdom from the well of enlightenment that is sent to me as and when it is required. On my own I can be quite hopeless."

"Well there is no need to be too worried, Gill, I have been doing a little research into how things work here. I have listened to your stories and understand the need for caution at times, but I have also identified the desperate need for love."

"Well yes… you are onto something there, but please remember there are those who will willingly take your love and not reciprocate."

Pondering on this prospect for a moment, she responds, "I had not thought of that." She looks a little saddened at this fact.

"It is a sad reality of life here but really not everyone is like that, there are many lovely people who are willing to open their hearts," I say in an attempt to help her regain hope.

Arianna sits forward and kisses me on the cheek. I blush slightly as she has caught me off guard. A ripple of magical sensations tingles right through my essence. This is a fabulous feeling that I never want to end, and I will treasure this moment forever.

She continues talking as if it wasn't as big a deal for her.

"So I have also learned about how people pay for things, and I also learned that people are individually identified through different measures; and how they are tested on their ability to achieve, like securing a good job, learning to drive a car or learning about a specific subject. It is amazing, isn't it?"

"It certainly is," I say, amazed at how fascinating and wondrous she finds everything.

The train pulls up and Arianna jumps with excitement.

"Can we go now? I would like to experience lots with you before I am watched over every moment by Mum and Dad's chaperone." She places the backpack on her back. The whole journey goes by really fast as Arianna asks question after question and I answer as best I can.

Before long we arrive at our destination. As we disembark the train I see a quiet-looking petite lady standing there. She makes her way towards us, wraps her delicate arms around Arianna and hugs her as tight as she can.

"Arianna, it is you, isn't it?"

Arianna is slightly taken aback by her as she is obviously not what she expected. And she fails to answer. The lady must pick up on Arianna's momentary reservation and so she releases her hold and turns to me.

"Gilbert, it is lovely to meet you, I have heard many wonderful things about you. I am Claire." She holds out her hand for me to shake.

I am chuffed that someone holds me in such high regard and I choose to hug her instead. To my relief she reciprocates. On witnessing my response Arianna hugs her also. They stand in each other's embrace for a time. There is a look of relief now on Claire's face and a knowing that she is making an initial connection with Arianna.

I look around the platform at all of the other people, some of whom have reached their destination, others who have yet to leave, some emotional farewells, some robotic office workers taking the same train to the same destination, something they probably now do every day without thinking. So many people, so many differences, all unique in how they came to be at this point in their lives standing on a platform in Madison Valley. My mind begins to wander and I pull it back to the now.

Claire and Arianna are standing peering over at me.

"So, Gill, you have a very important mission to carry out," Claire remarks to give me an opening to depart.

Jeepers, how could I forget? How can it not be forefront in my mind? I have been so distracted I have not given one moment's thought to the initial reason I am here. How could I forget about my assignments? I should probably have checked in with them already. I cannot believe my complacency, as it means so much to me to have a successful first mission and to the lives of those I will be visiting. I must catch a grip of my thoughts, they are whizzing all around me.

"Sorry, Gilbert, I did not mean to startle you," Claire says, clearly picking up on my anxious vibrations.

"Are you all right, Gill?" Arianna enquires, obviously concerned also.

"Yes, thank you, I am fine. Claire, you did not startle me, in fact thank you for the wakeup call."

"I am a messenger also, Gilbert, so I know what it takes to try and keep on top of things," she says empathetically.

"Yes, that's right, you are an earthly messenger, aren't you?"

"That is correct," Claire replies.

"Really, Aunty Claire, are you? It is okay to call you Aunty Claire, isn't it?"

"Arianna, yes really, and yes of course, that would be lovely."

"Oh, will you tell me all about it? Please, I want to know everything."

I share what I know of Claire's story.

"I recall hearing that Claire came to the Waiting Zone a shy young lady. Because of some childhood circumstances she had withdrawn from her physicality. She was treated as someone who had a disability and an introverted personality when it was that she chose to utilise her gift of transcending through the realms and connecting with others' energies in a different way. When she joined Arianna's mum on her Wish Giving mission, Claire came in contact with her childhood sweetheart and learned he did not desert her as she had been led to believe. She took over as the wish giving messenger because you had just been born and Mrs Boss needed to focus her energies on being a mum and wife. Claire was granted the honour of returning to earth and carrying out her missions from there as she had the extra gift of being able to transcend her energies between realms."

"Wow, Claire," says Arianne. "That is amazing that you can live in both realms, I bet that there are not many people doing that."

"You would be surprised to learn just how many gifted people there are, Arianna. Well maybe we should begin to make our way to the car and I can fill you in more," Claire suggests.

"Okay, well I really must be going," I say finding an opportunity to depart.

Arianna comes closer and looks me in the eyes. "You are not coming any further with me?" she asks in a sad voice as if I am abandoning her.

"I must embark on my mission, Arianna, but I will be back to join you when I release the beams and then we can spend some quality time together. If you need me you know how to connect with me. I will be there for you."

"You promise?" she says, holding out her little finger.

"I promise," I reply, then I take her tiny little finger in mine and it signifies our true bond of friendship.

"Goodbye, Claire, please take good care of her." My earlier premonition concerns me.

"I will, Gilbert, you take care also, and may I suggest a place of natural beauty would be a great way to realign your thoughts and prepare for the task you have ahead."

"Thank you for that, Claire, yes, I might just do that, it always guides my thoughts in precisely the direction I need them to go."

I can see Arianna is excited about her impending adventure so I choose not to drag out the goodbye. She is now safely delivered, and even though my heart is aching at the prospect of our being parted, I know I must depart. In an instant I transcend my energy to a magical haven.

CHAPTER NINE
Rumination

I arrive at a location that is vast, spanning further than my eyes can see. Trees reach high up to the sky, they are the greenest green I have ever witnessed. They are vibrant and so alive. The energetic vibrations I am absorbing by being here are dynamic. I lower my head to locate the exquisite scent that I am picking up. I turn around to see an array of flowers, every colour, size, and fragrance. The aroma they emit is unique. It would certainly be a magical scent in a bottle, it is one of those smells that would be priceless to capture. The infusion of scent and colours I am absorbing through my senses is a recharging combination, enough to heal many an ailment and recharge a drained energy supply. The strength and vibrancy of the strong trees that stand tall behind me and the softness of the abundance of flowers before me recharges me in this exclusive location that will tend to all of my spiritual needs.

I sit for a time in silence. I clear my mind from my past thoughts to make way for new fresh and focused thoughts to enter when I am ready to deal with them.

After some time I start to connect with my assignments. The gift of memory has been sent to me, and I recall each introduction briefly. Firstly, I will encounter Frank. He is in his sixties and has been experiencing slight memory loss for some time. He has begun on a spiritual journey, and I sense that he may need guidance to fulfil his desire to progress towards enlightenment as he has not had much faith during this lifetime. He was not interested in understanding the significance of progression of the spirit during his earlier years but as time lapsed it became more apparent that it is beneficial to connect with spirit. He is also the father of Carrie, my next case. She is a very young sufferer at only forty-eight. She migrated to the other side of the world and their connection has remained strong, but the loss of consistent loving physical interactions has taken its toll on both spirits. Their journey is important in successfully progressing towards their personal goals of sublime advancement. I shall work hard here, even though it will be challenging it will also be rewarding should I be able to unite their energies.

My third case is Joyce. She is in her seventies and lived a privileged life, gifted to her because she is so grateful for all of her treasures both physical and spiritual. She has faith in the universe and how it works, she knows that everything, good and bad, happens for a reason and her faith and acceptance of life's path has been kind to her. She has not had many lessons to learn until now. She is part of a women's circle group that comes together weekly to focus their powerful energies on specific people in need of positivity or love to eradicate some of the hate and fear connected to them. She has given a lot of love to others to help them and now she needs all of her love for herself. Will she be able to focus on her own loving requirements that in the past were fulfilled by others? I am feeling encouraged to share some love with this lady and so I close my eyes and project some loving energy her way. I trust that she will receive it well.

Next is Henry, a seventy-five-year-old actor who has lived a life of financial abundance, being loved by most people he meets because of his charismatic interactions in his personal life and through his on-screen connections. He is admired for all of his hard work and commended accordingly. Now that he is older and his work commitments have slowed he is unable to sustain the high cost of living he has come to rely upon. Throughout his life his ego has fuelled him and he could win medals for the fulfilment of his personal desires to advance through the ranks of fame. He will be remembered accordingly, however this does not leave much room for spiritual progression. Now Henry is paying the price of not addressing his spiritual needs earlier, as no amount of acting accolades will help him move forward this way. He is also dealing with financial distress so late in his years. This could be very challenging for me. I will do my best and hope for the best possible outcome for Henry.

My final file is a vast contrast to Henry's. Her name is Angela and she is ninety-two years old. She has unselfishly sacrificed her entire life to helping others. She is an earth angel in my eyes because she has the right balance between taking care of her own self-love needs and catering to the needs of others without imposing on their journey, instead assisting them to progress effectively. Angela wholeheartedly understands the spiritual progression of life and that our spirits come here to learn and advance. There is nowhere else in the spectrum of being where knowledge, wisdom and experience can be gained. She has had many a struggle and breakthrough in her time and experienced the call on many occasions. She shines brightly as she is so pure of heart. I await the honour of my interactions with this lady.

I now feel reconnected to my mission and energised to embark on it. I am grateful to Claire for the suggestion of taking some time out to adjust my thoughts. I do hope that she and Arianna enjoy bonding. I must now move forward.

CHAPTER TEN
Frank

I arrive at a hilltop location. A white one-storey home overlooks the countryside that spreads as far as can be seen. The house is grand with large wooden windows and a large entrance door that with a pillared patio out front. Two church steeples can be seen in the distance, indicating that a town is not too far away. This is an idyllic rural setting, an unachievable dream for many people. I sense that Frank is a strong, determined man.

My attention is drawn towards a shed. Not any ordinary aluminium shed, this shed has been built out of bricks and is as big as a small chalet. The door opens and out comes a man who has quite a strong physical presence. It is a presence that is full of strength and yet generous at the same time. He enjoys his domain, I can sense that. Behind him comes a dog, it is short and brown with a large darker patch on its back side. It whizzes past Frank and straight towards me, barking and twirling around in a panic as it obviously detects my presence.

"Rover, come here," shouts a deep voice.

Rover immediately pays attention to the command and returns to Frank. He holds great respect for his master.

"What is wrong with you, boy? Are you seeing things now?" Frank says, rubbing Rover's head and ears playfully.

I try to move closer but Rover is onto it and is barking around me again. Frank comes closer and grabs Rover.

"Oh Rover boy, don't tell me you are losing your mind too," he says as he lifts Rover up safely into his strong arms and brings him around the side of the house where there is a wooden kennel. Frank hooks up a lead that is attached to the kennel and Rover objects slightly but soon retreats to the wooden box where he lies peering sadly through the opening.

A car can be heard coming up the long steep driveway. Frank steadily makes his way around to the front of the house where a new car is awaiting him. The driver switches the engine off. It is a flashy sports car, racer red in colour with large alloy wheels and high performance tyres. Frank smiles when he sees it. I observe from his energy that he loves cars. Out of the car hops a young man. He is in his twenties, with brown neatly cut and styled hair, and of clean crisp appearance. He immediately waves to Frank and so Frank makes his way over to the car.

"Hello, can I help you?" Frank asks.

The young lad looks disappointed but tries to put a brave face on it.

"Hey, Granddad, do you want to come out for a drive?" he says in an upbeat tone.

Frank takes a moment to absorb what the young man has just asked. Then as if he suddenly remembers he replies.

"Oh yes, grandson, how did I not recognise you there? It is this flashy car, when did you get it?"

Despondent, the young man replies again, "Oh, I have had it a while, Granddad. Can I take you for a drive? You know that you like to get out for a drive."

"I do, don't I. Yes, I would really like to go for a drive," he replies and is about to get into the driver's seat.

"Whoa, Granddad, maybe I could drive this time. You can sit back and enjoy the ride," he says while guiding Frank into the passenger's seat. Then he quickly makes his way to the driver's seat and jumps in and locks the doors.

"I was thinking we could go for a nice drive up around the hills and pop into Amy's for some lunch. Would you enjoy that?"

Looking a little confused Frank replies, "Erm, yes, I think that would be nice."

I stay with them as they go for a drive into the hills. I watch Frank's face as he looks admiringly at the vibrancy of the surrounding countryside.

"So how is your mum, Jake?" Frank asks clearly.

Jake smiles and he answers happily and relieved, "Mum is fine Granddad, Mum is just fine."

"That's good to know," Frank responds and then he looks out of the window again.

"There's Amy's house," he shouts in excitement. "You did say we were going there for lunch, didn't you?"

Laughing, Jake replies, "Yes, we are, Granddad, and Mum is going to be there too, and the kids."

"Well, you know how I love a nice lunch," Frank replies without emotion.

The car pulls up outside a two-storey home that dominates the landscape in its magnificence and has panoramic views of the forestry below and towns in the distance. The front door opens almost immediately and out bursts a woman who I estimate to be in her forties, followed by a lady in her sixties, another girl in her twenties, and three small girls aged between five and two.

"Oh look at all of these women waiting for you, young Jake," Frank says happily.

"They are here to see you, Granddad," Jake replies while getting out of the car.

Frank stares for a moment and then manoeuvres himself out of the very low car when Jake opens his door and with a heave-ho from his grandson he is upright.

Everyone stands waiting in anticipation for a reaction from Frank.

"Why is every one of the lovely ladies in my life standing looking at me? What is the occasion?" he says, breaking the uneasy silence and to the relief of everyone.

"Happy birthday!" they all shout in unison.

"Oh great, it's someone's birthday, there will be cake," he says and everyone laughs.

"It is your birthday, Dad." The lady in her forties comes over and puts her arm around him.

"Amy, it is you. You shouldn't go to so much trouble for me but young Jake said that there was lunch."

"Yes, there is lunch, Dad," she says, laughing.

"Good, I am starving," he says to the entertainment of the crowd.

"Well has there been a day ever different?" comments the older woman.

Her voice grabs the instant attention of Frank. "Jane, is that you there?" The woman smiles at the recognition she has received and so she makes her way to Frank.

"Yes, it is me, Frank," she says, giving him a hug.

"You are getting old looking, love," he remarks. Everyone tries not to laugh.

"Oh Frank, and so are you, my love," she says in response.

"Would everyone like to make your way into the dining room? I will put on some music and get some food out," Amy says as she tries to change the subject of aging.

"Yes please," Jane replies in relief.

Once in the dining room the atmosphere becomes jovial. Frank is obviously very much loved by all of his family. He is the most senior person here and so head of the family. More people arrive with gifts and hugs for Frank. He is seated in the head of the table and seems very happy to be placed next to a rather large plate of sandwiches and cake. I notice the interior of this home is traditional but with a modern twist. There is obviously an eye for detail from the residents.

On many occasions family members try to begin and maintain a conversation with Frank, some with more success than others. It is hard on the family to experience the non-recognition that comes when someone they love becomes somewhat vacant and unfamiliar.

Suddenly Frank stands up and begins looking at everyone in the room. He moves to the next room, which is the kitchen, and looks at everyone there, then on to the living room. He is followed by a concerned Amy.

"What is wrong, Dad?" she asks, concerned by his behaviour. She stops him and looks at his face closely. She is saddened immediately by the blank expression on his face.

"Where is she?" he asks despairingly.

"Who? Where is who, Dad?" She tries so hard to get a reply.

"Carrie. Where is my Carrie?"

By now everyone has gathered in the living room. Apart from the music coming from the dining room there is silence and the atmosphere that was once filled with joy is now filled with dismay.

"Dad, Carrie lives far away. Do you remember she moved away a long time ago?" Amy says while trying to console her father with a hug.

It is not what he wanted to hear, and Frank pushes her away. "No, she didn't, she wouldn't leave me," he explodes in a rage.

"Frank, I know you are confused right now but that does not give you an excuse to be aggressive," Jane explains quite firmly.

Frank puts his head down and stands there without a reaction. Jane assists Amy to get up and some of the family return to the dining room.

"I want to go home," Frank says.

"That's okay, Granddad, I will bring you home," Jake assures him.

Quietly behind Frank, who isn't reacting in any way, there is a conversation going on between Amy, Jake and Jane.

"Someone needs to tell him," Amy says.

"What good would that do?" Jane responds.

"It may not do any good at all but it might give him some answers. He obviously wants to see her and he can't." Jake shares his thoughts.

There is a momentary pause and then Jane says, "What would you say to him? The daughter you so love and adore is losing her memory just as quickly as you are?"

"No, of course not, but there must be some way we can get it across to him," Amy responds.

"Let's see how he goes today and then we will arrange something if he is persistent," Jake adds.

Jake moves cautiously closer and puts his hand on Frank's shoulder. All of the time they have been talking Frank has been unresponsive. I choose to focus on his thought frequency to explore what is going on in his mind.

I feel that he is in a dream-like state. He is focused on another reality. It seems to be a reality of his past. It can be associated to reminiscing as he is revisiting a significant moment that has contributed to his now.

He is younger in this reenaction, maybe in his twenties. I see a lady who has similar characteristics to Jane but she is certainly different. Her hair is dark and she is of slim build and of similar age to Frank. She has vibrancy around her and seems to be attracting all sorts of attention. The setting is a bar or a disco. There are people dancing on the rectangular wooden dance floor. They are jiving around the place. Frank seems to be situated in a specific position while he watches the crowd. The clothes he wears indicate that he is more of a formal presence than the happy crowd so I deduce that he is some type of security in his black trousers, white shirt, and black tie. He is closely watching Jane who is sitting at a table close to the bar. She is joined at her table by another lady with black hair and two men who are very friendly in their interactions. The man who is sitting closest to Jane rises from his seat and goes to the bar. Frank makes his way towards the man at the bar but before he reaches him the man has collected the four short glasses and mixers and returned to the table to the cheers of Jane and her friend. One of the men asks Jane's friend to dance and she accepts the invitation. Jane sits watching as her friend dances and she starts to mimic dancing in her seat. She is singing and swaying to the music, and when she is approached for a dance she accepts immediately. Frank doesn't look too happy with what he is witnessing and this must be obvious to the other security guy who approaches Frank and informs him that he is to move to front door duty. Frank reluctantly retreats through the double doors. A short time later he witnesses Jane's dance partner go to the men's toilets. He makes his excuses and follows him. The unsuspecting man is shocked when he is pushed against a wall by a very hot headed Frank.

"If you go anywhere near my wife again you will have me to answer to, do you understand?"

"Who, Jane? Is she your wife, I am sorry man, she never said that she was married."

"Let this be your warning to back off!" Frank emphasises.

"Okay man, okay," he says with his hands held up beside each side of his head in retreat.

Frank backs away but as he does the man says, "You would need to keep her on a leash man, she is giving out the wrong message."

Just as he has the last word, Frank propels around and plants a left hook into the jaw of the unsuspecting man. He is thrust against the wall and loses consciousness as he slithers down to the floor. Frank takes one last look at him and then leaves the room. Going through the doorway he meets someone he knows.

"Hey, Frank, how are ya?" the tall dark-haired guy enquires.

"Yeah, good Noel, and you?" Franks responds.

"Good, Frank, good. Hey, what happened to your guy there?" he asks, pointing to the guy slumped against the wall.

"Drunk, I expect. I am going to get one of the other lads to help me move him," he says to his concerned friend.

Frank continues out into the foyer to call the lads to assist him. They come almost immediately and in no time at all there are four men in black ties and white shirts carrying the man out towards the front entrance. Jane, who seems to be going to the toilets with her friend, witnesses the incident and she gives Frank a disapproving look that is so filled with venom it would cut through ice. He continues with the task in hand and they place the unconscious man at the front entrance to sober up.

I have seen enough for now. Frank has obviously not dealt directly with issues of the past and this is only one example of probably many instances that he has experienced through his many years. His ego took charge in this case and he did not deal well with the issue in hand, which is that he was not comfortable with his wife's behaviour. Giving how she reacted when she witnessed the man being carried out she believes that Frank is in the wrong and not her. Two wrongs certainly do not make a right but they are an opportunity for learning. In this instance the main issue is being suppressed and overpowered by the strong influence Frank has in his position of authority.

Sometimes we do not deal with the emotions that are connected to the experiences we endure. When we suppress our emotions we halt the opportunity to spiritually grow. It is often at the end of our life that we regret these decisions as it is then we want to have advanced as far as we can in preparation for our passing. When someone experiences stillness of the mind they are often dealing with the emotions they have not dealt with in the past and which have slowed their progression towards enlightenment.

We are now back with his family. Frank seems more responsive as he looks around.

"Are you ready to go home now, Granddad?" Jake calls.

Looking up at his grandson he says, "Yes, son, I am. I don't like being in strange places."

They all look at one another. Amy appears to be especially disheartened as she puts a tissue to her mouth to hold back her cry as she dashes out of the room.

It is often very hard for a family to experience this coldness from their loved ones. The unfamiliarity expressed by the sufferer as they disconnect for a time from the emotional memories they have of their family and friends is often a burden on those who are close to them. On many occasions sufferers can become aggressive but that can be caused due to confusion and facing the emotions they have not dealt with previously.

I shall leave Frank for now, and I feel encouraged that he is presently enduring the struggle connected to spiritual advancement.

CHAPTER ELEVEN
Carrie

I have now been guided to Carrie. It was not a long trip for me as I can instantly relocate my entity around the globe. It does tend to drain my energy slightly though so I take some time out to recharge before I proceed.

I am in a busy built up area. The sea is not too far away, I can smell it in the air. Everything seems brighter here and, although Frank comes from a place that embraces the spirit, this place radiates spirituality. It is very strong; I can feel it enter my energy field. I imagine there are very many connected people here.

I am outside a home that is in the middle of a side street overlooking a bustling shopping centre. Trees screen the front of the home, I suspect to create shade from the heat of the sun. The front door opens and a young woman comes out. She is in her late teens or early twenties and she is saying goodbye to someone. Carrie comes to the door.

"Bye, love, will you call me later?" Carrie asks as she hugs the girl.

"Yes, Mum, I live here. Remember? Of course I will be back later."

"Of course you do, silly me. Be careful," Carrie responds.

I follow Carrie back into the house. She walks down the hall into the living room where she takes a seat on the large cosy rectangular lounge. She puts her head in her hands and says to herself, "Why is this happening to you?" Then she starts to punch a pillow in the corner. "You need your mind, you are a mum, and you need your mind because you still have so much to do," she says and then the tears just flood down her face.

They cease as quicly as they started as she appears to suddenly be entranced by something, just as Frank was. I decide to join her on her inner journey of revisitation.

I can see a very young Carrie, possibly in her teens. She is all dressed up and with a group of friends, both boys and girls, in a cosy living room; she seems to be the youngest of the group. They are drinking alcohol, wine and beer bottles are being whisked away by a tall organised woman who I presume to be in her early twenties.

"Don't spill anything on my carpet or you will be licking it up, Nigel, do you hear me?" she implores.

"Chill out, Francis, he'll not waste a drop knowing him," one of the other girls says jokingly to everyone' amusement.

Just as she has the words out Nigel spills some beer on the rug.

"You clumsy git, you are going to have to sit outside," she screams at him.

Everyone looks at one another when she leaves the room with all the bottles.

Carrie gets up to follow her and grabs some other rubbish on the way.

"Are you okay, Francis?" she cautiously asks when she enters the kitchen.

"It's not them that has the smell of stale drink in their house all week, Carrie, what about Elsie? She is only six, it's not on."

"Yes, you're right. What time is the babysitter coming?" Carrie asks.

"She should be here soon."

"Right, well I will get everyone to come to the pub with me and then you can follow us, does that sound good?" Carrie tries to remedy the situation.

"Oh, do what you want, Carrie," Francis snaps back at her and goes to leave the room.

"Hey, what did I say wrong? I am only trying to help." Carrie tries to find an answer.

Francis stops. "It is always me that is left behind to follow, you are all free to do what you want, and I have to sit waiting on a babysitter," she says, feeling sorry for herself.

Carrie doesn't respond and so Francis turns and keeps walking to the living room where she puts on some music for her guests.

I track Carrie's thoughts. What just happened there? she thinks. I tried to help and then I made things worse. There is no helping some people. She has it all, a reasonably secure home, a beautiful daughter and friends who are there for her but she doesn't appreciate any of it, I wonder why? Carrie then makes her way up the stairs to the toilet. She hears a little call from the bedroom with the name Elsie in bright letters on the door.

"Carrie," the little girl calls.

Carrie goes into the room. "What's wrong, Elsie, I thought you were asleep?"

"I can't it is too noisy," she says, frightened.

"Why didn't you call someone if you are afraid?" Carrie asks.

"Mommy told me not to get out of my bed," she replies innocently.

"Oh Elsie." Carrie gives her a hug. "It will be okay, we are all going out in a minute when the babysitter comes and then there won't be any noise."

"I don't want a babysitter, Carrie. I just want Mommy or you to mind me," she cries.

"It's okay, Elsie, you just try your best to go to sleep and then it will be morning and the sun will be shining through your window, and I will bring you to the park and for an ice-lolly."

Elsie's eyes light up. "Really, you promise?"

"I promise," Carrie says, holding out her little finger. Elsie hooks her finger into Carrie's, and they smile at each other.

Then there are footsteps coming up the stairs and Elsie looks scared again as she hides her head under the covers.

Francis barges into the room.

"What is wrong with her?" she asks in a dominating manner.

"Elsie is a bit scared and can't sleep," Carrie replies.

"You go to sleep this instant, young lady, or you will be sorry," she roars. "Do you hear me?"

"Yes, Mommy," calls a muffled voice from underneath the covers.

They leave the room and make their way back to the living room where the babysitter has arrived and everyone is ready to go.

I follow as they stop off at the nearest pub. The drink is flowing excessively and the group is getting quite drunk. Carrie is getting a lot of attention from men, which doesn't surprise me as she is glowing fun and energy feminine vibes. There is a karaoke and Francis has written Carrie's name on a piece of paper and given it to the organiser.

"Are you going up to sing?" *Carrie innocently enquires.*

"No, you are," *Francis responds, laughing and with a hint of malice, and then she takes a drink.*

Carrie's facial expression speaks volumes, to Francis's amusement. Then her name is called out, the organiser won't take no for an answer and the crowd starts chanting. Carrie just wants the ground to swallow her up. I tap into her feelings and she has high levels of fear and embarrassment. She eventually gets up and takes centre stage.

"Hello, Carrie, what would you like to sing for us all tonight?" *the organiser enquires.*

"Something easy," *she responds into the microphone.*

"Okay, my choice then," *the organiser responds in an upbeat way.*

The song starts and a very nervous Carrie begins to sing the words on the screen, each moment so painful to her. Her nerves are quite evident. Then there is a call from the crowd, "Come on, Carrie, you can do it". *Suddenly it is as if she is overcome by a moment where her fears and inhibitions disappear and she begins to sing her heart out, she gives the song everything she has got and then some. She really begins to look like she is enjoying herself immensely and the crowd is loving the* transformation and they are all singing and dancing along, cheering her on. She looks and sounds really good, to the obvious horror of Francis who looks to be very jealous. I believe she is not a positive friend to Carrie at all. The song ends and the crowd claps. Carrie goes back to her seat. She graciously smiles and humbly accepts all of the compliments with gratitude.

"Can I buy you a drink?" asks one guy who has quickly made his way to her side. Francis is horrified and Carrie looks to her. It is obvious that Francis is hot on this guy.

"Yes, you sure can, but you will have to buy my friend Francis a drink also. Have you met Francis before?" says Carrie, being a true friend, because I sense through her emotions that she likes this guy also.

"Yes, Francis and I are old school friends, isn't that right, Francis?"

"Yes, we are, Mike," Francis responds, smitten.

They have some drinks and the guy asks if they are going to the road house. Francis has taken over the conversation and so organises with Mike that they share a taxi with him.

Before long they have arrived at the roadhouse. The music is wanting to blast out of the windows and doors as it pulsates the walls. Mike gets out of the taxi and pays and the girls get out too. He also pays for their entrance to the disco. They enter through the doors and everyone turns to take a look at the newest arrivals. Francis makes it her business for everyone to see that she has arrived with Mike.

"Do you ladies want a drink?" Mike asks.

"It is my turn to get you a drink, Mike," Carrie insists as she makes her way to the crowded bar. In the meantime, Francis and Mike have found a spot. Carrie finally locates them with a handful of drinks. Carrie seems to love a beat as she moves to the music.

They stand there sipping at their drinks until they are almost finished. Mike has not offered to buy another one and so Carrie says, "Anyone for another drink?"

"Maybe Francis would like to treat us this time around," Mike encourages.

A slightly shocked Francis replies, "Oh yes, of course, where are my manners?" She reaches into her pocket and takes out a note.

"Carrie, will you be a doll and get us another round?" she pushes Carrie to agree.

"Ah, that's not fair, Francis. Carrie has already been to the bar. Anyway we will go and have dance while you go to the bar."

Francis is horrified and is finding it hard to swallow.

Carrie lowers her head, smiling but trying to avoid eye contact with Francis.

She and Mike are really having fun dancing on the dance floor. Francis has returned with the drinks but cannot leave them unattended and so she is forced to stand holding them. After a few dances Carrie and Mike return for a refreshment.

"Have fun?" Francis enquires.

"Yes, that was great fun, you can really move, Carrie," Mike says.

They drink their drinks, and Mike goes to the bar.

"Right, Carrie, you are ruining my chances here," Francis says.

"I am sorry, Francis, I was just dancing," Carrie responds.

"Whenever he comes back I am going to ask him out to dance, the slow set should be coming on soon, that should do the trick."

"Sure, Francis, no worries," Carrie agrees.

When Mike comes back he asks Carrie if she is ready to get boogying again.

Carrie jumps as Francis has just nipped her in the backside. "Maybe you should ask Francis out to dance, Mike, she is a great dancer too," she says, encouraging them on to the dance floor.

She watches as Francis is all over Mike trying to impress him. It is so obvious and Mike does not seem in the slightest bit interested. In the meantime, Carrie has been joined by another interested guy. They are talking and having fun together right through the slow set.

Mike and Francis return to their drinks. Before long the music comes to an end and the lights are brighter indicating it is time to drink up and leave.

Carrie smiles and says, "I must go to the ladies' room, please excuse me."

"Me too, I will come with you," says Francis.

They walk off to the ladies' room together. As they enter they get chatting about the night.

Suddenly there is a bang on their cubicle door.

"Francis Higgins, is that you I hear in there?" someone shouts in an unfriendly manner.

By the look on Francis's face she knows exactly who it is and why they are not happy to hear her. She doesn't respond and then she mimes to Carrie to stick with her and that there might be a fight. Carrie looks disappointed. I sense she doesn't want to. Francis opens the door.

"Oh Julia, how lovely to see you at the end of the night."

"Not as lovely as it is to see you, Francis, and smooching all over Mike too, well there are no limits to how far you go."

"You guys have broken up, Julia, you need to move on," Francis says in an uncompassionate tone.

"Oh, you have gotten all brazen now that you have someone by your side, haven't you, Frankie!" she taunts.

"Well, Carrie has put many a person in their box, Julia, so if you don't want to be the next one I advise that you move on."

"Ah you are trying hard not to be dorky, Francis, aren't you? Well let me tell you something, getting someone else to fight your battles for you doesn't cut it," Julia says.

Francis then pushes Julia against the wall and begins slapping her. It is not a pretty sight as Julia overwhelms her almost immediately. I can see that Carrie doesn't want to step in but she can't stand and watch as Francis gets bullied again. She gets closer and attempts to unhinge the lock Julia has on her friend. Julia swings her fist and Carrie ducks and she punches the wall instead. Julia lets out a roar of pain and lets Francis go.

"So you want to play dirty then?" Julia challenges and lunges at Carrie.

Carrie lifts her fist and plants it on her face. Julia falls to the ground unconscious. Francis is delighted and hugs Carrie. Carrie looks despondent; she really didn't want this to happen. There were a few other girls watching and they ran to Julia's aid.

"Come on, Carrie, before the bouncers come." Francis grabs Carrie's hand and pulls her out of the door.

They make their way through the dispersed crowd back to where they were standing and to Francis's disappointment Mike is nowhere to be seen. The bouncers seem to be coming towards them to either usher them out or because they have identified them. They choose not to hang around and quickly make their way outside.

There are a lot of people hanging around outside. One girl makes her way hurriedly towards Carrie and Francis. She has auburn curly hair to her shoulders and appears shorter than Carrie.

"Sis, I am so happy to see you," she says while hugging Carrie. She is all out of breath as if she has been running.

"You too, is everything okay?" Carrie responds.

"I need you to come with me quickly. Shelley is in a fight at the roadhouse pub, and she needs you to bale her out."

It's as if Carrie is overcome by something. I invade her thoughts to see what is going on. My sister needs me; we must always defend our family. We have a rep to protect. No one hurts my family and gets away with it.

"Right, let's go then," Carrie says, all geared up for a fight.

I have seen enough, I do not need to see any more brutality. I am surprised that this is part of Carrie's past as she seems to be a person so filled with love now in her present. But it is important that we never judge the path of another's soul. Carrie obviously feels this is her duty.

Back in the now I watch as Carrie sits there still entranced. In through the door to her living room comes a young girl. She quite resembles Arianna in her angelic looks and her pure aura. This takes me aback somewhat.

"Mum, are you there?" she innocently calls out; her voice is one that I have not heard before.

She enters the living room where her mum sits entranced. Concerned by what she sees she quickly runs to Carrie's side and wraps her arms around her mum.

"Mum, can you hear me, Mum?" she whispers in sadness and despair.

Carrie blinks and looks to her daughter. She struggles to get away from her embrace.

"Get off me or you will get one too," she shouts, to the horror of her daughter.

"Mum, it's me, Sarah. Please remember me, Mum," she pleads.

Carrie stares at her, totally confused by what she is suggesting.

"Mum, please try to remember. It is me, Sarah, your daughter. I won't give up on you, Mum. I know you will remember me," she says, coming closer to Carrie and holding her hand and then gazing into her eyes.

Carrie looks right into her daughter's bright blue eyes and then there is a momentary silence as she seems to be searching for something. Sarah sits there with her eyes open knowing that she must be patient. Suddenly Carrie's face changes, it is as if she has found what she is looking for.

"Sarah, it is really you. I was so frightened, I did something terrible. Oh, I am so happy to see you," she says to the relief of a heartbroken and concerned Sarah.

"It's okay, Mum, I am here now, I will help you." She hugs her mum so tightly, not wanting to let go.

"I love you, Sarah," Carrie says with so much feeling.

"I love you too, Mum," Sarah says and a tear slides down her cheek. She knows her mum is never going to be as she was and she knows that Carrie will become more and more distant. She has so much love for her mum, and she doesn't want this moment of connection to end. I do believe if time stopped right now and she had to live in this moment for some time to come she would not mind, she has her mum close to her and they are both united in an intimate moment.

I shall leave her for now and return shortly.

CHAPTER TWELVE
Joyce

I arrive at a location which appears to be a country home. There is a lush green highly maintained lawn that wraps itself around the large two-storey residence. The building itself is made from grey stone and the windows are large, white painted and with smaller individual glass panels inside the thicker frame.

I get the impression this is not a personal home; there are people in white uniforms pushing people in wheelchairs around and others walking with older people outside. I'm drawn towards a lady whom I recognise to be Joyce. She is sitting on a bench with a crocheted blanket on her lap. She is busy talking to the lady sitting next to her and appears to be quite content.

She is discussing how the trees sway to and fro in the wind and how amazed she is by the process. Then out of nowhere she says, "I was always a taker you see, I took away something precious so now the good Lord is taking my mind. When I did give back it wasn't enough."

"Oh, I am sure it is not like that at all," replies the lady.

"Oh, but you see, dear, it is very much like that. What you give out you will receive in return. Sure I don't even know your name, have I seen you before?"

"Yes, Nan, you have seen me many times before," says the young lady.

"Nan, is that my name?" Joyce asks.

"No, Nan, your name is Joyce."

"But then why do you call me Nan?" She looks ahead all of the time displaying no emotion. The young girl squeezes Joyce's hand a little tighter.

"Because I am your granddaughter, Nan, that is why."

"Oh," Joyce replies and then she gets back to chatting about the trees and how they are blowing in a certain direction. Her granddaughter does not appear to be too distraught. She seems to have gained a level of acceptance which leads me to ascertain that Joyce has been unwell for some time.

I begin to receive a flashback. I see an image of a very young Joyce in a police uniform. I allow my mind to transcend.

I find myself on a road. It is neither dark nor light so it is either dawn or dusk. There are a few scattered houses around but there does not appear to be any activity. A maroon-coloured saloon car is situated at the side of the road somewhat hidden from view. Joyce stands with other police officers. Their uniform is dark in colour and they have formal brimmed hats. They appear to be waiting for something and one of them is holding a red hand light. The energy around them is not positive, I feel the intention of their activity is not in the pursuit of good. They are all chatting to one another in an informal manner as they bide time. A low-

flying helicopter momentarily lands in a nearby field and disappears as quickly as it appeared. I can see movement in the fields but I cannot determine exactly what it is. Then flooding out onto the road are about ten soldiers in their camouflage uniform. They are prepped for the worst case scenario with their survival packs and intimidating guns.

A message comes through on a walkie talkie device.

"Target is fast approaching from the east. Take position," the voice orders through the little black box.

The police position themselves on the road and the soldiers in the ditches where they have their guns ready.

A car can be heard in the distance but not seen. This is strange as the road is so long and the engine noise is getting louder.

"They are coming closer, get ready," someone says in a panic-filled voice.

In the distance there are two dim lights that have become slightly visible. One of the male officers stands out in the road and circles the red torch indicating to the oncoming vehicle to stop. The car stops before it reaches the officer and sits for a few moments. The anticipation in the air is strong. All of the officers wait to react. Then just as quickly as the car stopped, it accelerates. It is apparent that the driver has no intention of stopping for the road block. The car picks up speed and heads straight for the first officer who jumps to safety in the roadside verge. The car then heads straight for two officers who are standing on the road. Joyce is one of these officers.

"Prepare the stinger," one officer shouts as Joyce pulls a gun from her holster.

"Joyce, don't shoot," the other officer shouts.

But it is too late, in a moment of sheer panic Joyce has pulled the trigger. As if in slow motion the bullet darts through the air straight for an unsuspecting target. It smashes through the window of the car and hits the driver. I watch as Joyce's eyes meet straight with her victim's. He is little more than a kid, about seventeen. I see horror in Joyce's eyes when she realises what she has done. This, of course, does not put a stop to the issue that there is an oncoming vehicle heading straight for her and so the other officer jumps sideways towards Joyce, saving her from danger. They both roll down a short bank and into a ditch. A stinger is flung across the road puncturing the tyres of the out of control vehicle. The car heads straight for the verge and flips over numerous times before coming to rest on its roof in the middle of a field.

All of the soldiers and officers run to the vehicle.

"He is still alive," one of the officers calls out.

The driver's face is bloodied and he is barely conscious. They try to get the driver's door open but cannot.

"It's no good, everyone move back."

There is smoke coming from under the bonnet of the car. It quickly worsens.

"It's going to blow, quick, get away from the car," another officer shouts.

"No, we can't just leave him in there!" Joyce shouts as she runs to the passenger side door.

"Leave the bastard, he's not worth saving," shouts one of the soldiers and tries to pull her back.

Joyce pushes him away and he falls over onto his behind. She then works fast and with super strength to drag the driver out of the car. Just as she gets him out one of the men comes to help her.

"Crazy bitch," he says and then begins to drag the young man to safety. Joyce walks behind them. In that instant the car blows up and they are sent flying in all directions. Joyce gets the worst of the blast as she is closest. The arm of her jacket has caught fire and she is trying desperately to put it out. In doing so she is burning her other hand.

She finally extinguishes the flames and then she runs to be at the side of the young lad. He is barely conscious. He looks deep into her eyes. She takes his hand, connecting now with her compassionate side and not the robotic officer that created this horror.

"Lady, tell my son that I will always love him," the driver says.

"You will be able to tell him yourself, you will be okay," she replies.

Struggling for breath he says, "You are the one who pulled the trigger, lady... you have taken my life...my son needs to know that I love him...you need to tell him."

Joyce drops her head. "I will tell him, I promise you that I will tell him," she responds to his dying wish.

At that his head falls to the side and he moves on. I see the energies leave his lifeless body and drift upwards towards the skies. I know he will now be in peace and love.

She screams, "No! What have I done?"

Frantically, she starts pushing her hands up and down on the boy's rib cage.

The officer who has been with her throughout the whole scenario tries to lift her off. "Joyce, it is no good, he is gone, let him go."

She struggles with him. "No, he can't be gone, I can't have done this," she cries, dropping to her knees beside the lifeless body. She lifts the man's head up onto her lap and strokes it.

"I am so sorry, I am so sorry," she cries, rocking forwards and backwards.

Her colleagues stand by as Joyce breaks down before their eyes. Some are clearly disgusted, others compassionate but no one attempts to comfort her during her moment of need.

The emergency services can be heard speedily coming to the rescue. It is too late for the young lad but is it too late for Joyce, I wonder.

This incident has obviously been a major turning point in her life. She has either harboured guilt about the reality of it all most of her life and tried to make amends, or shielded herself from the emotion of it all for the sake of her career. Either way this event has defined her existence in some way or I would not have been guided to this moment of her past.

For many of us our lives are defined by many significant moments that combine to make us who we are in our future. Our spirit grows and learns with each positive and negative experience. I get the feeling that Joyce has more than made amends for her wrongdoing; although what she did was morally wrong she may have served her penance and her spirit may have evolved past the darkness towards enlightenment. My concern is that her present situation is so that she can seek inwards to deal with forgiveness. I sense that all of her life since that incident she has been unable to forgive herself, whereas in order to free ourselves from the pain and guilt of past events we need to forgive and move forward towards freedom of our spirits. If we love ourselves we will learn from our mistakes and endeavour to not duplicate them. Joyce may have worn a police uniform but she felt the full moral effects of her actions.

I shall return to spend some further time with her in the now to ascertain if the knowledge I am receiving is correct.

When I return I see there appears to be an energy field around Joyce that I have not witnessed before. There is something magical about it. The energy is strong and positive and solely generated for her. I watch as the waves of magic caress her from head to toes and slowly back up again where they then levitate.

"Isn't that beautiful, Denise," she says peacefully to her granddaughter.

The young girl is so overjoyed that her Nan has remembered her name that she springs up and down in delight.

"You know my name, Nan, you said Denise," she exclaims.

A little baffled by the overreaction, Joyce replies, "Of course, dear child, what else would I call you?"

Denise hugs her Nan and kisses her cheek. "Oh, thank you, Nan," she gently says with tears running down her cheeks.

"Oh, my love, it is okay, there is nothing so bad to warrant so much sadness," Joyce says, comforting her granddaughter.

"These are tears of joy, Nan, I love you and before you leave again I want to thank you for always being there for me when I needed you throughout my life. To me you are my world, the best Nan ever."

Now tears fill Joyce's eyes and grandmother and granddaughter just sit there in a loving embrace. People walk past and say, "Aw." I suppose it is because there are not many displays of affection here. Patients can become so detached from their emotional connections with their families that they often don't connect on such levels. This leads me to consider that there are other energies at work in this scenario.

I effortlessly tune into the frequency of the magical energy that still surrounds Joyce. I choose to travel to its origin. While on my journey I feel nothing but peace, love and goodwill and I know that the origin of this magic is located in a thoughtful, caring place. I feel the strength of it, a united force.

When I arrive at the location I observe a serene atmosphere. The room itself is big enough to accommodate the twenty or so inhabitants. They are all standing in the middle of the room holding hands with their eyes closed. I am drawn to a particular lady who seems to be guiding the others.

She says in a gentle almost whispering voice:

"Joyce, we combine all of our loving energy and send it to you via the universal channels that be. May our love combined give you strength and peace to help you along your journey during this time. The more love we give, the more love that we have to give, our supply is never ending. Our love is yours right now, our beautiful friend, and may it stay with you in your heart and comfort your soul."

There is a pause for a few minutes. The ladies all stand holding each other's hands gently with their eyes comfortably closed and their heads relaxed down, their chins touching their chests. The energy that gravitates from each woman and congregates in the centre of the circle is mesmerising to witness in this powerful moment. It accumulates there above them all awaiting release.

The lady continues, "We now transcend our combined energy to you, Joyce, may it find you well and give you much needed light to see through the darkness." She raises her arms and each participant follows. "Our love to you, our friend," she calls.

The energy rises on command and in a flash it has dispersed.

There is silence for a time and then the lady leading the circle gives permission for everyone to relax and let go. They open their eyes one by one. Each of the ladies seems to have been *positively affected by what they have done and this is evident in the smiles on their faces and the array of energies circulating in the atmosphere. This is a very strong circle, the strongest I have ever witnessed. These women know and believe in the potential of their loving energy and they use it in a positive way, to heal others. What a gift and how fortunate Joyce is to have this support during her journey. This energy is strength, power to create miracles. Channelling combined energy in this way projects goodness to those areas that need it most. It can never be underestimated.*

I am happy to leave Joyce at this point; I have had enough insight into her past and her current influences for now.

CHAPTER THIRTEEN
Henry

I arrive at a park-side location. I am drawn to two women who are sitting on bistro style chairs having some refreshments at an intimate upper class street cafe. One of the women is significantly older than the other which indicates a bond other than friendship. The older lady is dressed very demurely in a pencil skirt suit and her glossy brown hair is styled up in a sophisticated way. She is very pristine, her makeup is flawless and her slim figure is perfect for her. It is evident that she eats only quality nutritious food as her skin glows and not one ounce of fat is to be seen on her face or body. She appears to have had a luxurious life. The younger lady is familiar to me. She too looks to be from an upper class origin. She is also well groomed but her attire is a more relaxed blouse and expensive jeans with pumps and her sandy hair is tied back in a ponytail. I now recognise her from the vision I had when I was introduced to Henry's profile.

"Mum, what are we going to do for him?" the young lady asks.

"My darling child, that man has caused me enough heartache in my life. I am not sacrificing one molecule of myself for him anymore."

"But Mum, he is not well, he needs our help."

"Why? Just because he is squandering his money and only thinking of himself? I am sorry ,love, but he has always done that. We just hid that from you when you were growing up."

"No, Mum, you don't understand. He is not familiar with things anymore. He doesn't know where he is at times. I have been called by the emergency services a few times because they have found him miles from home and delirious."

"That would be the drink, love," her mum spits out.

"But that is the thing, Mum, he wasn't drinking on any of those occasions. There is something very wrong and he won't listen to me. He shouldn't be driving a car; he is a danger to himself and others and as for the bailiff situation…"

Her mum turns her head in a stubborn manner, trying her hardest not to let her daughter break her decision.

"Please, Mum, just help me get him to the doctor's before something else happens. Please."

"Okay, Emile, but I am doing it for you, not him. Understood?"

"Yes, Mum. Thank you, Mum," she says, drinking her coffee quickly.

"What, now?" her mother exclaims.

"Yes, now, Mum, there is no time like the present." She stands to put on her jacket and then makes her way to the other side of the table to help her mum get her things together.

"Give me a moment please, love," she says poshly as she composes herself.

"Ready then, Mum, let's go."

"My darling child, have you ever considered that maybe it is you with the forgetfulness?" her mother says, raising her eyes in an attempt to trigger a response.

"Sorry, Mum, but is there something I am forgetting?"

"We must not forget to pay. Honestly, you do take after your father, you know. How embarrassing it would be to leave without paying." She pulls out a luxury leather purse and places a large note on the table, gesturing for the waitress to come. Finally rising from her seat she ensures that she has everything in place and finally flicks her cashmere shawl over her shoulder to the relief of her patient daughter.

I pick up from this conversation that Henry has not been the easiest person to share a significant part of this lady's life. She has obviously felt challenged by Henry during their time together and vice versa as she appears to have many rigid standards that she expects to be adhered to in her presence. Henry has spent most of his life in the spotlight and so anything untoward usually has a tendency to get scrutinised and highlighted. This lady thinks a lot of appearances and the impression that others have of her so maybe life under the watchful eye of the world's media was not the best circumstance for her.

However, we all come to earth to learn more about ourselves and each challenge is individual as it is an opportunity for our spirits to grow and advance towards enlightenment. Many people choose to run away from life's challenges, shielding themselves from the pain; whereas if they were to somewhat embrace the challenges in the moment, then reasoning, comfort and healing often follows as a reward for courage. Our bodies and minds are equipped to deal with so much more than we credit them for. Many people don't realise until later years that there are so many opportunities in life for personal learning. Or maybe it is that many of us are so busy focusing on other things that our spiritual wellbeing is not often considered until our latter years.

It is tougher to learn as we advance through life whereas if we are encouraged to listen to our inner guide from a young age, the journey through life may be a simpler more fulfilling experience as we will be guided towards our best, happy and most fulfilling life.

My vision earlier did not feature Henry himself just as this recent visit didn't either. He must be an elusive character who impacts on the lives of those around him, even when he is not physically present. I feel that his presence leaves residue wherever it shadows. Now with his mind experiencing obscurity it is time for him to face up to that which he chooses to avoid so that he can finally move forward spiritually in time for his departure from this eventful lifetime. I sense that he is not a bad person, he is an unfortunate one.

A a lot of people never consider the prospect of death and some who do often fear it, so they create for themselves an unrealistic concept of what moving on signifies. Each of us has been gifted with a life, our life is precious, and we are also gifted with the magic that is our body and minds. Inside each of our bodies is a magical core that guides us through our lifetime. Our inner spirit may not always be heard, but it is always there waiting for us to recognise its existence. When we first come into the world our spirit is pure, untarnished by the influences of life. The family we are born into then influences us, and this may determine somewhat how we connect with our inner self. Some of us will endure a tougher experience than others and this may seem unfair in some respect but those who take the time to move forward will be rewarded for the suffering that has hurt their hearts. No challenge is ever in vain. This wisdom has been gifted to me from the well of enlightenment, the universal source of wisdom that is sent to us messengers during our missions. It assists us in our comprehension of life as we carry out our tasks.

I feel that I must now pursue Henry and experience him first hand. With all of my might I focus my energy to connect with his current location. I do not know why but I am finding this virtually impossible. I try again but to no avail. It then occurs to me that his daughter and wife may by en route to find him and so because I have recently been directly in contact with them I will be able to hone in on their vibrational frequency and join them in their pursuit.

We arrive at an outlandish location. It is a backstreet bar with neon lights of girls with the sign Hooray Henrietta above the door.

"So this is where your father has spent most of his life and most of our money," Phyllis says in disgust.

"This is where I was told he would be, Mum, I am sorry but he obviously is crying out for help."

"Oh darling, that is not a cry, that is a selfish and seedy indulgence."

"Shall we just see if he is here? We have come this far, we can't turn back now."

"If it must be done then let's get on with it, I am certainly not letting you go in there alone."

They make their way towards the door. Beyond the doorway it is dark and coloured lights are glowing. On entering Phyllis brushes herself down and gasps in disgust when she is exposed to the stale smell of beer and smoke and the arrangement of the establishment. A man is behind a bar drying glasses, he has a rugged handsomeness about him. His eyes are hazel brown and match his well-groomed hazel brown hair and his six-foot strong stature. He calls out in a sarcastic voice.

"May I be of assistance, ladies? Looking for a job perhaps?"

Wrapping her cardigan a little tighter around her body, Phyllis states in disgust, "Most certainly not."

Emile giggles and then approaches the bar. "We are looking for my father, Henry Whistler, do you know where he is?"

"Oh, you are Henry's daughter?" he says intrigued and quite taken aback by her.

"Yes," says Phyllis, "and I am his ex-wife, could you please tell us where he is so that we can see him and get out of here."

"I haven't seen him in a while; in fact, I have been trying to track him down. I have been a bit worried about him lately; he doesn't seem to be himself."

"Yes, we know that," Emile replies, concerned. "Oh, I wonder where he could be."

"Well, he is not here, so let's get out of this dump." Phyllis gives a shiver.

"Thank you for your help." Emile holds out her hand to shake that of the barman.

"John, and your name is…?"

"Oh, yes, sorry. I am Emile, here is my card, and would you be kind enough to call should my dad come here today?"

"Most certainly, Emile, it would be my pleasure," he says.

"Emile, let's go," says Phyllis.

Emile smiles at the barman and then turns to follow her mum towards the door.

"Oh ladies, I did hear that he has been spending some time up at the cathedral recently."

"The cathedral?" Phyllis explodes in laughter.

"Maybe he is trying to redeem himself, Mum."

"Well let's go see for ourselves, shall we, this should be interesting." She waits for her daughter to open the door for her.

"Thanks for all of your help, John," calls Emile

"No probs, anytime."

As they are leaving, a half-naked woman comes out of a side room. She is a little defensive when she sees the expression of horror on Phyllis's face.

"What are you looking at, lady? Have you never seen a body before?"

In desperation Phyllis rushes outside and gasps for air. It all seems too much for her.

***

It takes very little time to reach the cathedral.

"It is beautiful, isn't it?" breathes Emile

"It truly is but only your father would have us venturing from a brothel to a cathedral in one morning."

"Mum, it was not a brothel."

"I feel quite unclean now, do you not? I thought that I brought you up better than that, Emile, I really did."

"Oh, Mum, give over," Emile laughs.

"Well let's keep moving then," Phyllis says impatiently.

They enter this grand and architecturally magnificent building through two large doors that are made of the darkest wood and decorated with carvings so intricate in detail that I am convinced they had to have been carved by gifted loving hands. A melodious tune is being played by a lady seated near the front of this gigantic room on a little raised platform. Hundreds of long pews line the three aisles.

There are a few people gathered at the top of the main aisle and Emile encourages her mum to follow her. Phyllis is obviously uncomfortable in this environment, but she follows Emile regardless.

There are about twenty people scattered amongst the first few pews. They are all kneeling with bowed heads. Emile quickly slips into a pew behind the others and her mother joins her.

The music stops and there is silence. The energy I feel from all of these devoted people is filled with peace and love. They are here doing a little bit of goodness for themselves and others. They don't need to shout it from the rooftops, they are satisfied to be in the knowing that they are being true to their beliefs and sending some goodness out there into the world to reach those in need.

There is a special glow surrounding some of those who are kneeling. I am guided towards thinking that they have been truly enlightened. One lady in particular glows with radiant beauty that shines from right within her tiny frame. The gathering raise their heads from their humble praying position. I move to where I can see them all. As I do the glowing lady stands and turns around to face the others, but I still cannot see her face. However, I can see that Henry is sitting beside her. He looks up to her in adoration. Suddenly the glowing lady begins to talk in the most calm and heavenly voice.

"My friend Henry has come here today in search of guidance. He feels lost in this vast world. He feels confused as all that is familiar to him is now not so familiar. He has sinned in his time but now he is seeking forgiveness and has asked us to help guide him towards enlightenment."

She turns to Henry, cups his face in her hands and says, "Henry, you have it within you to move towards enlightenment; you need only believe it and open yourself up to the possibility of connecting with your inner guide who will direct you along your path. Forgive yourself for all of your wrongdoings; it is okay to do so as they have been part of your earthly learning. Your inner spirit guided you here, to us, so that we could support you. It has been there all along but you did not choose to listen, now that you are willing to listen you have nothing to fear anymore."

Henry smiles in response, as if he is relieved of some of his burdens by hearing this.

"Let's all join together one more time and pray that Henry is guided towards enlightenment, he has taken the first steps himself and may he be guided along the rest of his path with ease."

She turns around, and I am taken aback. The face is so familiar, I should have realised from the energy I felt when I first saw her. It is Angela. She is my next assignment. Of course I know that people are drawn towards one another but this has caught me off guard. This angel knows that she is enduring the same harrowing journey as Henry and yet she puts another person's needs before her own. If only there were more Angelas in the world today the selfless act of sharing love through helping another in their moments of need may be experienced more.

Henry is in good hands here, and I finally got to experience his energy first-hand. He is a man of little needs and yet he has had so much material wealth throughout most of his life. This is not the food that he needed to nurture his soul and it is now that he seems to have connected with his guide and is searching for his spiritual breakthrough.

Angela is already there. She has obviously experienced her breakthrough early in her days and chose to live in peace and help others along their path to enlightenment. It is now time for me to connect with Angela and her journey in a bid to ascertain why it is that she needs my guidance.

I look to Emile and Phyllis before I leave. Emile is approaching her dad and giving him a hug. Phyllis's energy appears to have changed; it is now a more compassionate aura that surrounds her. She will have much to learn during this time also. I shall leave Henry now in the arms of his daughter and ex-wife. Now the breakthrough can commence, the struggle is almost over.

CHAPTER FOURTEEN
The Visit

Adjusting my focus to Angela has not occurred as smoothly as I expected it to. This is really quite bizarre given the close proximity of her presence. This shows that we should not always expect things to happen as we anticipate them to in any given moment as this is the quickest path to disappointment. I have learned that everything happens for a reason and sometimes divine intervention blocks our flow for a reason that may not be apparent initially but will reveal itself in time.

Behind me I feel a presence; the energy is so intense yet familiar. I try to turn and yet I feel I have no need to. This is a bizarre sensation.

"Boss," I call as I recognise his energy.

Right in front of me appears The Boss.

"My presence will be felt here, Gill, can you make your way outside?"

"Yes, of course," I reply, even though I imagine that something important is occurring because Boss's expression tells a story all of its own.

I take one last look over at Angela and wonder why it is so hard to penetrate her energy field. Why does she protect herself from me? She glances in my direction with a solemn gaze. There is something this angel has endured and not released the pain. She needs me, I know it, and when she sends a little smile in my direction my hunch is confirmed. It is as if she is aware of my reason for being here and is letting me know that it is okay, she knows I must go for now. I send a smile back in the hope that she knows I will return. Angel tears stem from heartaches that have the power to transform on a vast scale as they touch the hearts of many and remain for a lifetime with those who endure them first hand. Oh goodness, I suddenly remember that Boss is waiting for me outside. I must depart.

When I arrive outside, Boss is quite unsettled. I have never seen him like this, he always displays such strength and focus yet now he is pacing and fidgeting.

I approach him and ask, "Is everything okay, Boss?"

He takes a few more paces and then stops to meet me. "Something has happened and I need to reassign you."

Concerned by his actions I encourage him to sit with me on a nearby bench. "Can you share with me the details of this new assignment?"

"Yes, of course, but I need you to connect with your stem of knowing. The trust that everything happens for a reason, and that reasoning may not be apparent at first but all will become more transparent as you progress towards completion. It is important that you only focus positive energy onto this replacement."

"Yes, of course, Boss. What replacement?" I hope he will soon enlighten me about what has occurred.

For a few moments he stares out into the distance.

"Is there something wrong, Boss?" I enquire cautiously.

He looks straight into my eyes as if he is searching for something. I realise he is searching for trust and faith. "I need you to trust me on this one, Gilbert."

"Always, Boss. But is it all right for me to say that you seem a little uneasy about the choice you have made?"

Lifting his hands to his head and rubbing his eyes with his palms while strongly massaging his head with his fingers—a sure sign of a troubled thought—he says, "I have an emotional connection to your new assignment. I know it is not her time yet and she needs to be guided back to her physicality. She has not reached her potential enlightenment and she has an important role to play in the transition of someone special. I cannot say much more than that as it may hinder your role in the process."

I nod in agreement and choose to trust that I am going to be guided through the process. This is my first lone assignment and it is not following the protocol I became accustomed to during my training. I shall learn a lot through this experience.

Boss hands me a new folder. It is sealed with a gold stamp. I take it from him.

"This contains all the details of your new assignment. I know you are up to this, Gilbert. I have been watching you closely and trust in your connection to your spirit guide and the wisdom you encompass. Listen to your guide at all times and you will always make the right decision. I cannot interfere further in this assignment as my heart is connected to it and hinders any judgements I make. You are on your own with this one."

"I understand, Boss."

"Good, then I shall leave you to it," he says as he turns to walk away. Momentarily he turns back and adds, "Oh, and Gilbert, thank you." Then he disappears into the crowd of people marching past.

I sit there on the bench in slight disbelief at the turn of events. I look at the file and wonder when I need to open it. I try to remind myself to trust and have faith that I will know, my inner guide will let me know. Although right at this moment I feel as if my spirit signal seems to be slightly overshadowed with the fear of failure because I don't want to let Boss down. On the other hand I don't want to abandon Angela either. I do hope this is just an initial blip.

I try to open the file but the lock will not release. I try again and again and it is not shifting. Now I feel unsettled. What is going on? I try to calm down and when I feel more composed I decide to take some time out to go within and connect with my inner guide. A sense of calm overcomes me and I can see things more clearly. I am guided to move on and not open the file at this point, it is not yet time to.

I walk down the many steps that are laid out before me and when I reach the bottom I just stand there. A bus is going around in one lane of a nearby roundabout and I am drawn to a small open top car that is approaching. The driver seems distracted. He is using dramatic hand movements to his passenger, he isn't paying enough attention to what is happening around him and he isn't slowing down. I am too far away to do anything but watch. A person shouts to get the driver's attention but that distracts him further and he doesn't stop in time. I clearly see the horror in his passenger's eyes. She mouths 'Stop!' But the collision is inevitable and horrific to witness.

The bus's brakes screech to a halt but not in time. The car slams into the side of the bus with an almighty crash. The front is crushed and the driver's head is lying cushioned from harm on the inflated airbag. It appears that he is going to be okay as he lifts his head and begins punching the airbag in a rage before getting out of the car. The lady passenger is unconscious and some blood trickles from her brow indicating an injury. There is no airbag on her side of the vehicle. Her hair colour is really what stands out; it is the deepest red that I have come across in my time.

Everything stands still as everyone tries to realise and process what has just happened in front of their eyes. The bus door opens and the driver appears. He takes one look and starts to vomit; the shock of it all has taken over his body.

I feel an overwhelming pull towards the lady passenger. As I get closer I am overwhelmed by panic and my mind begins to spin into a tizzy. I feel connected somehow. *Was I supposed to stop this from happening?* I cannot think straight and so I must not make any rash decisions. I must try to reconnect with my intuition to guide me through the situation.

I observe a man dashing quickly out of a nearby car and he rushes to where the lady is located. He checks her pulse and calls for assistance and begins CPR on her immediately.

It isn't long before the siren of the emergency services can be heard approaching, the human rescuers who dedicate their lives to helping people maintain the best level of physicality possible. Medics are all about the human form and assist a positive spirit to heal a body, often to miraculous levels. These are all vocations with loving qualities of giving unselfishly to others that must be commended.

There are many helpers around the lady now, and I begin to compose my elusive thoughts and emotions that overwhelmed me for a time. I know better than most that panic can often be quite debilitating to a rational thought process. I notice there is something not right. The lady's body has begun to glow. The others around her must not see it as they carry on with what they are doing.

I watch as her essence begins to leave her body. My assignment file suddenly drops from my grasp and lands open on the ground. I am astonished to see there is only one page and it has big messy writing that reads: *She must not pass on yet. It is not her time. She has a job to do.*

I stand there in shock. No details, just a note. I am numbed again but this time I take control of my thoughts. I need to act quickly or it will be too late. I call, "Stop!" and she turns towards me. I quickly pick up the file and scan it before dashing to her side.

Someone shouts in the background, "Her pulse has stopped!"

Then he pulls out the defibrillator and prepares to send surges of electronic energy through her body in order to shock it back into life. The medic shouts, "Everyone clear!" Little does he know that no amount of charge will bring someone back who does not want to return.

I turn to the essence. "Siobhan, it is not your time, you must return."

"But I feel so free," she exclaims. "It is a wonderful feeling."

"Yes, and you will feel it once again and maybe even better if you return to your physical vessel," I say, desperately trying to encourage her back.

"There is nothing there for me anymore, I am ready to go."

"I am not supposed to tell you this, but you have been chosen to fulfil an important duty before it is your time."

"Me? Really? Chosen?"

"Yes, you must listen to your inner guide and follow your instincts accordingly; wisdom will be channelled to you as you need it."

This seems to have engaged her thoughts.

In the meantime, I look towards her physical vessel only to see they have stopped working on her.

"She is gone, there is nothing more that we can do," says one paramedic.

"Okay, well then I shall call time of death to be 3.25pm," replies the other reluctantly.

Everyone surrounding her body bows their head in respect.

"What? What's happening? They can't have given up on me, I need to go back...right?" she says, realising that she actually does want to return. Man cannot make a totally reluctant spirit return, especially when they don't restore themselves before the body ceases to exist.

"You must do something….this can't be it," she says, with her fiery red hair shining through in her flushed cheeks.

All around the scene of the accident the crowd of onlookers has been moved back and police now accompany the paramedics. The driver of the car, a rough-looking character whose energy is quite toxic, is causing a scene, with the bus driver blaming him for the crash.

The police intervene and bring the guy's attention to what has just occurred. He freezes as the realisation of her departure from existence sinks in.

"No way!" he yells.

He pushes his way past the guard and to her side. There is no real emotion being released from his energy field, he locks everything away. I take another look at him but again I cannot get a good view as his hair hangs over his face, I feel like I have met him before. His energy is darkened by a shadow of anger, and I must protect myself from it. I focus back on Siobhan.

"You have been chosen and so I shall use one of the special gifts I have been honoured with delivering. I shall help you back."

Gratitude and relief overwhelm her and she hugs me.

"Thank you, thank you."

I am a little uncomfortable with this sudden interaction and so I quickly move forward, somewhat flushed. I guide her spirit to a space a metre or so away from me.

I have to use a precious beam that was allocated to Angela so that it can guide Siobhan back to herself in a miraculous recovery. This almighty element of divine energy has the potential to bring so much enlightenment to the receiver as they voyage on their journey back to eternal life. I hope Siobhan treasures this gift and utilises its residual energy to help others who need to be touched by divine love to aid their advancement.

"Could you stand there for a moment?" I ask, reaching into the holding container to retrieve a precious *Beam*. I look to Siobhan as she waits patiently to inhabit her body again. I must move quickly because complications may occur due to my lack of attentiveness.

"Be sure to keep aware of the signs that will be sent your way, you have been given a second chance at this life, use it for progression."

She smiles and I know it is time. I take one last look at the magic of the beautiful beam before I release it. The beautiful beam that was allocated to Angela's glowing soul but that now has been utilised to enable Siobhan to return to her physical self a more enlightened soul; and all because of the unremorseful actions of a darkened soul.

The beam launches from my grasp and in an instant it disappears. I watch as Siobhan receives it. She instantly gravitates back into her body with a glow of beautiful celestial energy surrounding her. The body that paramedics had given up on and that now breathes again.

"Look, she is breathing," someone screams.

There is a moment of excited panic as everyone crowds around, excitement that soon transforms into disbelief.

"This has got to be some sort of miracle. Right?" one paramedic says to another.

"Well, let's say I have never seen anything like this before, but we need to get her straight to hospital, she is not out of the woods yet."

They start to move her towards the awaiting ambulance.

"You said she was dead," an aggressive voice penetrates the atmosphere of relief.

"Yes, we did, and she was," the paramedic replies.

"You will be saying there was some kind of divine intervention next to try and weasel your way out of it, well I am not letting it go. I will want justice for your negligence."

The driver is ignored and then a policeman approaches him again.

"Could we have a moment, Sir?"

"What? Who? Me? It is those attempted murderers that you should be questioning; they would have her in a grave by now."

The police officer tries to reason with him but to no avail as he becomes agitated and more aggressive.

The ambulance leaves, and he has to be restrained for a time.

"Sir, we understand that you are feeling shocked but there is no need for this behaviour. You will get yourself an added charge for unruly behaviour. You need to come with us to the station for questioning about the incident, so you can either get into our car and we will escort you to the hospital afterwards, or we can hold you at the station for longer to deal with the added charge. Your call, what is it to be?"

Withdrawing, he responds, "Okay, I hear you," and obediently makes his way to the car.

Darkness now shadows this situation, and it need not be the case. It saddens my heart to witness such uncompassionate behaviour when love and positive actions are needed to create a successful healing atmosphere for Siobhan. The beam assists with her spiritual wellbeing but her physical recovery will take time.

I must now depart but I have that knowing feeling that it is not for long, my job here is not complete. I wonder why but as I am open to the possibility of all types of circumstance, I expect the reason will soon be revealed to me. I do contemplate though that maybe Siobhan may need further guidance to return from her sleepy disposition. She had left her body for a longer than expected time and issues may arise from this.

CHAPTER FIFTEEN
Meeting Within

The time has come to release the beams, well, what is left of them. Each of them have matured and connected with their allocated assignment since we arrived on this realm. The power of this connected energy has assisted each of their counterparts along their inner journey. Those who witness the outer changes do not have the privilege of observing the inner enlightenment that is occurring. This is sad as it is those who have to watch the process who suffer most. The journey within is personal to each person as they revisit past events to work through unresolved issues. This can be intense but it is vital as it makes way for forgiveness which can set a spirit free from past events that have hindered their spiritual progression. Those events may be directly connected to the life they are living now or past events that have not been fully dealt with; however, each is important in a person's journey and so must be dealt with in the now, thus facilitating progression towards their highest potential for spiritual enlightenment.

I am going to go against protocol here in a bid to save some precious time by summoning all of the kindred spirits to join in one meeting place. It is not a physical meeting place but a spiritual one where I will summon all of these lovely people together and we will all be present inhabiting one single energy. An internal meeting place, so to speak.

This will be the first time this has been piloted as a Memory Taker position, but I must be innovative on this mission to ensure I capitalise on every precious moment. Mainly because I have had so much time absorbed with other aspects on this trip, and I don't want vital moments to pass.

Each member will not be present in physical form, only in spirit in their subconscious minds, and when they return they will have been gifted with a peaceful *knowing*. They will project their energy to another space and I will meet them there. A dreamlike state of wonder is how I like to think of it, an internal workshop.

I take position; I focus and create a safe place for us all to congregate. There is a perfect magical place that I will be using. It is between all consciousness and the realms of reality and it will play host to pave the way for a perfect new way of advancement. I do hope my innovation pays off and makes amends for my time management incompetence.

Looking at the magnificent beams, I choose two and hold those before me. The energy they encompass sends a shiver right through me. They take on a presence all of their own. I summon Carrie and Frank; their energies are already directly connected to each other and so it should be an easy connecting transition for them to travel together.

I hold out the beams and focus my mind on my intention, which is to summon my first two assignments to my side. Pausing in this moment I can feel magic at work. The sensation sends ripples through me. The beams have truly worked well doing their job as they are both quick to return. Both Frank and Carrie stand and look at each other in amazement. It has been many years since their spirits have been able to directly connect. They have encountered many lifetimes together in many different connecting roles. This lifetime they have been directly connected through blood but disconnected through distance.

"Great to see you, Carrie."

She hugs him tight. "Oh, Dad, you wouldn't believe how great it is to see you." Their hearts are aglow. Carrie looks over at me. "Have you made this happen?"

Nodding, I reply, "Yes."

"I can't thank you enough; I have really missed this bond."

"You are welcome," I say. To be the facilitator of such a reunion makes me happy.

I leave them to reunite for a moment and I pull out the third beam, which seems slightly tarnished, as if it has lost some of its glow. It is taking on a life of its own and has an assignment allocated, so I allow it to go ahead with its duty. I await the presence of the allocated assignment, and I soon see that it is Henry who is to join us. When he arrives he still seems dazed and confused and so I spend time focusing some of my energy to support his. After a moment he has rebalanced.

"Hello, Henry," I say in an attempt to see how he is.

"Hello," he replies, looking around. "Where am I?"

"Don't fear, Henry, I will explain all to you soon enough."

After a quick welcome to the group I summon the last person.

Joyce arrives with her head lowered; I have the impression that she has always been hard on herself as guilt has consumed her conscious and subconscious mind for many years and hindered her gifted power for goodness. Instead she has allowed her choices to haunt her life instead of learning from them and choosing remorse and self-forgiveness. These are gifts to our soul and humanity as they give us the strength to move forward a stronger and better person. She didn't stay true to herself and her belief system and she has beaten herself up about it ever since. This has hindered her spiritual growth as she has ceased looking for happiness because she never felt she deserved it. It is her enlightenment that has suffered as a consequence. I hold out the beam and it moves to a position that it would like to launch from. Within a split second she is before me.

"It is so beautiful here; am I dead?" she exclaims.

"No, Joyce, you are not advancing yet," I reassure her.

"Am I here so that you can save me? I am feeling so lost within myself. Can you help me?"

"Yes, you are spot on, Joyce; we are all here to achieve peace and enlightenment."

"Oh, thank you," she responds.

I have now summoned all of my beams, four in all, as I had to use Angela's beam to save Siobhan. Although the reasoning for this compromise is not apparent yet, I need to trust that everything is happening as it should be, even though Boss seemed unsettled about it. I have to stand in faith and not let doubt creep in, as it will shadow the greater good. Trusting in the process is the only way to go.

The only object left in my box is the magnificent crystal. It does not glow as of yet so I do not know its purpose but I am sure I will when the time comes for it to work its magic.

"Okay, everyone, can we all gather around, please," I call out.

Four unsuspecting souls stand before me, and I hope I have the ability to guide them towards enlightenment. If I get my job right here at this moment they will now be at peace internally and that will be reflected externally. This will be pleasant for them and for those who are closest to them. They will notice a sudden calmness that surrounds their loved one. This is a beautiful thing, and although it means it may not be long before their passing, it does mean the remaining time they experience will be more pleasant for all involved.

They will have advanced to the next stage along their journey of enlightenment and moving towards the light of eternity will no longer be something to fear for them. It will be something they look forward to because momentarily with me they are at peace and have the opportunity to experience contentment with the sheer serenity of being.

I have a sudden overwhelming niggle, one that is pulling me away from here, but I cannot abandon the task at hand as I am at a zenith part of the process so I have to shrug it off and continue.

"Hello everyone, my name is Gilbert, but you can all call me Gill. I am a messenger sent to assist you along your path of enlightenment. Things may seem quite unsettling and confusing right now but I am here to gift you with the information you need to move forward peacefully. You all want that? Right?"

They all stand nodding their heads. "Yes, please."

"Lately things have been going wrong in your physical life and it has been frustrating for you. Am I right?"

Again more nodding.

"Well, I am The Memory Taker, and I have been sent to guide you towards enlightenment. Do you know what that means?"

They gaze to each other in search of an answer.

"Well, it means that you are coming to the end of your physicality but to reach your true spiritual potential before you make your way to heaven you have been gifted the opportunity to reach your highest potential in spirit. This will enable you to move forward the best you can be. Is that clearer?"

"Yes, somewhat clearer," Joyce replies.

"Great. The let's begin. Each of you has the potential to reach high levels of spiritual enlightenment before you ascend, but you have placed blocks in your life that have limited this potential and that is why you now experience the shadows of your mind. This allows you the time you need to vacate the physical world temporarily and turn inwards to work on the things you have been avoiding in life before you move forward. Does that make sense?"

"In a way it does," replies Henry

"Okay, well let me put it like this. What do you feel here in this space you inhabit in this moment?"

"Peaceful and happy," says Carrie.

"At ease," replies Frank.

"Lighter," says Henry.

"Wonderful," says Joyce.

"That's great because this is just a small insight into how you are going to feel when you move on from your physical self."

"Wow," replies Joyce enthusiastically. "Can I go now?"

"When it is your time you will go, Joyce. You still have a little work to do before then, but I promise you that it will be worth it as it will free you to enjoy the potential that is sheer tranquillity."

"It sounds amazing."

"It truly is. I have not fully yet encountered it as I left before my time, but when my time comes I know I will be very privileged.

I am just in a position of being more aware and certain of it than you all are."

"If you have not been there then how do you know? Where do you come from?" Carrie asks curiously.

I can sense that everyone else is also thinking the same, so I take a moment to explain.

"I am a messenger from the Waiting Zone. It is a place where those who leave physicality before their time go to wait until it is their time to ascend. We all work as messengers in different roles, carrying out duties we have been honoured to be bestowed with. I like to think of it as a second chance to secure my place in the tranquillity of heaven. Does that make it any clearer?"

"Yes, I think so," Joyce replies.

"But what has that got to do with any of us?" asks Frank.

"My job is to help each of you to be your best possible self so that when your time comes you will be able to move forward straight away. My journey is different because I have detoured."

"So we don't have to wait then?"

"Exactly," I say, relieved at the clarity they now have. "The next process may take time as I will work with you all individually, but we will stay with the group so we may all learn from each other's journey. Is that okay with you all?"

I await approval from everyone. Henry seems reluctant.

"Henry, we are all here because we have stumbled along the way, you do truly deserve your place here."

Relief flows over him and he takes a step forward in the group.

Now it is time to enlighten these beautiful souls.

CHAPTER SIXTEEN
Gathering

I gather us all into a circle, and we connect together as one. This is a powerful entwining energy that links us together at a higher level. We continue to stand there in silence feeling the energy for a period of time in a meditative trance, connecting with our highest self on an escalated level.

I softly begin to speak. "I would like to begin by sharing with you all some very powerful words by the insightful John Lennon."

I feel the vibration of our circle lift in anticipation of the words of wisdom I am about to share.

"We need to learn to love ourselves first, in all our glory and our imperfections. If we cannot love ourselves, we cannot fully open to our ability to love others or our potential to create. Evolution and all hopes for a better world rest in the fearlessness and open-hearted vision of people who embrace life."

Sensing hearts opening, I leave them all with those words for a few moments, allowing their meaning to be fully absorbed.

"Do you all feel like you have lived your life fearlessly and with an open heart?"

"Not wholeheartedly," Carrie replies.

"Thank you, Carrie. Well you are not alone. Most of us live our existence connected to some element of fear and this can lead to us closing our hearts to protect ourselves and those we hold dearest. In doing this we are closing ourselves off to growing in spirit. It is okay to make mistakes as it is through those mistakes that we learn more about ourselves. Each experience we have is an opportunity to grow. When we approach each situation with an open heart and eliminate the fear we may have connected to it, then we are trusting in the process of being and assisting natural spiritual progression to take place. Many of us have developed an inherited defence mechanism towards protecting our feelings, when it is ever so important to have the freedom within us to feel when we are progressing in spirit. Once we feel we can manage those feelings we can grow more naturally. We also often tend to live our life's truest purpose when we allow our heart to guide our mind. These feelings can never simply disappear by ignoring them, instead they are often hidden deep down with our soul where they can fester and damage our spiritual progression. They will niggle at us and in more serious cases they end up defining the person we become and may even make us ill. Can anyone relate?"

"Yes, I can," Joyce replies.

"Me also," Henry responds.

Carrie and Frank both nod.

"You see, everyone can relate. Forgiveness is a very big part of moving forward. Forgiveness of ourselves and others sets us free to move forward in our power," I say, hoping it will be absorbed quickly.

"But how can you possibly forgive everyone?" asks Frank.

"I certainly understand how you could think that way, Frank. I too had things that I needed to forgive that I found challenging, but it was when I did forgive that I discovered I could move forward in my own power. Living in past hurts can only drag you down and damage your ability to reach your highest potential."

I gift him a moment to ponder on that.

"Okay, as we stand together I am going to go around the circle to assist you all with pinpointing the most significant block you have in your life in a hope to enlighten you and help you free yourself from the burdens of the past. When I call a name I would like you to listen carefully and connect to the past energy that the gem is calling you towards. It may be unsettling, but it will be worthwhile, trust me."

I am receiving some dubious responses; it is as if they are not one hundred percent comfortable with it. A beam begins to glow brightly.

"It is Carrie who is first," I say and she steps forward.

"Carrie, I am being giving the indication that you are harbouring guilt and sadness about some of the choices you have made in your lifetime, am I right?"

Carrie's energy becomes very dour and she confirms my thoughts by nodding her head and then she lowers it.

"Carrie, I get the sense that you are a person who has always been led by spirit. You live with an open heart and make the choices that you feel are right at any given moment in time. You cannot live in past regrets as they will hold you back from shining your bright light with all who come in contact with you. You made your choices and must trust that this was the right path for you. Every single human makes choices throughout their existence. Choices that impact on the way their life flows and even who they share it with. You feel as if you sacrificed so much of your time for someone else and they didn't value it. If you do something for another person with expectation, that is a true recipe for disappointment. I would say to you that you did not just make the sacrifice for them. You made it for yourself too and you made the most of following your heart because it led you to greater heights than you could ever have dreamed of. Is that correct, Carrie?"

"Yes, that is correct," she replies with her head held higher and a bright realisation in her heart.

"It is now time for you to let go of all of your past regrets and set your spirit free to grow. Your life has been as it was supposed to be. Those that your heart has missed you will see again. Be proud of you, everyone who loves you is very proud of you. Isn't that right, Frank?"

"It certainly is, Carrie. We have always known that you have loved us, and we are proud that you followed your dreams. Even though we always miss you we somehow always feel that you are with us."

To hear that from her dad sets Carrie's heart free. She has experienced a breakthrough in front of our eyes and she is shining. It is amazing how a few heartfelt words can eliminate many years of doubt.

Frank's beam glows indicating that I can now access an insight into his block.

"Frank, it is your beam that now glows. I am guided that you have issues with forgiveness. You can be resentful towards others but also towards yourself because of the actions you have felt that you must take to resolve matters, especially in your earlier years."

Yes, but that is the past," he responds defensively.

"But it is significant as it has been a block that has held you back from making your own breakthrough. You accepted that this was the 'norm' and therefore you remained in the struggle instead of choosing to move forward in your own inner power towards the breakthrough stage of enlightenment. It is not a tangible thing and so you hid it deep within and harboured it there for many years. It is only in your later years that your spirit is challenging you to address these issues and even then you are reluctant."

"Maybe, but sure, why does that matter?"

"It matters, Frank, because you have the opportunity to ascend as a more enlightened soul. This is something you have not explored as you have not often connected within until now, but you have the potential to make that breakthrough by eliminating the block you unknowingly created during your lifetime. It was placed there in your early years as a way of protecting yourself. You went through a lot of emotional upheaval when you were young. Without consciously being aware of it you were on the defensive for the rest of your life, protecting what you had with a forceful hand, creating for yourself a badge of honour that you could be proud of and that you pass down to your children and so on. Now it is time for you to let down your defence as you are safe and your family are safe. You need not feel angst anymore, you must now think only of you and what your spirit needs and that is to release all of that pent up defensive emotion. Go on, Frank, set it free and then you will be able to set your spirit free, you can do it."

At that moment there is a sudden release of fiery energy that shoots upwards, catching us all off guard as it beams all around before escaping into the abyss. Franks drops to the ground and Carrie dashes to him.

"Dad, are you okay?" she calls.

Frank opens his eyes and smiles at her. "Yes, I am more than okay, love."

I sense that he is lighter and that there has been a great weight lifted off his shoulders which had often pinned him down during his life. He will certainly feel a greater sense of freedom now.

Now it is Joyce's beam that glows bright. I have awaited this opportunity ever since I received the flashback to her past.

"Joyce, you have now been asked to step forward," I say gently. This news seems to have taken her off guard but she raises her head and makes her way towards me. She gives the impression that she has been ready and waiting for this moment for a long time. She looks straight at me and smiles.

"Joyce, I had a preview into that moment when your life did a U-turn. Before that moment you had purpose and drive for your career and what you believed to be your calling. What you thought to be your reality changed because of the actions you took and this has been very hard for you to deal with ever since. You have let this one incident define the way your life since has progressed. Am I right?"

"Yes, you are right, and I am ready for your guidance," she says, determined to make a positive difference for herself.

"Joyce, forgive yourself!"

Tears flow from her eyes. "How can I? I did the worst thing ever, and it can never be forgiven."

"Of course you can be forgiven, Joyce, you simply must forgive yourself or you cannot set your spirit free. It is okay, you have given so much back and you did not let the young man pass on in vain. You have been a guardian angel for his child and dedicated most of your life to ensuring that he was not forgotten, but it is time to forgive yourself. It was not your intention for him to die, that was just the tragic outcome. You have learned many spiritual lessons along your journey, but to move on to the breakthrough you simply must forgive yourself; it is okay to do so."

I move closer to her and allow my energy to hug hers. I can gently feel her letting go of her self-hatred and her aura changes to a more peaceful energy.

"Now see, that wasn't so hard, was it?" I enquire.

"I feel so filled with peace."

"And so you should, Joyce. It will take a while for you to totally forgive yourself but open your heart to it and your self-love will flow back in abundance to you. What better way to ascend."

So three beams have been put into motion and only one is left: Henry. He has been very subdued throughout the gathering. I do hope that having a group gathering has not imposed on his ability to move forward. There is only one way to find out though so as I wait for his beam to glow I try to engage the group as a whole. I am startled by an overwhelming feeling of uneasiness but it is not directly focused on this group and so I dismiss it, hopefully not to my peril. This group needs to be my main focus right now as they need me the most and we have reached that moment where we are almost there.

Henry's beam begins to glow, and he responds with anticipating energy.

"I am ready to hear it," he says, expecting the worst.

"Henry, why do you sound so defeated?" I ask in response to his solemn tone.

"Well, I have not been a good person throughout my life, and I have abused everything that was gifted to me."

"Henry, on the contrary, were you not the pioneer of the children's aid foundation that went on to help millions of displaced children in their time of need?"

Henry's head rises. "Yes I was."

"Henry, did you not gift millions of people the pleasure of watching you act in inspiring roles on both TV and film for over fifty years?"

He smiles a proud smile. "Why, yes I have."

"You may have indulged in some wasteful indulgences in your lifetime, Henry, but you have gifted the world so much and you should not focus on what you have taken from it. You will be remembered for what you did for others more so than what you indulged in. You are a good person who also needs to forgive and respect himself. You did do wrong due to infidelity but you have paid the price for that as you subsequently lost the love of your wife and have suffered depression as a result. However, you are loved very much by your daughter and many other people and you should cease from shielding this love from entering your heart as it is genuine and will help you heal. This type of healing love is miraculous in its capabilities, and you need to open your heart to it and stop being so hard on yourself. You do deserve it."

"Do you really think so?" he asks, quite liking the prospect of liking himself as he has been disgusted with himself for so long and it has been destroying him bit by bit.

"Yes, I know so. Now close your eyes and breathe. Breathe right down to the pit of your stomach. Come on, everyone, let's do it together. When we breathe to our full capacity we are clearing our minds and opening our hearts. Henry, by letting the love flow inwards your spirit will heal beyond belief, so don't close your heart. Let all of that love flow with you on your journey."

I watch for a moment as each of these wonderful people stands before me with an open heart, and I know that only good can come from them allowing this to happen without fear. They feel safe here and that is how it should always be. Everyone has the potential to visit their safe place inside at any given time; if more people did it then they would be happier and more centred.

"I will leave you all now to return to your consciousness. You will feel more at peace with who you are and accepting of why you are experiencing the darkness. Try to share your inner peace with your loved ones by being happy as it will give them peace also."

Things will be clearer from this point on for each of my assignments and they will be more at peace with their situation now that they are not filled with so much fear. I will educate them on the process of enlightenment, and the gift of understanding quite often leads to inner peace and acceptance.

I suddenly hear a loud call inside my head.

"No!"

It is Arianna.

CHAPTER SEVENTEEN
Connections

    I quickly transcend to a new location that appears to be a hospital room. This is not where I was expecting to locate to, and I am startled and concerned. There are monitors everywhere and the constant beeping of machines dominates the ambience as they act as a guide to the wellbeing of the patient lying there before me. It is Siobhan and she is either asleep or in a coma. I suspect the latter as she is surrounded by machines. She lies there unresponsive apart from the heart monitor that shows she is indeed alive as it pulsates the loudest noise that can be heard in the room.

    Storming in like a tornado with the purpose of destroying everything in his path is the young man from the accident scene. I cannot shift the feeling that I have encountered him before. If only I could get a proper look at his face I might be able to locate him better in my mind. I try to manoeuvre to where I can see him but to no avail. I shall have to wait until it is time, I suppose.

"Mum, are you awake?" he says into her ear. "I need to talk, Mum"

My thoughts are suddenly distracted from the current reality.

Arianna, I have to find her.

My mind goes into panic. My gut instinct is telling me that I must stay here right now. I have an overwhelming feeling to trust my inner guide.

The young man is still talking. "Mum, I need you to tell me what I need to do? What you told me, it is not true. It can't be."

Siobhan just lies there unresponsive. I can sense agitation from the man.

"Mum, she still acts as if we are just friends, surely it has been long enough now, and I can't keep being the nice guy with no benefits. There is no way what you said can be true; I need you to tell me that. I need you to tell me that now, Mum. Wake up."

There is still no response, and he seats himself in the visitor's chair beside the bed and places his head in his hands.

The door then opens and to my utter shock and yet also my relief, in walks Arianna. I cannot believe it, and oh how I have missed her radiating energy. My heart skips a beat, and I immediately yearn for some closeness with her. She doesn't seem to sense me here, which disappoints me as I crave a connection from her. I have to accept that she is not directly connected to my energy right now, although it deeply saddens me to acknowledge it.

She smiles as she walks in and makes her way to the bed, where she conveys caring emotion towards Siobhan as she places her hand on hers. Love immediately fills the room; I even observe the energy of the young man alter.

"How is your mum?" she gently asks.

He finally lifts his head from his hands, and it suddenly comes to me that this is Jake. How did I not put two and two together sooner? It is him that I saw in my flashback, it is actually happening and Arianna must have no idea.

Can I stop it from happening? Am I supposed to intervene?

So many thoughts swirl around in my mind, and I am unsure what I am expected to do. I am filled with emotion and I try to allow it a few moments to subside. After quickly composing myself I draw my attention back to the room and the current reality.

"She is the same," he responds, hostile.

Arianna moves around the hospital bed towards him. She stands humbly before him and says, "I am sorry but I am not ready yet."

This must have been the harrowing, "No!" that I heard so intensely.

He sits with legs wide apart, elbows on his knees and his head lowered. Finally he responds by lifting his hand to hers. She quickly grasps it and he raises his head to look at her.

"It's okay, babe, I understand," he says unconvincingly, well to me anyway.

"Really?" she innocently responds.

"Yes, really," he says, pulling her onto his knees and kissing her. "You are worth waiting for."

She seems so happy, but it is hard for me to watch her being so vulnerable and naive on so many levels.

"Come on, let's get out of here and do something fun," he says, jumping up with her in his arms. Her tiny frame is no challenge to carry around for Jake with his strong physique.

"Are you sure that you don't want to stay with your mum?"

"No, sure they will call if there is any change with her, and anyway I have that gig on tonight."

"I didn't know if you would still be going."

"The show must go on, beautiful lady," he says as he whisks her out of the room.

Oh, it makes my skin crawl to see how smooth he is and how Arianna has fallen for him. I feel that she is seeking the goodness in him and this is what her heart truly wants to find.

I look over to Siobhan and see a flicker in her eyelashes so I dash to her side. The flicker quickly turns into a blink. Her eyes are open and she is still but conscious. I feel as though I have witnessed a miraculous moment that sends ripples right through my energy field.

She looks over in my direction and struggles to point her finger towards a drawer. I open it and inside there is a letter in a white envelope with Jake's name on it. I lift it out and deliver it to Siobhan, who grasps it tightly and points towards a leather jacket draped around the chair Jake had been sitting in.

"You want the jacket?" I ask

She blinks hard in response. I bring it to her and she places the letter in the inside pocket. She then slumps, closes her eyes, and is unresponsive again. It is as if that moment took all of her energy away.

A moment later in through the door charges Jake with purpose. He looks to the chair and then looks to his mum's bed where the jacket lies beside her. He looks confused but decides to disregard anything that hinders his focus and so he grabs the jacket and leaves.

I need to know what is in that letter. So I too leave, following Jake like a detective. Arianna is waiting at the front doors to the hospital. They loiter there for a moment before being moved on when Jake lights up a cigarette beside a sign that says, 'No Smoking'.

They make their way to the car park and I recognise the car that they get into from my premonition back at dispatch. It further affirms that the inevitable is one step closer. Oh, how I don't want this for Arianna. If only she chose to love me and not let her curiosity of the human world overcome her. But the reality is that she is curious and until that curiosity is satisfied she will never feel truly fulfilled. It is still hard for me to watch.

I take a moment to quickly reconnect with my assignments. I channel my energy towards each of them, and I know they are all moving forward since our meeting. That gives me some time to stay close to Arianna for a while.

It is getting late in the afternoon, and we seem to have arrived at a concert arena. The energy is manic and everyone is buzzing. There is a huge stage that everyone appears to be navigating towards. The closer everyone gets the more congested it becomes and movement is restricted. I do not enjoy the feeling of being trapped so I move into a more open space and try to navigate my thoughts to Arianna so I can locate her. The music is getting louder and the crowd is also loud and it is quite distracting.

Finally I see the car pull in through a side gate. It is now occupied by six people all crammed in. Jake just abandons it where they are and hops out. A young girl spots him and screams, "Oh my god, it is Jake!" This instigates tumult of screaming and a tsunami of teenage girls descends on the car. The rest of the guys get out of the car and the screaming increases.

There are now hundreds of screaming girls all around them and they are signing autographs and posing for selfies. They all love the attention. I make my way around to the back of the car. Arianna is still inside and she looks sad. I seize the opportunity and hop into the car beside her. The clothes she is wearing do not show her true inner essence. A short denim skirt, black boots, and a grey t-shirt with *KillaBees* emblazoned across it. Then, just when I felt all was lost, she abruptly sits upright and scans the car. It is as if she has just had a shiver down her spine and she shakes it off. I place my hand on hers as it rests on her lap. She looks down but seems happy to embrace my energy. I look into her eyes as she looks past me to see what is going on outside the car. It is still chaos. In her eyes there is something missing, something distant, something that has changed, and my heart saddens. The Arianna who energised me with her sheer being every time we were in the same space is now broken. I so want to be the one who fixes her, but will she let me? Or will she choose to stay broken? I know that is up to her.

For now I choose to access my heart's energy, and I radiate it onto her. I watch it perk her up and her cheeks become aglow again. This is a magical moment, I can feel it. Arianna begins to slowly lift her head upwards; it is as if she can feel me again, as if she can see me again. My heart flutters at the prospect of a connection, a connection that I crave. She begins to slowly smile and her face is almost aligned with mine. She has her eyes closed then…Knock knock. A tap on the window by one of the guys from the band distracts Arianna's attention, and she quickly scuffles to get herself together and out of the car.

Jake appears to have walked on without her with all of the teenage girls following him. Arianna follows the crowd. This seems so wrong to me, Arianna has such magic that she should be leading the crowd, not following behind like an afterthought. My hope is that she acknowledges her self-worth again and stops letting Jake disregard her when it suits him. She is a princess and deserves to be treated special indeed. I do not understand the control he has on Arianna's heart. I hate to see her so solemn and her heart so dull but there is something there, something deep rooted that connects her loyally to him.

Arianna runs behind the group of girls to catch up with Jake before he accesses the VIP area without her. The gates close just as she makes her way through the crowd of screaming girls. There is a large man standing there, and he won't let her past.

"Can you let me in, please? My boyfriend has just gone in."

"Oh, really, young lady, and who may your boyfriend be?"

"Jake, of course…"

He laughs. "Yes, yours and thousands of other young girls here today."

"No but…" Arianna pleads.

"Sorry, young lady, if you don't have a VIP pass you don't get past me, no exceptions."

Arianna walks a few steps away and drops to the ground, puts her head on her knees and cries. She is humiliated and feels deserted; I hope that as she has hit such a low point she will begin to see some sense and stand up for herself. Just then the door opens and Jake pops his head out.

"Babe, are you coming or what?"

Arianna jumps up with a smile of relief and gratitude pasted all over her perfectly constructed face. Her faith is now restored in Jake, and this makes my heart ache. She makes her way to the gate and passes the security guard. He is holding back a crowd of screaming girls who have spotted Jake. The security guard nods and tips his cap to her in a gentle salute. She smiles back in forgiveness. The door closes behind them as they make their way back stage.

The energy is crazy and lots of things are going on. There are small areas sectioned off where bands and their entourage prepare or chill out. Adrenaline is high and there is an underlying feeling that I can't dismiss. It is that feeling that something wrong is happening. There is the external appearance of fun and happiness, but when you look a bit deeper darkness is at work and in the group Arianna is with Jake appears to be main man. I fear for her innocent heart; it is bound to be tarnished by some of the things she witnesses here.

They are all sitting around on chairs and beanbags when a rolled up cigarette is lit. It starts to be passed around and I watch as each person takes a few puffs from it. It is not long before it reaches Arianna.

"Here, lady," a young girl says with her eyes all out of focus and in a provocative position.

"Oh, okay, thanks." Arianna takes it. She holds it in such an awkward manner and passes it straight on to the next person so it catches the attention of the girl who passed it to her.

"Hey, lady, are you too good to take a puff from the peace pipe?" she says, trying to sit up to confront Arianna.'

"No, of course not, it is just that I don't smoke. It is not good for my lungs," Arianna says innocently.

"Well then you can't possibly be part of our group, we wouldn't want to tarnish those clean lungs now, would we?"

"But is it not okay that I don't want to, is that not my choice?" Arianna desperately looks Jake's way for support.

"Hey, babe, just take a puff, it will be a whole lot easier and who knows, you may like it...we all do, don't we, guys?"

"Yeah," everyone hollers in unison.

"Ari, Ari, Ari, Ari..." they all start to chant on Jake's lead.

The joint is passed back to Arianna who is now looking very vulnerable. She reluctantly holds it between her finger and thumb and scans the group. She looks at Jake and he nods for her to go on and do it. She watches it slowly burn down a little more.

"Come on, or there will be none left," one of the guys shouts.

Arianna closes her eyes, pulls the joint towards her and takes a small drag which she unknowingly inhales. She breaks out in a fit of coughing, and she can't stop. Everyone claps and then laughs at her reaction, including Jake.

There is sadness in Arianna's eyes and she dashes off to a portable loo until the coughing calms down. She is in there a few minutes and tears are welling down her face as she feels betrayed. Then a knock comes to the door and her face lights up with hope, only to be disappointed again when she sees a girl standing there.

"I won't be much longer," Arianna explains still gasping for breath.

The girl hands her a bottle of water. "Here, this will help," she says with a smile.

Arianna is grateful and smiles while taking the bottle.

"You're not from around here, are you?" the girl enquires.

"No, I am staying with my aunty for a little while."

"So, how did you meet Jake?"

"I was taking a walk in a park close by and he came to say hello. He was different than he is now though, he was really nice."

"He is with his group, and they all act different when their egos combine."

"I don't like it," Arianna replies, lowering her head.

"Yes, I used to feel the same about Jez when I first started to go out with him. I suppose it is all about whether you like him enough to overlook some of the crap."

Arianna ponders for a moment.

In the background they hear, "Are you all ready for a fun time?"

The response is a multitude of fans screaming in excitement.

"Well, we are the *Killabees*, and we are here to rock this place." More screaming follows as the music begins.

"Hey, that's the guys. Do you want to come out front with me, and we can watch them together? I'm Amber, by the way."

Arianna smiles. "Sure, that would be cool. Thanks, Amber."

Amber grabs her hand and drags her to the VIP area at the front where they dance happily together.

I will leave Arianna for now as I have some valuable insight into where she is at, and I need some time to process it all.

CHAPTER EIGHTEEN
Detour

    Seeing Arianna falling head over heels with an uncertain love has reborn unsettling feelings within me. Feelings I have hidden deep down for some time so I can protect my heart from the wounding it encountered. Reminiscing with Arianna about the love I believed I had and how it all shattered before me so quickly has brought me to this point.

    An overwhelming feeling has engulfed my spirit and instigated the urge to take action. This is something I never thought I would want to do on this journey. I need to see her, even if it is from afar. This is very disconcerting as never, since departing from my physicality, have I had a desire to return to that emotional place. Even though I have been filled with forgiveness of my past somehow I still harbour deep emotions that I am finding it tough to shrug off. I know I have learned the lessons my spirit needed to experience from it all, but I have an inexplicable knowing that I must return because there is more I need to see. This is an unsettling yet intriguing realisation.

I have two options here. I can choose to ignore the urge and never know and therefore suppress the feeling of pain; or alternatively I can listen to my inner guide and choose to trust that I am to follow my instincts. I choose to listen to my guide and in that instant I know things are about to change forever.

I focus my energy to once again connect with the woman I gave my heart to in what seems to be a lifetime ago. I do feel an element of fear as my instinct ignites to protect my heart.

I arrive in what is my hometown. I am brought to a quaint little cottage surrounded by a picket fence. There doesn't seem to be anyone around but I choose to look inside anyway.

I am a little taken aback by the pictures of Jane that are scattered around the room and on the wall. They are not what I expected as her husband has been replaced by a four-year-old girl. Again I realise not to expect, as life and circumstance can change things quite quickly at times. There is joy in Jane's eyes and that relieves me. She looks radiant and less conservative, motherhood must have softened her.

Then I come across a photo placed on a side table that is going to change everything for me. It is one of those moments that cannot be erased and in one split second a current reality is altered. It has a profound impact on me; the sensation could be likened to being run over by a steam train! Dropping to my knees I quickly grab the photo. I look again and again to absorb its contents. My heart is galloping and my mind is racing with all types of scenarios.

There right before my disbelieving eyes is a photo of my mum, dad, and the little girl. They all seem so happy, and the more

I look at the child the more clearly I can see it. It is my eyes that look back at me. This little girl is mine, I know it with all of my being. Why did I not realise it sooner? Jane's husband was infertile and could not give her the child she so longed for, and yet I did. For the first moment since leaving my physicality I am beginning to question whether I did the right thing. I would love to be this child's dad. I had never contemplated being a dad before but I know I would have been a great one. Wow, the reality of the implications of my actions is sobering, and yet my heart is aglow that I helped create someone so perfect.

I sit for a time just looking at her picture and getting to know every feature and freckle. I am then hit with an amazing desire to meet her or at least see her, to witness how her character is growing.

Oh my goodness, so much to absorb in such a short time. My reality has just been enhanced and to think that I hid away for so long from discovering this treasure and all it took was one leap of faith to reveal such a spirit-enhancing realisation.

I go back outside and I channel into Jane again. I am guided toward the old school house. If I remember correctly it is used as a childcare centre. Excitement ripples through me as I make my way there. Upon entering, I see lots of children happily playing in the different sections of the large room. Then I see Jane and it brings feelings flooding back to me. Not all of heartbroken love, confusion, and rejection that consumed me before; what I feel now is more bearable. I choose to embrace this new-found perspective. I know things could have been different between us, especially in comparison to the drastic premature outcome I chose.

She is leading a group of children in a wiggly dance, and she looks to be having fun releasing her inner child. The children appear to love it, and they mimic her every move while giggling at the silly ones. It is so nice to see her so free spirited.

I scan the room to see if the little girl from the picture is around, but I cannot see her anywhere. I scan again but still no sign.

I realise that she looked older than the children in this room and so she may be at school. I had channelled into Jane's energy and not the little girl's. It is still nice to see Jane and as I go closer to her she stops what she is doing and quickly looks around as if she can sense me close by. This is a sign that she is still deeply connected to me.

I leave and again I arrive outside in the town square. I close my eyes and visualise the little girl. Nothing happens, and it saddens me. I try again but to no avail. I stand there not knowing what else to try but my heart is desperate to see her. In the wisdom I have accumulated I know that if nothing happens it is for a reason, and I am not to push or act in haste because if I do I may miss something wonderful.

Then it happens. As I lift my head I see lots of children come into the square with their parents. School must be finished for the day. Then there she is in her little school uniform with braids either side of her adorable freckled face. I run to be close to her and watch as she obediently holds onto the side of a buggy, skipping happily along. She looks so happy.

"Nan, can we go to see Mum?"

Nan! That means my mum...

"Of course, my dear, don't we always," says my mum. Suddenly she stops. "Hold on, dear," she says to the little girl.

I stand up and look to her; she looks older and there is something that glistens in her eyes. She looks around as if she is seeking something. Then she looks right in my direction and says softly, "Gilbert, is that you?" She catches me off guard as I would never have thought she would connect to me so quickly.

I lift my hand and touch her face and she raises her hand to mine. I know she cannot see me, but she can definitely feel my presence. We both cherish a special moment.

Then in an instant the little girl shouts, "Mum!" and she runs off.

My mum shouts, "No, Anna, no!"

As Anna runs onto the road a school bus is heading right in her direction. I cannot let the inevitable happen so I run as fast as I can and shove her with all of my might. She is propelled to the other side of the road with only a grazed knee to show for it. I look to my mum as she stands with her hands covering her face. I look to Jane as she runs to our daughter, and I look to my little girl sitting crying because she has a grazed knee.

Anna, Mum called her. Anna, that is a perfect name for her. I watch as Jane tenderly lifts her into her arms and makes her way back into the hall. She is closely followed by my mum pushing the buggy. She does look way too old to be pushing a bug...Oh, the buggy! It has just dawned on me that in there is my brother and I haven't met him yet. This is all so much for me to absorb. To have felt so isolated from everyone, not feeling like I belong, and then to so unexpectedly and in such a short time feel connected again. And, of course, I am not here anymore to enjoy the fruits of my labour. This is the first time I have ever begun to regret my actions, it is certainly a reality check. I take a moment to absorb this realisation.

While I do this I watch Jane nurse Anna back to smiling again with a Minnie Mouse Band-Aid that is applied with a healing motherly kiss.

Pulling myself together, I make my way to the buggy. My little brother lies there so peacefully and when I peek my head in he smiles and giggles at me. He looks exactly as I did when I was small; he is bound to be a reminder of me every day for my mum. She has been so strong. I realise how much she has been through and yet she still moves forward being so positive. I can see in her eyes that she holds pain close to her heart every day.

I become distracted as I overhear Jane say to Anna, "Anna, you should never dash off without Nanny or Mummy with you, you could have been run over. Do you remember the green cross code that we talked about together?"

"Yes, Mummy, I am sorry, Mummy. I won't do it again."

"Okay, but maybe we need to practise it a bit more later on today."

"Yes, Mummy. Mummy, someone pushed me and I fell."

"At school, my princess, that's not nice."

"No, Mummy, when I ran across the road, so that the bus didn't get me."

I watch Jane and my mother look to each other in a knowing way. They feel my presence, and I don't want to disrupt things anymore for them so I will move on.

I cherish my time here and now it is my duty to find a place where I can fit into it all, even if I do inhabit a completely different spectrum. I take comfort in the knowing that everyone is well. I listen to the calls that indicate it is now time for me to leave for a while as I am being drawn to my assignments.

CHAPTER NINETEEN
Ascending

I make my way to a place of no distraction, a tranquil place surrounded by serenity and peace. There are some beautiful places in this world, but today I have chosen a meadow. All that can be seen in every direction on this beautiful blue-skyed day are fields filled with flowers. The field that I sit in now is a full of yellowness; adjacent to this one is a field of red then pink and so on. I feel as though I am inhabiting a rainbow as the array of colours merges, assisting me to believe in the true magic of life again with the enchanting energy this vision creates before me. I really needed this energy boost so that I can give my best to my assignments. I feel as though I have neglected them on this mission. I can only hope that I have provided them with enough personal insight at our group encounter to help guide them towards their highest potential ascension.

I continue to sit until the sun begins to lower in the sky. It produces its own array of colourful wonder and subsequently it slowly darkens the colours of the land surrounding me.

I am rejuvenated though and my heart is rejoicing, so I am grateful. I can now approach this impending final task with a love-filled heart. Because I have taken the time out that I needed to recharge myself I can now be confident that I will present my best possible self when I encounter these wonderful souls.

Awaiting an intuition call from my first prepared assignment I remind myself that I may encounter many unprecedented scenarios from this point. I must not have any expectations from any of my assignments or their families. Each one is unique and every situation is different. This is often a time of sadness for those left behind yet those who manage to ascend positively from this scenario can now bask in the freedom of spirit and wisdom they have learned in their darkness. If only those who are so close to them knew that what occurred as a result of the darkness was the highest potential light for their loved one. Often because they have been there for them they have felt support and had the courage to reach their highest ability.

Joyce

I feel that I am being drawn towards one of my assignments. It is time for them to move forward from their physicality. I am brought to a large family home. There are quite a number of cars outside but no noise spills out from the open front door where a man in his mid-thirties stands smoking. I have the feeling I have seen him before but again where and when elude me for now, I may have to work on my own memory as it is wavering.

On entering the home I witness many people sitting around and some busy ladies, serving tea and biscuits to those who seem to be in a time of contemplation. It is as if they are waiting on something, and I can only conclude that they are here because a passing is imminent.

I make my way up the winding staircase and I am drawn to a room at the end of the hall. I enter and there lying in her bed is Joyce. On seeing me she smiles. It is comforting to know that my presence is received well. There are people nearby but I move as close beside her as I can. She closes her eyes and we connect on a more soulful level.

"Joyce, how have you been?"

"Oh love, it is good to see you here. I don't think I can hang on much longer," she replies slowly in relief.

"Have you had any enlightening moments since we chatted last?"

"I have spent a lot of time within, and I have been thinking as much as I could. The one thing I have come to realise that brought my heart to peace was that although I was a catalyst in the death of that young man all those years ago, it was ultimately beyond my control as it was his time to move on from this earth. If it had not been me that was involved it would have been someone else. My life has actually been enhanced by the deep sadness that I felt as it made me a more compassionate and caring person, this I would not have changed for the world. I have also had so many wonderful people enter my life through my connection and the dedication to right my wrongdoing. I feel more at peace with it all than I ever have done. I feel as if a huge weight has lifted from my chest, and I can finally forgive myself. I can now let it go and know that it did not define me as a bad person, it in fact was the turning point for me to ultimately become a better person."

"Joyce, you truly have come a long way in such a short time. You do deserve peace, and you do deserve your place in heaven. May your enlightened spirit guide you there when you are ready to depart."

"Will you stay with me? I would feel better if you did."

"Yes, of course, I will stay close by so know that you are not alone."

"I will say my goodbyes here, and I thank you for all of your help in freeing my soul."

"It has been my pleasure."

I watch as she awakens from her dazed state. She slowly opens her eyes and those closest to her rush to her side.

She smiles at them and tries to speak but nothing is coming out.

"Hello, Mum, it is good to see you," says a woman in her fifties who has been holding her hand tightly since I arrived.

"I..." Joyce struggles to say what she wants to say.

"What, Mum, what are you trying to say?"

In this moment I feel that I have to intervene. I close my eyes, and I focus with all of my energy for Joyce to have a short time where she can say what she wants to say to her family.

"I love you all, and I want you to know that although it has appeared that I have suffered, I haven't. I am now free and at peace. I am happy, and I want you to be too." With that she closes her eyes and drifts off from her consciousness.

"Mum, I love you too," says her daughter with an open heart as she kisses her mum on the lips.

In this moment Joyce lifts from her body and is now spirit. Her entity gravitates above her body and she watches as her family rally around her and some tears of loss are shared. She watches as they comfort each other, and she places her hand on her heart as it touches her so much to witness this display of loss. There is a lot of love surrounding this moment. Just then a beaming light appears from above, and Joyce looks to it.

"It's so beautiful," she says, smiling.

"It is, Joyce, now allow yourself to go, and you will move forward towards the divine tranquillity that awaits you."

I watch as she ascends. This is the most beautiful thing to experience and it is a quite personal and individual one for each person. I now wait for the special beam to return. It will not be as bright as before because it has used its energy guiding Joyce towards her realisation. The final part of my job for this assignment is to return the beams to dispatch so that their energy can be renewed.

Joyce's is one of the most beautiful ascensions I have witnessed. I am proud at this moment that I have been part of the process and as she got to say goodbye to her loved ones. They will have closure, which will assist them in the grieving process, especially knowing that she is now at peace. There could not have been a better ending for her really under the circumstances.

Her beam is released and as it magnificently makes its way back to me I am ready to receive and safely return it to its holding vessel. I am ready to move on.

I begin to feel another pull. It is bizarre as I feel divided. It is as if I am being pulled by two energies. I focus my energy on the strongest to see where it brings me.

Frank and Carrie

I arrive in a town. It is a small town with an array of shops and bars lining a main street that spreads at least half a kilometre. It is bustling with people, many of them stopping to chat and happy to see each other. I notice that people smile at each other and say hello as they walk past. This is a friendly town.

I attempt to locate my assignment, and it is proving to be a challenge. I am distracted by the friendly atmosphere that surrounds me; it is like a breath of fresh air. This would be a nice community to be a part of.

Then finally there he is, Frank. He is standing beside a car, and he is looking quite pale. He falls over on the pavement. Instantly, numerous people surround him. One person takes control.

"Give him some space, please," he shouts.

Frank lies there lifeless. The guy checks his pulse and then begins CPR on him. Other people call the emergency services. Another woman says, "I'll get Lucy, that's her dad. She works in the hair salon over there." Then she runs off in the direction of the salon on the other side of the street.

"Dad, Dad!" Lucy comes rushing towards him. The crowd that has gathered makes a clear path through to her father.

"Is he going to be okay?" she asks the guy who is performing CPR.

"I hope so," he says, desperately trying his best to keep the rhythm going.

Just then an ambulance comes up the street with its siren wailing. Everyone moves from its path.

"So what do we have here?" the ambulance medic enquires.

"This is my dad and he has passed out," Lucy informs him.

"Okay, so does he have any pre-existing medical conditions that I need to be aware of?"

"Yes, he has Alzheimer's."

Thank you, that helps. We will do our best for him."

It is not long at all before they have him on a stretcher and into the ambulance on the way to the hospital. He is being made to hold onto life right now through the passion of others to save lives. This is a wonderful thing when the person who is being saved wants to be. In this case I sense that Frank is okay with it as he has always loved his life and although shadows have invaded his mind, inwardly he has become more enlightened. His everyday physical existence did not provide him with this as he was too busy with his duties and other distractions to discover this element of existence. Luckily, this is a more spiritual experience and so physicality is not a necessity. However, to reach maximum glorious advancement after life it is always advisable to explore a more enlightened spiritual experience when we are going through life because life itself often sends us challenges that enable us to learn. If we choose to ignore the opportunity to learn as we go, this can often result in us living a more challenging existence because lessons continue to be sent in a desperate bid to help our spirit grow.

After arriving at the hospital Frank is brought straight through to the emergency department. From there he is moved to a ward. He is still not conscious. His family come in to be by his side. Two people having a conversation that I feel that I have to hear.

"What?" Lucy says, shocked, putting her head in her hands.

"I know, love, it is not easy to deal with but we have to have faith that they are going to be together again at last," her mum comforts her.

"But Mum, this can't be, they can't have the same condition at the same time and both now be reaching the end. I love them both," she wails.

"The distance is what hurts my heart. I know that you all are here for your dad so I am going to go and be by Carrie's side."

This confuses me, as I have not been called to Carrie's location yet. It suddenly comes to me. That is why I felt pulled. It was happening for both of them at the same time even though they are at opposite ends of the earth. Their hearts are connected as they experience this together.

I quickly choose to create an external meeting place for our spirits to connect so that we can work through this together.

It is not long before we are all standing together again.

"Sorry, guys, I did not realise that you were both searching for each other."

"It is okay, we are here now," Carrie says, beaming. She is glowing brighter than I've ever see her beam. Frank too appears to be lighter in his presence now than in our previous encounters.

"You both seem brighter, can you share your experiences since we last met up?" I ask.

"Do you want to go first, Dad?"

"Me? Okay then," Frank responds.

"Go ahead, Frank."

"Well, when I listened to you last time I didn't think I had much left to learn in my life. I thought I had learned most things as I have lived a full life filled with ups and downs. I know I have done wrong in my life but never without reason, so I struggled to see what it was that I needed to learn. It is obvious that I was never going to be a priest and live through God so I did the best I could do by providing for my family and ensuring they had a stable home to live in. This is what I wanted to do, but I know I sacrificed a lot to achieve this expectation of myself. It has always been my family that I made with my wife that I work hard for. It is my life and I have never seen past that. I would do anything to protect them and myself from what I perceived to be harm and shame. It came to me one day when I was walking in the field with the horses that I have often felt disappointed and sometimes betrayed when the kids, and maybe the wife too, didn't do things that I felt were right. I was working so hard for them and it hurt me. I didn't show it much but it would eat up inside me. Even though I tried to make it go away I couldn't. I didn't say anything often because it would be disregarded or laughed at and that made me feel even worse than not saying it. I could handle it myself. I have realised that all of those things don't go away. They stay inside and explode in different ways, often on someone who really doesn't deserve it, but by then it is too late and the things that come afterwards then have to be dealt with. I have taken a lot on board myself as I felt I had to because I was the strong one. This is a lot to carry around in a lifetime, and I know I should have let others carry the load too when they wanted to. By doing it all I took the ability away from them to be able to deal with life in a way they can manage. I know I need to let it all go and I have. Life didn't need to be so tough at times as people and family are in your life because they can add something to it and share the burdens too, which makes it better. If we don't allow that to happen then it can create clashes in personalities. Live and let live is something I never understood until now."

"My goodness, Frank, you have seen the light."

"I think so. Thank you for helping me."

Carrie holds hands as her eyes filled with love gaze to her dad.

"Dad, that is really good, I am so happy for you."

"Well, Frank, you must have done plenty right for your family because look at Carrie, she is beaming brighter than most stars right now."

"She is, isn't she?" he says with his heart filled with pride.

I feel as though I have just borne witness to the true love of a father. This is a magical life energising moment.

"Carrie, please enlighten us."

"Oh, where do I start? So when I realised what was happening to me I was very sad. Sad to be leaving my children who need me and sad to be leaving the life I love so much. I searched for a reason why this was happening to me when I am so young. I still don't have the full answer to that, but I know I can be at peace with it because it is not for me to understand. I need to accept and make the best of what it is, which is an opportunity to prepare for moving on, my time here is now over. I know that throughout my life I have been stubborn, I have pursued things just because I felt it was something I had to have in my life. I pushed until I got it. I believed that *anything worth having was worth fighting for* but I realise now in reflection that some things were not meant for me, and yet I still pursued them with so much intensity that it not only affected me but those around me. I have made huge decisions in my life that have had huge implications. I suppose it is knowing when to call it quits but still remain open, that when the time is right the opportunity will come around again if it is meant for me. I suppose what I have learned is to accept what isn't meant to be and embrace what is. This has eased my mind and spirit and I suppose resulted in me glowing right now."

"You have certainly embraced the wisdom bestowed upon you, Carrie. Well done to you for keeping an open heart and letting it in."

"I have to say that the process has been easier knowing that I am connected to my dad through it, thank you."

"You are welcome, Carrie."

"So what happens now?" Frank enquires.

"I will be returning you back to your physical presence, and you will have the opportunity to say goodbye to your loved ones. Then when you are ready you will ascend. I will be there to guide you and collect your beam. Carrie, I must also inform you that your mother is dashing to be by your side, which may be something for you to consider before you leave."

"Thanks again," Carrie responds.

They both return to their physicality, and I reflect on how much they have both learned. I feel that their connection, after so much time apart, has made their situation easier to bear.

I am called to Frank first. He is lying in the hospital bed surrounded by his family. They are all so concerned and love filled. Frank lies there unresponsive for a while. Then he slowly opens his eyes.

"Dad, can you hear me?" calls a man in his forties who resembles Frank.

Groggily, Frank responds, "Yes, son, I can."

"He's awake!" his son shouts, and a crowd of people come rushing to his side along with some nurses who are calling, "Give him some space, please, he needs some space."

"It's okay," Frank whispers to the nurses and they ease away.

Frank looks around the room and smiles. He then mumbles, "I am happy to see you all. Good life. Tell your mum..."

Immediately buzzers from the life support machines begin to ring, and the nurses buzz for assistance. Frank has already left his physicality as I watch him ascend before my eyes and his beam is released. This man doesn't wait around. He just gets on with the job in hand.

After working on him for a short time one of the doctors announces his time of death. There are tears from his family as they have now been given the news. I can sense that they have been uplifted by his final words though; it is always nice to have closure.

As I expected it is not long before I am by Carrie's side. She is at an airport location with a young lady who takes me aback with her sheer glowing beauty. It is Carrie's daughter Sarah who was a gift from the Waiting Zone that Boss was talking about earlier. She can sense my presence very strongly, and so I must keep my distance. Carrie is seated in the arrivals lounge as her daughter stands and paces the entrance to the arrival gate. Then there she is, Carrie's mum comes walking towards them with her arms stretched. "Nan!" Sarah squeals as she runs to her. Carrie lifts her head and seems to have recognised who it is. Her face beams with the emotion of the moment.

"Mum!" she screams as she scrambles to get to her feet. Both Sarah and her grandmother look at each other in amazed disbelief as they did not expect such a welcoming reaction. Carrie hugs her mum and won't let go. Her mum doesn't want her to let go ever as she holds on just as tight. Then in an instant Carrie releases her grip and is instantly detached from the moment again.

Sarah is saddened by this.

"Don't be sad, love, it is okay," her grandmother comforts her.

"Nan, I don't know how to tell you this but we have just heard that Granddad has passed away."

Her grandmother goes quite white and needs to sit down.

"I didn't know when would be the best time to tell you, but I know that you need to know."

"It's okay, love, I knew it would happen soon, but I am just a bit shocked is all."

"He did come around before he passed away, and he asked for everyone to tell you that he loves you."

Her grandmother grabs a pendant on a chain that hangs around her neck so tightly. It is as if it is an instant comfort to her. "Ah, bless him," she says as a tear trickles down her cheek.

Behind them is a scuffle. It comes to my attention that it was where Carrie was seated.

Her mum and daughter run to her side, battling to get through the crowd.

"Let me through, it's my mum," Sarah screams.

Carrie is lying on the ground. She looks up and the crowd appears relieved and begins to disperse. She holds up her hand.

"Mum, I waited for you," she gently says.

Her mum quickly grabs Carrie's hand while her daughter lifts her head and places it on her lap as she slides below her.

Carrie looks towards Sarah.

"You are special, always live through love."

Sarah begins to cry and Carrie kisses her hand as she slowly passes away.

"Mum, no," she cries, hugging her as tight as she can as she knows her mother has gone.

Tears drip onto Carrie's peaceful face.

I watch as this time Carrie leaves her physicality and ascends. She takes a moment to smile at me and when she looks to her tearful daughter she touches her heart and blows her a kiss. Sarah immediately sits upright and shivers and as she gazes upwards it is as if she can see her mum rise. A little smile appears and she too touches her heart just as Carrie is doing. At that moment Carrie turns around and focuses on her destination. She is at peace with knowing that it is her time to leave and that her dad awaits her.

As the emergency services assess Carrie's remains her mother and daughter hug. They will be comforting to each other during this time as they are suffering a double loss.

"They are now together," Carrie's mum shares with tears trickling down her cheeks.

"She came back before she left," her daughter says happily.

"Live through love," Carrie's mother says.

The gift of these last final words will have a profound impact on the way Sarah continues to live her life. I feel that it was love that Carrie tried her best to live through during her life but was often challenged and her heart ached. As I connected to her past energy my heart ached even though her energy was filled with love. This pain can be soul shattering but Carrie found a way to shatter the shackles and work through it and she wants her daughter to never feel as restricted as she did.

I hear Carrie whisper to my subconscious, "To live with an open heart is a gift that keeps magic alive."

Just as those words are finished her beam quickly returns and she has now ascended. I can't help but smile for her.

Henry

Collecting the beams from three of my four assignments makes me ponder on how close I am to this mission being completed. Only one more beam to collect from my main assignments. I have no idea what happens with Siobhan's beam, although I don't expect to be able to leave without it. I shall not ponder too much on this fact as I am sure I will be informed and guided when the time comes.

I am drawn to my new location. Henry comes straight into my thoughts so I know it is he I will be assisting. The first thing I notice is that I am inside a familiar home. There are Christmas decorations all around that bring this home to life. A warm glow from the fireplace heightens the cosy ambience created from the eight-foot pine tree that towers in the large living room; it is aglow with white lights and colourful hanging decorations.

I now place the home. It is the house that I first encountered during Henry's initial visit. It was under totally different circumstances as the bailiffs were here. I am rejoiced to witness that it is now a love filled home.

Two people are snuggled up on a luxuriously cosy sofa as their children happily colour in Christmas pictures in their pyjamas at a nearby table.

"How wonderful is this, love," the guy says to his wife.

She kisses him and then says, "It is perfect, my love."

"To think that everything fell into place for us to own such an amazing home it is unreal. Who would have foreseen it?"

"What is meant to be will always be, my love."

"I am so proud that it is your family home and that our children can grow up here just as you have."

"I cannot think of anything more wonderful, Jack. Dad would be so proud if he was aware of what we did to save this house from redevelopment."

They hug as they are united in their love for each other and the challenges they have overcome. They are now enjoying the fruits of their labour; this is always a special moment for anyone who sticks with something until the end. Not everyone has the strength to endure the course, but this lovely couple have come through triumphant.

I recognise her now as Henry's daughter who I encountered previously. She truly loves her dad.

"Mum and Dad, look, it is snowing," a very excited little girl screams as she runs to the window. It is getting dark outside and the white snow can be clearly seen settling on the ground.

"Come on, Junior," the man calls, and the boy excitedly joins them at the windowsill.

I watch this picture perfect moment as the love surrounding this family is apparent and further enhanced by the perfect beauty of the moment.

"I reckon tomorrow will be a great day to make a snowman, so it is a good time to go to bed so that we have lots of energy for snowman building in the morning," says Jack.

"Yay," shout the two little children.

"Dad, can I ask you something?" the little girl sweetly enquires.

"Of course, Rosie, what is it?" he responds, lowering himself to her level.

"Dad, can we make a snow woman too?" she asks with a serious little face.

Laughing joyously Jack whisks his son and daughter up into his embrace. "We can make a snow family if you want," he exclaims.

"Yay," they both cheer.

"Say goodnight to Mum," Jack says, tilting them both down to give their mum a bedtime kiss.

"Good night, Mum," they both say together and give her a good night kiss. One on each cheek in unison.

"Good night, my sweet peas," she says, rising from the settee to meet them.

Jack then leads them playfully out of the room. "So what story are we going to read tonight?"

"A snow one," the little boy excitedly requests.

"Yes, a snow one," the little girl agrees, equally excited.

"A snowman one it shall be," Jack says and up the winding staircase they go.

"I will just check on Dad when you are getting the kids to sleep, Jack."

Jack smiles back to her and winks.

Strangely, as I stand there a beam comes to me, and I capture it in the beam box. I don't understand how this has occurred, so I quickly follow her to where Henry is.

On entering the room I sense that Henry no longer inhabits his physical form. His daughter runs to his side.

"Dad, can you hear me, Dad?"

There is no response from him and she hugs him.

"I am sorry that you were alone, Dad, I love you," and she hugs him tightly and kisses him on the lips. She grabs a nearby chair and sits with him, holding his lifeless hand.

Suddenly on a nearby locker she notices a notepad with some writing on it.

"Oh Dad, you left a note," she smiles while reaching for it.

On it is a squiggled message. *Forever in my heart. Peace, love, happiness. Love you xx* and the third *x* is incomplete indicating the moment he passed.

I can feel that Henry is very much treasured in memory. I sense that he is humbly proud of his family's efforts on his behalf. They know he loved them always even though it didn't always feel like it when during his lifetime his behaviour showed otherwise. But he sought forgiveness for his actions and his family's response showed that he was forgiven. His remorseful heart was set free to ascend.

He didn't connect with me before departing but I have come to understand that he has been a man of few words, and he has continued to honour this trait through his ascension also. I can feel that he transcended successfully and his note shows his openness to expressing affection, which he was blocking himself from when I first encountered him.

It is now time to move on from my assignments with the beams safely back in my care. They are drained but will recharge again on my return. I am awaiting receipt of one, which leads me to reflect yet again how saddened I am that the beautiful Angela has not been in receipt of a beam. I am sure she has been a wonderful support to Henry during his enlightenment. I will keep her close to my heart in the hope that should she need me, I will be summoned to her side and although it will be without a beam I can only hope that will be enough.

Now it is time to check on Arianna. I have not been as tuned in to her as I should have been, because I needed to ensure that I completed my mission successfully. But as I await the return of my final beam I have reconnected and an urgency has overcome me that she needs my assistance.

CHAPTER TWENTY
Necessitating Arianna

    I arrive to an area that seems peaceful. I had braced myself along the way for the worst case scenario so this is a welcome setting to encounter. It is a parkland location and it is early morning. There are a few joggers and some people walking their dogs but otherwise it is quiet. Maybe it is the calm before the storm and then again maybe not. I do not know what to expect due to my previous encounters with Arianna's earthly journey and the premonition that is due to become reality at any moment. I attempt to locate her.

    I seem to have arrived in an apartment. I peer out of the window to see that it is situated on the first floor of a hotel block that overlooks parkland.

    The apartment is quite modern but nothing makes it personal which indicates that this is not a home; it is a temporary residence. It is certainly in need of tidying up. There are some little magical components that are drawing some nice energy in the form of a crystal or two hanging from blinds and some hand painted art that expresses love in a high form. It is like a warm glowing light in the corner of a darkened room. I get an overwhelming feeling that Arianna is here so I decide to look for her.

As I make my way to the next room I am aware of the lack of noise, well, apart from the street noise seeping through a window that has been left ajar.

I go into the room and see Arianna sitting on a chair in front of a mirror. I am horrified at the presence I feel surrounding her as she is lacking her glow and she looks so tired and drained. She is really skinny and she looks so sad. I have never seen her like this before. What a drastic transformation in such a short time, her beautiful radiant energy is gone. My heart reaches out to her, I want to whisk her up in my arms and be her hero. I physically ache witnessing this.

Then it happens.

"Gill, is that you, Gill?"

My heart leaps into my throat.

"Arianna, can you hear me?" I ask in hope.

Her head turns to me and her eyes open fully wide from the half closed position they depressingly lay in moments ago.

"Yes, I can, I knew that you would come, and that you would save me," she says, relieved.

I cannot believe I have let things get so bad. What must Boss be thinking? He is bound to be as disappointed in me as I am in myself.

I wrap my arms around her and she responds as I had hoped by exhaling a sigh of relief.

"I didn't think it would be like this, Gill," she says, down hearted. "I have never felt so sad and alone before."

"I know, it is not something that I wanted you to experience either, Arianna. But sometimes when we reach our lowest low that is where we find the seeds we need to reach our highest high."

"You are so wise, Gill, but I don't feel that right now."

"Of course, no one does. That's where faith comes into play."

"When he is around it is as if my heart is enchanted, there is a deeper force connecting me that I don't know about. I can't help myself and I know that I shouldn't, I know that it is wrong and I should run away but I don't have the strength to, Gill. I need your help."

"You are not the only one to have succumbed to temptation, Arianna, so don't be too hard on yourself."

"Then there is the note..."

Just as she has the words out of her mouth the apartment door opens and Jake shouts, "Babe, are you up yet?"

Arianna's whole demeanour changes in an instant. She becomes rigid.

I call to her, "Arianna, try to shield yourself from it."

But she no longer hears me. She gets up, puts on a fake smile and walks out of the room.

"Yes, babe, I have been up for ages."

"Yeah right!" he sarcastically replies.

"Jake, can we go out today?" she pleads.

"I told you, babe, you don't deserve to go out for a while after the last scenario. Showing me up like that. Don't you know that I am a well-known star, and you could do my rep a lot of harm if you do that to me again." He moves closer and kisses her mouth. "Now you wouldn't want that to happen, would you?"

"No, of course not, Jake," she responds obediently.

"That's my girl, now I am feeling a little peckish, and I just got some supplies in. Will you rustle me up something nice?"

Quickly moving towards a little kitchen area, Arianna replies, "Sure, Jake."

I follow her and try to get her attention.

"Arianna, you need to get out of here. This isn't right."

No reaction.

"Arianna, can you hear me?"

She whispers without moving her head and trying not to move her lips. "Yes, I can."

"So the next time he goes out we are leaving. Okay?"

"Okay, I'll try," she replies with minimal movement.

"Did you say something?" Jake accuses her.

"No, babe, just talking to myself," Arianna replies nervously.

"Well don't, I am trying to get in some tunes here and you distracted me," he says, agitated.

I won't distract her further as I don't want to make her feel fear anymore and I am not leaving her side until I get her out of here. So I wait. Even though it pains me to watch how he disrespects her and tries to control her. He has trampled all over her inner beauty, and I can only hope that she finds her glow again. Oh, it frustrates me so much to think that he has created an invisible jail for her. I can't believe that she is afraid just to get up and walk out of the door. This is so physically easy but totally off limits in her mind as there has been a fantasy barricade set in place that she is too fearful to cross due to the control he has of her.

He doesn't seem to have any intention of going anywhere. He just sits and drinking beer and smoking weed. He has Arianna sitting beside him and his arm is firmly placed around her shoulders. Then after what seems ages he falls asleep. I watch and wait for some time to pass and Arianna doesn't move a muscle. I come closer and whisper, "Arianna."

She jumps a little and Jake begins to stir but luckily he rolls over and releases her from his lock.

"Don't do that," she whispers.

"Sorry, but hey, it got him to let go of you."

She smiles.

"So do you have anything you really need to bring with you?"

"I can't go," she says, scared.

"Yes, you can, I am here to help you, now is the best time."

She nods and quickly but quietly makes her way to the bedroom where I found her earlier. She slowly opens the top drawer of the dresser and takes out a little bag. Then she leaves the room. She fearfully looks over to make sure Jake is still asleep.

"It's going to be okay. I am with you." I try to comfort her, placing my hand in hers, and she responds by holding mine back. My heart is a-flutter.

We make our way over to the door and she stalls. She doesn't move.

"Arianna, you need to open the door," I say, guiding her to the task in hand. She reaches for the door knob but pulls back.

"I can't," she cries.

Jake hears her and stirs again. Arianna nearly jumps out of her skin in fear.

"Listen to me, Arianna. You can do this."

She settles down, and I begin to guide her.

"Now lift your hand slowly towards the doorknob and with the other hand gently unlock the latch." To my relief she has taken a deep breath and is responding. "Good, now place your hand on the door knob and gently twist it."

She slowly moves her hand to the doorknob and then she turns around to see if Jake is still out cold.

"Twist it," I say, egging her on, "you can do it."

She does so and as soon as the door opens she quietly makes her way out into the hall and smiles with relief. Freedom is close and she runs to the elevator and presses the button. It seems to take a lifetime for the doors to open. And all of the time she keeps checking the area. Finally *ping!* the doors open. Arianna takes a step back when she sees one of Jake's band mates standing there. He shouts loudly and appears to be stoned.

"Hey Ari, where's the man?"

Quietly, Arianna replies, "He is in the apartment, I am just going out to get a few things."

"Cool…don't forget the beers."

"I won't," she says and as he staggers past she slips into the lift. When the doors finally close she lets out a huge sigh of relief.

"You did well," I reassure her.

"I am not out yet," she replies.

"Have you tried to leave before?" I ask.

"Yes, it didn't end well, but I have you with me this time so it will be okay."

"That's the spirit, Arianna." I place my arm around her, and she snuggles into the comfort and safety of it. The elevator, although very small, feels like a safe place to be right now.

The doors open with another *ping!* and straight away across the spacious foyer we can see the large glass doors that lead out onto the street and freedom.

We cautiously make our way out of the elevator as people are waiting to get in. Together we quickly walk hand in hand across the open floor. There is a reception desk to our right, and I notice one of the receptionists trying to get Arianna's attention.

"Keep looking at the doors, no matter what."

The receptionist shouts, "Miss Arianna, miss!" He is waving his hands but Arianna does not look at him, she keeps walking towards the doors and with every step she gets a little faster.

He begins to come after us with a portable telephone to his ear.

"Ignore him," I say, urging her on. "You are so close...keep going."

And that she does, I am so proud. By the time she reaches the doors she is running and as she approaches the doorman politely opens the door for her.

"Stop her!" the receptionist shouts.

"Keep going, young lady, don't look back," he calls as if he knows of her situation.

She takes a moment to smile at him in gratitude and then continues to run out onto the footpath and navigate her way across the busy road to the parkland.

There is some shouting from a window on the upper floor. It is Jake.

"Stop, Ari, don't do it!" he shouts. But she begins to run and doesn't stop to catch her breath; she keeps going until she is two streets away where she feels safe. She then stops, panting, and tries to slow her breathing.

"It feels so good to be out of there." She smiles at me and I see her glow slightly return.

"I bet it does."

"So, what is the plan now?" she asks.

"Well I reckon that we should go to Claire's, she will take care of you."

"No, you can take care of me, Gill. I can't let her see me like this."

"Of course I will, but we also need someone on the ground to help us."

"I don't know about it, Gill."

"Well we need to go somewhere until it is time to go back to the zone."

"Oh, I hadn't thought about going back to the zone."

"Hadn't you?"

"No, but it would be so nice to go home," she says dreamily.

"So Claire's it is?" I cautiously confirm.

She looks to me. "Okay, if you think it is best."

"Great, so we need to get some cash so that we can get the train."

"Already sorted," she says happily and pulls out the little package she went to recover from her room. "I am prepared this time." She pulls out a new brand new white t-shirt and disappears behind a nearby tree to change. She brushes her hair and wipes all signs of makeup from her face. Her hair is now looking natural again and the black eyeliner and dark make up is gone and replaced with a more natural complexion. Oh, it is so nice to see her looking fresh again.

"What's that?" I ask.

"Oh, that is the note I was telling you about. He ripped it up so that I couldn't see it, but I got it out of the bin. His mum wrote it."

"Can I read it?"

"Sure," she says, handing me a small clear zippy bag with a jigsaw of ripped paper in it.

As she hands the torn up note to me I don't attempt to put it together yet, even though I really want to. "I will do it later, it is best that we get going now."

"Yes, sounds good to me." To my surprise she pulls out a mobile phone. "I will let Claire know we are on our way, will I?"

"Arianna, you mean to say that you have had a mobile phone the whole time with Claire's number on it, and you have never used it. Why?"

"I had to keep it safe and hidden, Gill, just like I had to hide the note."

She has definitely thought it through. The train comes and we board it. We find a booth for both of us and it is not long before Arianna falls asleep. I can't help but ponder on what she has endured in the time I have been detached from her. I know the objective of her coming to being was that she experience life and learn life lessons but her experience seems to have been really harsh. Dare I say it is as if she has been touched by the dark side and if that is the case they will not stop until they have darkened her soul, especially as she is the daughter of the Waiting Zone boss. Oh, I do hope that this isn't so, and how did I not think of this before? I feel totally responsible and neglectful of the situation. We do have to get to Claire's as Arianna needs earth angel guidance. Claire will help her to cleanse. I have to believe that this will be okay; I can help fix this and get Arianna home more enlightened.

We are close to our stop and so I wake her up. The train slows to a halt and Claire is waiting for us on the platform as she did before.

"Oh my love, are you okay?" she asks and wraps her arms around Arianna.

"I am sorry, Aunty Claire," she replies apologetically while resting her head on Claire's shoulder.

They begin to make their way to the car park and I follow.

"Gill has to come too," Arianna says, stopping and turning around.

"I am following you, don't worry," I reassure her.

She turns to Claire and says, "He is my protector, you know. I am safe when he is around."

This makes me feel very proud.

"You are one very lucky lady," Claire responds.

"I am, aren't I," she states and rests her head back down on Claire's shoulders. Her energy seems to be drained and in need of revitalising.

We soon arrive at Claire's lovely home. First she makes Arianna some soup and then takes her to her room to rest.

"The children will be back soon, Arianna, try to get some rest when you can as they will be excited to see you."

"Oh, how lovely. Yes I think I will have a lay down. Thank you for my lunch, Aunty Claire."

"You are welcome, my dear."

In no time at all Arianna is asleep again, and I sit in a chair in her room watching how peaceful she is, a small smile on her face. I am so relieved that she is safe.

I think of the note and it may be a good time to stick it back together. But I find I cannot concentrate on it and my thoughts begin to roam. I am feeling an overwhelming urge to visit Angela. *How can this be?* Maybe it is time for Angela to ascend, and she needs my guidance. It shouldn't take long and Arianna is peacefully sleeping, so I allow my thoughts to continue to focus on Angela. The note will have to wait.

CHAPTER TWENTY-ONE
Angela

In such a short time there has been so much that has happened. I have been niggled by guilty thoughts that Angela has missed out on the potential of the highest ascension, which she well deserves. With all of this niggling at my heart and mind I know that is why the time has come for me to visit her. I close my eyes and ears to the noise of the surrounding world and focus on her location.

I arrive at an old building situated behind the cathedral we visited earlier. There are many people gathered outside who seem to be praying and there are many tears. The sound they are creating is really quite haunting. The energy around the crowd is very dull as sadness penetrates the atmosphere. As I look towards the building I feel a glow coming from within so I enter.

The halls are filled with nuns rushing around. I am guided towards the stairway so I move in this direction. When I reach the top I see that a distinct magical glow is coming from one of the rooms at the end of the hall.

On entering I am consumed by love. I sense that Angela will not be on the earthly realm for much longer. I watch her as she lies in her humble yet cosy bed. She is propped up with pillows surrounding her tiny frame, her eyes are closed and she seems peaceful. There are a few sisters in white and black gowns and habits keeping themselves busy by rearranging things in the room.

Angela opens her eyes and looks my way. The nuns run to her side but yet she looks past them and maintains her gaze in my direction. Only those who are divinely connected can see me with their hearts. I feel pain in her heart and she calls me closer. I go as close as I can and she whispers as loudly as her frail body will allow.

"I knew that you would return. I need to show you something," she says and then closes her eyes. I follow her into her thoughts as she has now unshielded her energy.

She guides me to a picturesque location. I see a two-storey farmhouse with fields around its circumference. There are animals in the fields contentedly grazing on the lush green grass.

I move toward the back of the house to see that there is a tractor parked at the back door where I expected a car to be. The back door opens and a little head pops out and back in again. To the side of the door there is a row of wellington boots in all different shapes and sizes lined up beside the step. I go inside. I see a busy country kitchen, the warmth from the Aga hugs me as I enter. A huge wooden kitchen table dominates the centre of the room. There is a man sitting at the head of the table, directing the movements of the five children that are running around.

"Listen to your father, children," a woman calls from beside the cooker. She is stirring a big pot of porridge. The children quickly listen and take their places at the table. The man smiles at the woman and she smiles back. Their hearts are in unison and are still so much in love even with the pressures of raising a family. I suddenly realise that the woman is Angela.

She is busy preparing lunch for her family. "I'm hungry, Mam," one little boy calls out.

"That's good, Sam, because we have lots for you to fill your tummy with. Would you like to help me bring it to the table?"

His little face beams. "Yes, please," he says as he jumps up from his seat and is by his mum's side in an instant. Angela passes him a bowl full of freshly peeled boiled eggs which he carefully brings to the table. She carries over a large salad bowl and some freshly baked bread, then a plate of meats and a jug of milk to wash it all down. I notice that all of the children sit patiently waiting for their mum to join them at the table, which is when their dad says, "Well what are we all waiting for, let's get stuck in." To the delight of the children they all fill their plates with a bit of everything and soon it is transferred from the plate to their tummies.

"Thank you, Mum," the oldest girl says while gathering up the empty plates and bringing them to the sink for washing.

"You are welcome, my love," Angela replies in her angelic voice.

"Mum, can we go out to play?" two mischievous-looking boys ask.

"Yes, you may, but do not go far as your father needs you to help him on the farm shortly."

"Yeah," they cheer as they make their way outside.

I can see that Angela has such a loving family. She glows in providing the love and security they need. The telephone rings and she gets up to answer it.

"Hello, Angela speaking…Oh hello, Ruby… no, I haven't given it much thought really, I am needed here and so this is where I must be…no, I don't feel like I need a break…of course it would be lovely to see you, but as I said I am needed here and happy to be here…yes, of course I will give it some thought…nice to chat with you too, Ruby…goodbye."

"You really could have a nice break with your sister, love, we will manage here."

"Harry, I have no need to be swanning off across the water for a break that I do not need. I am happier here with you all. This is where I want to be. Ruby is quite welcome to visit us, if she wants to see me she can come here. She just wants to show off her new house and fancy lifestyle. I am happy for her because it makes her happy, but she can't see why it is family that makes me happy."

Harry stands up and lovingly kisses his wife's head. "I just don't want you wearing yourself out, is all." She stands up to meet him, and he puts his arms around her. They have a cosy cuddle and the remaining children are giggling in the corner at this show of affection.

"You all fill me full of energy for each day, my darling, not the opposite. Now we had better get moving or the day will be over before we know it."

"What did I ever do to deserve such a wonderful woman as you?" he says and gives his wife a quick hug before he dashes out the door to finish his day.

***

I am moved forward slightly in time. Everyone still looks the same and so I conclude that it is not long after the scene I have just witnessed. Strangely though, Angela is all dressed up in an outdoor coat as if she is going somewhere. I would have assumed the shops but then I see an old brown suitcase at the back door.

"Harry, are you sure I should go? I don't know why but I have a feeling that something isn't right."

Putting his arms around his wife in a loving way, he says, "Please stop, you're fretting my love, we will be fine."

"Ah Harry, you and the children are my world, I don't see the need to remove myself from what makes my heart sing to experience something that doesn't."

"Think of it as a time out to recharge yourself and then you can come back with renewed energy."

Dropping her head in defeat she agrees. "Okay, I shall try to relax."

"Don't forget to enjoy yourself, you don't know how long it will be until you get the opportunity again. Now say goodbye to your mum, children." Harry says.

They all surround her and hug her and tell her how much they will miss her and how much they love her. Tears well in Angela's eyes, and I sense that she does not want to leave her beloved family and yet with the best of intentions from others she is being left with little alternative than to give in to their requests. A car is heard pulling up outside.

"That's the taxi, love, you had better get going. Have a lovely time at your sister's birthday. We will miss you, but we will be fine."

"Oh Harry, I love you, I wish I didn't have to go, my spirit is telling me not to."

"Allow yourself this, Angela, and then it will be back to the daily routine in a few short days, and you will never hear another word from your sister about going to visit."

Beep. Beep. The taxi sounds its horn impatiently. After a few more cuddles from everyone Angela picks up her suitcase and makes her way to the taxi. Seated in the back she waves at her beautiful family who have now congregated outside in the rain. As the taxi pulls off she quickly turns around to see them all. Two mischievous boys run after the taxi and down the lane until they reach the bottom where they stop and wave their little arms so fast to see her off.

Angela has tears in her eyes as she is reluctant to leave her family, she rejoices in caring for them so much. It is what she loves to do most and some people just don't understand that.

***

She has now landed safely and is soon disembarked from the airplane with bags collected and now she is walking through to the arrivals lounge. Angela looks to be out of her comfort zone and stands out in her country farm attire. A woman of the same height comes rushing from the sidelines and wraps her arms around her, taking Angela aback.

"Oh Angela, you're finally here," says the lady, who looks similar to Angela and so I perceive her to be her sister. She is dressed in the finest of fashion and her blonde hair is styled to perfection for the era. She holds out Angela's arms and says, "Oh my darling Angela, I will have you looking and feeling a million dollars in no time at all."

Angela has still not spoken but her facial expression says it all, she just wants to reboard the plane and return to her family where she feels as rich as any millionaire.

"Come on, let's get you home, you must be shattered after all of that travelling, I hope you don't suffer from jet lag, it can be a horror."

Angela attentively follows her sister to the car park and gets into the passenger side. On the journey there is excitement from Ruby and a solemn response from Angela. I don't think she can help it; she has an aura of grief surrounding her.

It is getting dark, and it has been a long day for Angela. Not long after bypassing the city with its light beaming out into the night sky from the tall buildings and vibrant energy that surrounds a city of culture they arrive in a village. Street lights line the main road and picturesque period homes are scattered all around. We pass a shop that is closed for trading and a pub that has a warm glow and traditional music emanating from its wooden framed window.

"That's the local pub where the party is being held, they have a lovely function room at the back, we can pop down there for some lunch tomorrow if you would like," Ruby says to Angela, in an attempt to break the silent and morbid atmosphere.

"That would be nice," Angela responds with a small smile.

At the end of the street there are two white pillars with black gates open and welcoming any incoming traffic up a tree-lined lane. On one of the pillars a plaque says 'Hammersmyth House' in gold letters. At the top of the lane there is a large two-storey period home. It is lit up like a Christmas tree, with lights glowing from each of the windows that is picturesquely inviting in many ways.

"Is this your home, Ruby?" Angela asks politely.

"Yes, my darling sister, it is, do you see now why I wanted you to come and be pampered by us? I have waited so long to show you and maybe next time you could bring all of your family, there is lots of room for you all." She beams so proudly.

"That would be nice," Angela says again politely.

When they pull up outside the front door a man comes out to help Angela with her things.

"Hello, I am Mike, Ruby's better half. You must be Angela, so nice to finally meet you. Ruby has told me ever so much about her big sister," he says, shaking Angela's hand firmly and speaking in a friendly yet overwhelming manner.

"Nice to meet you also, Mike," she smiles back.

After a short uncomfortable moment where no one utters a word Mike says, "I shall get the bags; you ladies go on ahead in and put your feet up."

As they enter Ruby talks about the decor and styling and how she wants to help people design their homes more tastefully. Angela agrees and follows her to a huge modern kitchen.

"Can I get you a drink?" Ruby enquires.

"A cup of tea would be nice," Angela replies timidly.

"Oh come on, Angela, you are on holidays now, you can let your hair down and with no kids to wake you in the morning you can sleep in as long as you want to. How about a glass of wine?" Ruby says in an attempt to liven her sister up.

"A cup of tea will be fine, thank you," Angela responds politely.

Ruby smiles equally politely and fills the kettle.

"If you don't mind I might go to bed after tea, Ruby, I am quite tired and I feel that a sleep might be good for me."

Ruby dashes around to the side of the counter where Angela is seated on a high stool.

"Oh Angela, I am sorry for pushing, I am just so excited to see you, it has been so long. I know that you must be tired and missing your family. I am sorry." She gives Angela a more heartfelt hug.

Angela hugs her back and then replies, "Yes, I do miss them so much, Ruby. I have never been away from our home this past decade and it is all very unfamiliar for me. I am sorry too."

They hug again.

"Why don't you go on up to bed, and I will bring you up a cup of tea, and then you can unwind and have a good night's rest."

"Thank you, that would be nice."

Ruby shouts, "Mike, love, can you show Angela to her room, she is very tired and needs to rest."

Eager to help, Mike directs Angela to her room and the awkwardness seems to have mellowed. He guides her to her room and quickly leaves her to it. The room is cosy with a big double bed and a dressing table with a mirror and cushioned seat. The decor is timely and everything matches. Angela smiles as she looks around at the room with everything in its place and barely touched by human hands.

Placing her suitcase on the bed she opens it and takes out some night clothes. Her long nightdress has an array of little flowers on it and a white section of cotton and lace that covers the chest area, with three buttons to maintain modesty at all times.

There is a knock on the door and Ruby brings in a tray and positions it on the bedside locker.

"Goodnight, sis, and enjoy your tea, I shall see you in the morning. I have a good day planned for us tomorrow."

Goodnight, Ruby...and thank you," Angela says from the heart.

Smiling, Ruby leaves the room and Angela gets herself dressed and snuggled up to drink her tea. In no time at all she has turned out the lights and is sound asleep.

When the telephone rings a few hours later she sits bolt upright in the bed. She doesn't move an inch. She can hear a muffled voice replying to the communication on the other end. A harrowing spine-chilling scream can be heard from Ruby. Slowly footsteps can ascend the stairs. Angela still sits straight as a poker in the bed. The footsteps reach the top of the hallway and make their way towards the door. Under the door there is a glow from the landing light. This highlights the shadows of the feet at the other side of the door. A little tap at the bedroom door and after a moment the latch is opened and Ruby enters with tears streaming down her face. Angela turns to face her sister.

"I am so sorry, Angela, I am so sorry, this is my entire fault," she wails.

Angela just looks at her, knowing in her heart that something terrible has happened but for just one more moment not knowing what it is will keep her in a different timeframe, one when everything was still perfect.

"Angela, something terrible has happened" Ruby cries. Mike is standing behind her trying to hold her together.

Angela then breaks her silence and says, "Tell me, tell me what has happened. Who is it? Tell me."

Mike and Ruby look at each other and Ruby breaks down, unable to respond to her sister's request. Mike holds Ruby up and says, "There has been a fire, it doesn't sound as if there have been any survivors."

"A fire, a fire, where?" Angela screams.

"A fire at your house, Angela, I am sorry but as far as we know nothing could be done in time."

She drops to her knees on the floor. "No, my beautiful family, this can't be happening." She gets up from the floor. "I must be there; I need to be there now. Please bring me to the airport." She begins to throw on some clothes.

Putting her hand on her sister's shoulder, Ruby says, "Maybe it is not a good time for you to fly, Angela, the shock…"

Angela pushes her hand away. She turns around to face her sister directly and says, "I am going home to my family now. If you are not going to get me to the airport right this instant then I shall find a way there myself." She then lifts her suitcase and makes her way out of the room.

"I will bring her," Mike says.

"Thank you, I shall go with her, she needs me even if she thinks that she doesn't," Ruby responds in a daze of disbelief.

"I can come too if you would like. We can get some flights at the airport."

"Yes, you're right, I must get her home straight away." She turns to Mike. "Oh Mike, her home is gone, her family is gone, how will she ever…?"

Mike grabs hold of her and pulls her close to him. Tears stream from her eyes as the reality of it all sinks in.

"We mustn't keep her waiting," Ruby says, quickly pulling back and wiping her tears away.

When they make their way downstairs Angela is standing with her suitcase at the front door. She is just staring at it and is swaying to and fro. She has gone inwards in order to survive until such time as she can grasp the reality of it all. It is all too much to comprehend, the feeling that nothing will ever be the same again, the pain of the loss is unimaginable. The not knowing what actually happened. Everything that you live for, work hard for, everything that makes your heart happy, for that all to be gone in a phone call, that cannot feel real for anyone.

I understand how Angela needs to be there, she needs to see for herself, she needs to hold her children, she needs to understand what has happened and most of all find out if it was because she was not there when they needed her most. Most importantly, she will feel guilty that she did not listen to her inner guide. She may even believe this tragedy has occurred as a result of her not listening to her spirit when it was telling her not to go. That is bound to be very hard to live with.

I stay with them on the long and turbulent journey to Ireland. One of Angela's neighbours has come to pick them up from the airport. Angela has still not uttered a word. She is blocking off her emotions in order to survive each moment, each one a step closer to the reality that awaits her—her worst nightmare come true.

They turn into the laneway where a day ago her children ran to wave their mum goodbye for a few days. Angela could never have comprehended the outcome of her departure, however I sense that deep within she knows her inner spirit was trying to guide her against going and yet she succumbed to the requests of others.

Sitting upright and holding her composure she continues to look out of the window. I do not sense any emotion emitting from her heart. Her thoughts are also blanked out, she has frozen all of her sensory abilities. Driving closer to the remains of her home that only a day ago stood majestically at the top of the hill, Angela begins to show signs of consciousness. When the doors of the car are opened the smell of singed materials and earth is potent. It is a dull day with a slight mizzle assisting in extinguishing the smouldering mound that is piled before us.

There are a few people here, the local doctor and priest among them. They both approach Angela. These good-willed pillars of the community are here to ensure that those directly affected by the tragedy are assisted spiritually and physically.

Angela stands rigid looking at her home, the love-filled nest that she worked so hard to create and fill to the brim with love and joy. The loving sanctuary where ten years ago her husband carried her across the threshold and to which she brought home each of her newborn children. Yesterday must feel so alien to her now as she attempts to fathom exactly what has happened.

"Sorry about your loss, Angela," the priest says, taking her hand.

Angela smiles sorrowfully but gratefully back at him.

"Angela, I too am very sorry for your tragic loss," the doctor says.

Then there is silence.

"What happened?" Angela asks.

They look to each other. Then Fr Hubert obliges. "Angela, the fire took hold too fast for anyone to escape. The fire fighters did all they could…"

"I get the picture, my babies had no chance," she says, unable to listen to more.

"Tragedy like this takes its toll on our body and mind and so I took the liberty of prescribing you some pills to help you deal with the immediate shock. Please also know that I am only a phone call away should you need me," the doctor says.

"Yes, I am also never far away, my dear lady," Fr Hubert adds.

"Thank you, Dr Hobbs, but I shall not be requiring any prescription; I shall be allowing myself to feel each moment of mourning for my gorgeous babies. They did not deserve to be taken like this; they have done no wrong and did not deserve to suffer such a harrowing death, and one that could have been prevented had I been here to protect them."

"Angela, you mustn't blame yourself," Ruby wails. It all is too much for her to bear. She has been sobbing uncontrollably from the moment they saw the remains of the house.

"Why, Ruby? Would that be because if I don't blame myself then you will feel less guilt about badgering me to come visit you?"

Ruby just wails louder.

Angela remains composed. I sense a deep-rooted sadness yet an acceptance of the process of life.

I feel her call me, so I return to the present. Facing her I think of how this angel subsequently went on and now shines in the lives of so many. Deep in her eyes, the gateway to her soul, the pain of her loss is still visible. She could have used it as a reason to be saddened for the rest of her days but she hasn't. Instead she has utilised her immense loss to connect with others in the most positive way possible.

"You came to help me advance to full enlightenment, didn't you?" she enquires softly.

"Yes, you have almost reached full enlightenment already, Angela, it is time to forgive," I reply.

"Enlightened I may be but no matter how much I have embraced anyone who may need me as my substitute family, I still harbour the pain of that loss." She drops her head.

"Angela, you are a living, breathing human being with a heart of gold. I know that you were eternally grateful to have experienced the true joy that having your own family unit gave you. When they were taken from you it was their time to move on, but their energy stays with you and I know that you have often felt their presence. You had so much to offer others and so much to learn for yourself and your spiritual advancement during this lifetime and that is why it was not your time. Deep down you know that you will be reunited with your beloved family and so that is why I now ask you to allow me to help you lay your pain to rest because you no longer face it alone. I have been gifted with the honour of alleviating your pain and replacing it with love and the excitement of knowing that you will soon complete your journey through this lifetime and receive the divinity that is rightfully yours. Do not let any darkness shadow your truest spiritual potential, Angela."

"Your words are like music to my ears, my dear. I suppose my reservation comes from advancing higher than those I mothered. I never got to hold them in my arms and say goodbye."

"You had no need to say goodbye, Angela, for they await your coming."

A smile spreads across her face. She knows that although her human mind and body will suffer further as she withdraws from her earthly journey, she trusts wholeheartedly that she can now advance peacefully towards her highest potential as it will only be a short time before she is rewarded in the heavens.

"I am grateful for your coming, dear; I know that you came back to me of your own doing."

I smile at her angelic face that is showing some signs of pain. Then as if with a bolt of lightning I feel a sensation overcome me, and Arianna pervades my immediate thoughts. Angela needs me to focus my energy on her right now to assist her in advancement and the magical crystal I have received for Angela is awaiting transition but I must honour my feeling and go straight to Arianna. I sense fear and danger.

"Angela, I must depart now but I will return soon." I try to speak in a calm and composed manner, but it doesn't quite happen as I intend.

Angela sleepily gazes at me and nods. I do wish that I didn't have to abandon her again. Maybe it will be third time lucky and I will finally get to assist her during our next encounter but alas this time it is not meant to be. Yes, this thought sits well with me, and so I begin to transcend my energy to Arianna's location immediately.

CHAPTER TWENTY-TWO
Déja Vu

I quickly arrive back to see someone with a dark hooded top in Arianna's room. She is still asleep and is not aware of their presence. There is a lot of noise from the children running around so it is easily understood how he has been undetected by Claire. I also see a window open so that must have been the point of entry. I am determined that it will not be the point of exit for Arianna.

I am horrified to see a needle and I try my best to stop the intruder injecting its contents into Arianna's arm but my efforts go unrewarded.

Arianna begins to stir from her deep slumber and as she opens her eyes she is instantly groggy. Whatever was pumped into her has taken affect. The intruder attempts to lift her. I cannot possibly let this happen and, overcome with a rush of emotion, I push him hard. It works and the person seems to be freaked out about what has just happened. He attempts to lift her again, and I conjure up the same emotion and do the same thing again. This time I am successful in banishing him from the room and I use the rest of my might to close the window.

I go to Arianna who is coming around but she has a different aura. I try to talk to her but she no longer hears me. Whatever he has given to her is strong and it has instantly infected her pure spirit.

She is conscious but has a different look in her eyes and it is as if she has been possessed. She opens up her drawer and puts on a black t-shirt and jeans and leaves the room without even combing her hair. My energy is very low after the altercation I have just had but I do my best to keep up.

She storms to the kitchen where Claire is preparing dinner and watching her children play happily outside. Then it happens. Déjà vu!

"Where is he? I know he is here. I can feel him," she says to Claire. This takes Claire totally by surprise.

"Arianna love, what is wrong, what has happened to you?"

Arianna changes her approach. "Aunty Claire, I have to go see him, he needs me."

"Arianna, it is my duty to protect you during your stay here. Jake is not in a position to be a positive influence in your life right now, and I want you to stay away from him, if you don't things will just get worse instead of better."

"But I love him," Arianna says, crying into her hands.

Claire approaches her and puts her hand, which is covered in washing up bubbles, on her shoulder. "Arianna, that is not love you are feeling. You know deep down that it isn't if you would only listen to your spirit. You are letting your spirit be overshadowed and controlled by lust, desire, temptation and ego. I have seen it happen to so many people; please don't let it happen to you."

Arianna looks at Claire and in that moment she has connected directly with her spirit, she has broken through the darkness.

Then the back door slams open and three children come running in.

"Mum, there is a man out the front and he is shouting for Aunty Arianna, he looks strange and we are scared."

Claire looks to Arianna.

"Jake!" Arianna grabs her rucksack and makes a dash for the door.

Claire gets there first and closes it tight, blocking her exit.

"Move, he needs me."

"Arianna, stop and think, don't do this," Claire pleads.

But Arianna has that strange look back in her eyes. "He came for me, he loves me," she says, then shouts, "Jake, I am in here!"

She looks at Claire and says, "Sorry, Aunty Claire, I have to go or I will never know."

Then she dashes out through the door where I am standing. As she passes me she comes to a halt and looks around, pausing for a moment from her mad dash. Then in through the front door comes Jake who is all rugged in appearance.

"Ari, come on, I am waiting for you." He sounds agitated.

Arianna gives herself a little shake and runs towards him; she follows him out of the front door and all that can be heard is the slamming of car doors and a car speeding off with music blaring from every open window.

I look to Claire who has three frightened little kids hugging her legs. She looks directly at me and her eyes are filled with helplessness.

Her attention is then distracted by the three little faces peering up at her with quivering lips. She quickly shakes herself into another mindset, with a little of my assistance for I absorb some of her anxious energy to help her mentally adjust from worried aunty to caring mum mode.

"Okay guys, don't worry about Aunty Arianna, she has someone who is going to help her. So who wants ice cream?"

They all cheer, "Yay, me, me, me!"

I need an immediate energy boost so I can assist Arianna. I attempt to connect with the natural supplies of nature and to my surprise an energy boost enters me in an instant. I felt a glow and it reenergised my core instantaneously. I know that it was sent via a direct source and I am grateful.

I channel in on Arianna's energy and for the first time ever I feel heavy hearted to do so. I cannot connect. I know she has been overcome with poison and controlled by something dark but why has her purity been shadowed so much? I can't help but wonder. Then again maybe it is not for me to know the why. I am just part of the greater picture and in order to have a successful outcome I need to commit to my role in the process wholeheartedly. I left her and look what happened. She needs me to be there for her continuously. *Arianna needs me.* I like that thought.

My heart begins to glow, and I feel so much love for her. I know her true spirit is still in there; I believe I can help her glow again. Everything happens for a reason and, even though I do not fully understand why yet, I am sure that I will in time, and I will be glad that I kept following my heart guide and saw this through without giving up.

I open my heart and attempt to reconnect. I have arrived back at the flat. There is music playing and everyone is drinking. Arianna is dancing around seductively, and Jake is lying on the sofa with his mates cheering her on.

"Yay, that's it, babe. Just keep dancing."

One of his mates turns to him and asks, "So why would you not let her go, mate?"

"She is special, man, and she is mine," he says proudly.

"But Jake, you could have any woman in the world. You are going to such great lengths to keep this one."

"You would never understand, man, never understand," Jake responds.

At that Arianna stops and holds her head as if it is in a spin. "I need to lie down." She walks off into the bedroom where she lies on the bed and passes out.

"Okay, everyone out!" Jake shouts.

"Ah man, that party is just getting started."

"Out!" he shouts continuously while physically tugging at each person to get up and leave.

"Okay, okay, see you tomorrow then," says one of his band mates.

"Yeah, man, back on the road tomorrow."

Everyone leaves and Jake closes the door. His demeanour instantly changes as he leans against the door with a disturbed intention plainly visible in his demeanour.

He walks towards the bedroom but stops half way to take a swig of beer. I seize the opportunity to distract him from the plan he has directed towards Arianna. I conjure up all of my might and push the bottle out of his hand. Beer spills everywhere and the bottle smashes on the ground.

"Holy shit!" He seems a bit freaked out but pulls out another beer.

I do the same again.

"What the hell is going on?" he shouts towards the ceiling.

I begin to prod him continuously and he jerks every time.

"Piss off whatever you are, go away!" he screams.

Knowing what he has done to Arianna and, even worse, what he is intending to do, I can't stop. I am getting great satisfaction in scaring him.

Eventually he has had enough and he runs out of the room. I make sure that the double lock is on the door and then I go to check on Arianna. She is sleeping soundly. I finally feel that I can loosen up a bit, which is a relief in itself. I will stay close to Arianna tonight and no matter if I am called away I will not get distracted again.

I sit in the chair and watch her as she sleeps. She is not totally peaceful as she jerks and frowns. I can't even imagine what she is experiencing due to the venom that has filled her veins. Finally she calms down and her expression becomes more peaceful.

As I sit there the note comes into my mind. Now is the perfect opportunity to try to read what is written on it. I take it out of my pocket and place the pieces on the dresser. I begin to put them together like a jigsaw puzzle. It is a slow process as it is in small pieces.

Finally after some time I think I have it. It is a little faded but I attempt to read it anyway.

'Jake, my dear son, your desire for this girl must stop now. She can never be yours. You are from the dark side and she is from the light, please don't shadow her spirit. It may be hard to comprehend but she is directly related to you. I too am the fruits of her father's loins. You must let her go.'

It takes me a few moments to work this out. *He knows he is related to her so why has he not let her go?* This is a forbidden desire on his part, and he is obsessed with controlling her against his mother's wishes. I wonder if this is what caused the accident.

I look out the window and see that it is beginning to get bright. *I need to get Arianna out of here* is my immediate thought. To my relief, she begins to stir and I attempt to connect with her.

"Arianna, Arianna," I say softly.

She seems a bit groggy but she responds with a tired, "Yes."

"We need to get out of here, do you understand what I am saying?"

She nods but seems unable to open her eyes.

"Arianna, try to open your eyes. Can you get up and wash your face?" I say, encouraging her to keep moving.

She doesn't seem to have much energy, so I place my hand on her back directly opposite her heart centre and pump some pure energy into it. She is soon up and in the bathroom washing her face and sorting herself out.

The realisation hits her that she is back in the apartment. She looks down at her clothes horrified and says, "How did this happen again? Where is he?" She begins to become more cautious.

On entering the bedroom she spots the torn up note laid out on the dresser. She makes her way to it but as she does there is an almighty bang at the door to the apartment and it swings right open and then slams shut.

"It's Jake," she says, scared, and she does not know what to do. He comes charging into the room.

"Don't be scared," he says when he sees her cowering in the corner.

"What do you want, Jake?" Arianna cries.

"You are meant to be with me, Ari, we are destined to be together. You are bound to have realised that by now."

"No, Jake, I don't feel that."

"That is not what you said when I rescued you from your aunty's place."

"Jake, you did something to me, because I don't remember a thing."

"Don't say that. You know that you are meant for me."

Arianna shakes her head and as he approaches her he spies the ripped up note laid out on the dresser. He scoops it up in his hand and throws it into the air and his attitude totally changes.

"So you have read it," he accuses her.

Arianna doesn't answer.

"She doesn't know what she is talking about. She is going crazy," he says.

"What do you mean?" Arianna asks, knowing that she may never get the opportunity to read the note now.

"There is no way we are related," he shouts, pacing the floor. "If she hadn't of went on and on about it she wouldn't be lying in the hospital now, would she?"

"What do you mean? Did you..."

"Did I what? Make her crash? Is that what you are trying to say?"

Arianna lowers her head.

"Right," he says, walking towards Arianna and grabbing her by the arm.

"Where are you taking me?" she asks.

"You can ask her yourself," he says, dragging her out of the room.

As I have no intuitive urge to stop this from happening I do not intervene.

CHAPTER TWENTY-THREE
The Final Beam

We soon arrive at the hospital. I follow as they make their way back to the same room as before. Siobhan is lying sleeping. Her recovery has been a very long process due to the extent of her injuries. After reading the note she wrote to Jake I can only conclude that she is dealing with emotionally charged ailments also.

They both walk in and stand at the bedside. Siobhan stirs a little and she seems to come around momentarily.

A doctor enters the room and brings with him a radiant atmosphere that overcasts the dreary silence in the room.

"Hello everyone," he says brightly.

"Hello," Arianna responds politely. Jake doesn't say anything nor does he turn his head to acknowledge the doctor who is looking at him awaiting a response. He soon realises that he is not going to get one and he glances at Arianna who gives him an apologetic smile.

"Right, okay," the doctor continues. "Well, your mum obviously has a lot of healing still to do, but you will be glad to hear that she is on the road to recovery. She is responding really well to all treatments, and I imagine she is aiming to get out of here and back home pretty soon if there is a support system in place."

"That is awesome news," Arianna replies.

Jake finally speaks to the doctor. "What do you mean support?"

The doctor looks to Siobhan who is not fully awake yet, but he is being cautious anyway.

"Maybe we could chat about this outside the room?" he suggests.

He goes to the door and holds it open waiting for Jake to follow him into the hallway. Jake grabs Arianna's hand on his way past and ensures that she is by his side.

"Well, your mum has been through quite an ordeal, and we have fixed her up to the best of our ability so she is now out of danger. We can't see any reason why she can't go back to the comfort of her own home and with the support of her family and outreach services she will be back to her old self in no time."

"But I am going on tour tonight. I can't possibly mind her," Jake announces.

The doctor looks to Arianna.

"I will," she says softly.

Jake looks to her. "You can't. You will be on tour with me."

"Your mum needs one of us right now, Jake, so why not do the right thing for her?"

He stands there, overcome with a dose of what seems to be conscience. Reluctantly he replies, "If it is the only way," and then storms down the hallway.

Arianna looks through the window of the room and sees Siobhan looking back at her with a gentle smile.

"Great. I will begin the paperwork then," the doctor says. He makes his way towards the desk and informs a receptionist that Siobhan will be going home, Arianna will be her primary carer and all necessary support networks should be implemented.

I had never anticipated this happening but how great it will be for Siobhan and Arianna to spend some time together. Boss will be proud of this moment. Arianna does not know the connection she has to Siobhan and it is not my place to inform her. Her unselfish heart is still untarnished. Even though she has been exposed to so much darkness at the hands of Jake she is still willing to put that aside to help someone in need without knowing that there is any other connection other than the connection she has to Jake. She truly is an amazing person.

I feel that it has all been a process. Everything happens for a reason and until that reason manifests, it is sometimes hard to bear the process.

1 month later

This month has been a welcome break. Although it has been physically tough for Arianna I can see that she has flourished throughout this time. Siobhan is also almost back to herself and they have both built an amazing bond that will never be broken.

They are both sitting out on a patio and the sun is shining on the water feature that is positioned in the backyard and it is creating a rainbow.

"Oh look at the rainbow," says Arianna.

Siobhan smiles. "Isn't it beautiful? I have always thought of rainbows as magical smiles from Mother Nature, reminding us of the amazing natural beauty that surrounds us."

"Oh, I love that thought," Arianna replies.

"Arianna, I cannot thank you enough for the past month. It has been so wonderful in so many, many ways that I wouldn't even know where to begin."

"I have to say that this has been the best experience for me too. It has helped me to understand that the most important things in life are balance, love and the simple things. This I did not understand before."

"Yes, many of us never come to understand those precious commodities until it is often too late or something drastic happens that makes us appreciate them more. It is sad really, isn't it?"

"Yes, is truly is."

They both sit and ponder.

"I am very grateful for the time we have had together, Arianna."

Arianna smiles and with her heart she beams, "I too am very grateful, Siobhan. I will treasure this time always."

"That is very nice to hear, my love."

Just as they sit there with their hearts united and aglow the telephone rings and Arianna says, "I'll get it if you like."

"It is okay, love, I will get it. I need to get about more anyway, it is not as if you will be at my beck and call forever."

She lifts up the telephone and says, "Hello..." but is cut off from saying anything more. The next thing we hear is, "Yes, that is me." Then everything is silent and Siobhan sits heavily on the seat beside the telephone table.

I can faintly hear someone calling, "Are you still there?"

"Oh yes, yes, sorry I am still here. What happened?" she asks. Her face is now white as a sheet as she listens.

"Okay, thank you for ringing...yes, I do have someone with me right now. Thank you. Goodbye."

Sensing that something is not right, Arianna rushes to her side.

Siobhan replaces the receiver and reaches for Arianna's hand

"What is it?"

"It's Jake. He has been found dead in his New York hotel room."

Arianna drops to her knees. "No, it can't be."

But from her aura I sense some relief through her sadness. The same applies to Siobhan's energy. I watch as their eyes meet and the understanding is clear without them saying a word, then they move in to hug each other close.

"Arianna love, I have something I believe it is time for me to share with you."

My stomach does a twist. Is she going to tell her about their bond? They return to their seats on the patio, and Siobhan pulls her chair closer to Arianna's.

"What is it, Siobhan? Whatever it is you can tell me."

"I know, my dear, but it is hard for me to say."

Arianna holds Siobhan's hand and looks into her eyes. "Please tell me, I need to know."

"Okay love, I will." She her lemonade before she begins.

"I know that Jake was not good to you, my love, and it breaks my heart to know so because you are so pure of heart. Before we crashed we were having an argument about you. You see, Jake has not been a good boy throughout his life. I often wondered where he got his dark streak from as I have always known that he was a gift to me after I experienced a loss. I never let myself stop believing that there was a really good boy inside but then I saw how he treated you and other people in his life just because he was famous. His dad was not a good person but he certainly was not dark, so I have always come to the conclusion that he got it through me as I was a really bad person in the past until I saw the light. Then when I saw the light again a lot of things became clearer for me."

Arianna is listening closely but it is clear she does not understand why there is a connection to her in all of this.

"The reason I am telling you this now is because I suppose he can't affect you or me anymore, my lovely. You see his granny has visited me after her death and that has changed so much for me. She told me that my real dad visited her. She said he had left the earth as he thought we had gone before him, and that he was waiting for us in a place called the Waiting Zone until it was our time to pass on."

Arianna sits back and says, "You know about the Waiting Zone?"

"Yes, just what my mother told me before she left."

"I have come here from the Waiting Zone."

"Yes, I know that now, because the first time I saw you I knew you were the one that my mother talked about."

"How did your mother know about me?" Arianna is trying to process it all and seems quite shocked.

"Oh, I knew that it may upset you, and I didn't want that to happen."

"It is okay, Siobhan, I just never thought that you had any connection to me other than through Jake."

"Yes, I know that, my love, and to see that your heart is truly pure, that even thinking I had no connection to you, you would come into my home and take care of me because I was in need whereas my own son wouldn't, well I know that you are special indeed."

"Anyone would have done the same," Arianna replies.

"On the contrary, my love, no they wouldn't. They would have tried to run as far away as possible, especially with how he has treated you."

"I believe that there was good inside Jake too."

"That is lovely; I do wish that you had experienced it more often."

Arianna smiles and says, "There is something more, isn't there?"

"Yes, there is but only if you want to know."

"I do, I feel that it is important."

"Yes, it is special to me, and I hope special to you."

"That sounds intriguing."

"Well, you know how I said that I knew as soon as I saw you?"

Arianna nods.

"Arianna, I am your sister."

"What? How? I mean that is lovely but how does that work?"

"It is a lot to process, isn't it?"

"Sure is."

"My dad fell in love with your mum in the Waiting Zone where you come from. He felt guilty that he would not be there to meet my mum in heaven and so he visited her briefly before she ascended to explain why."

"So you are my sister?"

"Yes.

"So that means that I am Jake's…"

"Yes, and I tried so hard to tell him but he thought that I was going crazy so I wrote him a note."

"So that is what was in the note. I found it in his jacket and gave it to him but he ripped it up before I could see it."

"I was afraid that that might have happened."

"He changed after that you know, it is as if something switched inside of him."

"Do you mind if I ask if you and he ever…?"

"Have we ever what? Oh, you mean sexual relations? No, we never did anything as I wasn't ready at first and then the note thing but it all makes sense now."

"Oh well, at least that is something." Siobhan seems relieved.

And if she is relieved, well I am ten times more relieved. This has shifted something within me. I know that I have been and always will be there for Arianna, but to know that Jake has not been gifted with her special treasure, well my heart is aglow.

"Do you know what though, Siobhan?"

"What, Arianna?"

"It has just occurred to me that the reason I have felt such a deep connection to Jake was because there was a deep connection there even though I wasn't consciously aware of it. Knowing this really does help me understand a lot of things."

Siobhan nods. "I am pleased that you have had this realisation, Arianna, and of course had you not met him you may not have met me."

"Yes, everything happens for our greater good, doesn't it?"

"It most certainly does."

They both raise their glasses and toast to Jake.

"Here is to Jake who has now moved on, may you find peace in your new home, son."

"To Jake." Arianna clinks her raised glass against Siobhan's.

They ponder on that for a moment and then something magical happens. Siobhan's beam is released. *Does this mean she is going to pass on?* is my initial thought. But seeing that she is sitting there drinking her iced tea with a peaceful expression on her face, I am more inclined to consider that she is no longer in need of its guidance and that she has broken through the threshold of healing that she needed to reach.

The beam rises from her and shines so brightly. I watch as the warm glow shines serenity onto both Siobhan and Arianna. Arianna can feel it more intensely and looks up directly at it and smiles a knowing smile. The beam then whizzes to me and I collect it, safely returning it to its temporary home.

"Have I ever mentioned my Auntie Claire to you?" Arianna asks.

"No, you haven't," Siobhan replies, looking a little puzzled at the dramatic change in conversation.

"I think it is time for us to pay her a visit, if you are up to it," Arianna suggests.

"It sounds like a lovely idea. Does she live far away?"

"Only a train ride."

"Okay, well why not?"

"Great! I will let her know that we will be visiting her soon. She is an earth angel, and she will be so happy to meet you."

I sense that I know what Arianna is trying to achieve. By seeing the beam she understands that it may soon be time to leave and knowing that Siobhan lives a quite isolated life she doesn't want her to be alone. Also, Claire does not have any immediate family around so she may benefit from having Siobhan in her life.

My spirits are quite high by witnessing what I have here. Although Jake passing on may be a sad moment for Siobhan and Arianna to endure I feel that they have embraced the life affirming meaning from his being connected to them both.

CHAPTER TWENTY-FOUR
The Crystal

It is almost time to return, I can feel it. This mission has been filled with so many happenings that I have found it difficult to keep up at times. I know that Arianna and Siobhan are in need of some time so I have left them together while I pursue an undertaking that is close to my heart on this mission. That is to help Angela move forward towards full enlightenment so she can ascend to her highest potential which she is so well deserves.

The final treasure that I have to distribute is the most magnificent crystal. I take it from its box and hold it in my hand. I immediately feel the energy feed up my arm. It is so powerful and it will do wonderful things for Angela. She has missed out on a beam but I know the crystal will serve her wonderfully.

Crystals have so much to give to us all. The energy they create is miraculous and can assist us with many endeavours throughout our existence. This crystal is especially unique as it has been super charged with the ability to meet the vital needs of the recipient.

I have returned to where she was last located only to find that she is not there. I have not left her for long and I have not felt the urge to be by her side. I soon realise, of course, that is because I was not channelled through the beams like the others. Oh, why did I not realise this? Am I too late?

I am being drawn to the church where I first encountered Angela. There is a funeral happening, and I see a picture of Angela beside a coffin. I am too late. The emotion I am experiencing weighs heavy on my heart as I feel that I have let her down yet again.

I am drawn to listen to the priest speaking about her.

"Although this angel has departed this life through the most difficult of circumstances to comprehend, it is important for us all to remember all of the amazing and wonderful things that she gave to so many of us every day and that a little piece of her will live forever in our hearts. Could we all please lower our heads for Angela, and share a prayer in these few words for this beautiful lady."

He continues, "To our beloved Angela, we know that your heart ached so very much every day for your beloved children but under your wing you have nurtured thousands more during your lifetime that consider you their mum. It all became too much at the end and you chose to leave us before your time, as the note you left in your final moments states. A lifetime of heartache is a hard cross to bear. Your heart told you that it was time and so as you have always lived a life true to your heart, you felt that you must stay true to it. May the love of God guide you towards his arms where you will be reunited with your lost loves. Amen."

Everyone repeats, "Amen."

From this I conclude that Angela took her own life in the end as she left before her time. Maybe I am to bring the crystal to the zone and assist her there, free from all distraction. She will not have long before it is her allocated time to pass, so I will need to return to the Waiting Zone at my earliest convenience.

I return to Arianna. They are now at Claire's house and Siobhan, Arianna, and Claire are all sitting out the front of the house watching the children kick a ball around the garden.

"This is a wonderful life you have, Claire."

"Yes, I certainly am blessed in many ways, Siobhan."

"Does your husband get the opportunity to come home often?"

"Yes, he is home every night, it is chaos when he walks through the door, isn't it, Arianna?"

"Yes, it really is," she replies laughing, "but a good type of chaos."

"That sounds lovely," Siobhan replies.

Claire grins. "Lovely is not the first word that comes to my mind, but you are welcome to stay and join the mayhem if you would like to."

"Oh, I wouldn't like to impose." Siobhan is a bit flustered.

"You would not be imposing at all."

"Well, if you are sure…"

"Well, that is that sorted then, I shall set another place for dinner," Claire says happily.

Everyone smiles.

It is time we were going back to the Waiting Zone so I try to get Arianna's attention but again she is off frequency with me. This is happening quite often now, and it concerns me.

I attempt to channel into Claire's energy and she hears me and says, "Excuse me, ladies, I won't be a moment."

I meet her inside.

"Claire, could you please let Arianna know that our mission is complete and it is time for us to return?"

"I will certainly do that, Gill," she says and as she turns to walk out she turns as quickly back again.

"Gill, do you see anything different about Arianna?"

"Yes, many things, Claire, but I suppose that is why she came here in the first place."

"That is right but I feel that she has become more humanised than spiritualised during her stay here."

"Yes, I do see that, Claire, but was she not highly spiritual before she came and it was humanity that she wished to experience?"

"That may be right, Gill, but I can't help but have some concerns that her humanisation has made her cross the line just as I did."

"Oh, I had never thought of that being a possibility but of course it is, as you have done it, Claire."

"I may be wrong but I just needed to make you aware of the possibility before you proceed with the process of returning."

"I can't possibly go back without her, Claire. I am already leaving loved ones behind that I never knew existed until this mission. I can't lose her now as well."

"I am sorry to hear that, Gill. You seem to have experienced an unprecedented journey yourself this mission."

"You wouldn't believe it if I told you. But do you know what?"

"What?"

"I have learned so much along the way."

"In my experience the opportunity to become more enlightened heightened when I was in the Zone."

"Forgive me, I do keep forgetting that you were there."

"Yes, I certainly was. Now let's try to get this beauty back home, shall we?"

"That would be great."

We both make our way outside to where Arianna and Siobhan are in full flight conversation.

"Arianna, can I speak with you a moment?" Claire asks.

"Sure," Arianna replies.

I am waiting for them as they come inside. I have heightened my energy in the hope she will connect instantly.

"Is that you, Gill?"

"Yes it is, you can sense me so that is great."

But to my utter disappointment she doesn't hear me. How am I to get her back home if she doesn't hear me?

"Claire, she can't hear me, will you tell her what I am saying please?"

"Yes, of course, Gill," Claire replies.

"You can hear him? Why can't I?" Arianna seems confused.

"I will tell you what he is saying."

"Okay."

"Hi, Arianna, this is Gill. I have now collected all of the beams and it is time for me to return to the Waiting Zone. It is also your time to return, are you ready?"

"Yes, I am ready, Gill. What do I need to do?"

"We need to get to the hill where we first arrived. Do you remember it?"

"Yes, but that will take a while. Have we got time?"

"I know so. Claire has said that she will drop you off."

"Oh, okay."

"Arianna, the vortex is closing for us, we need to go back now."

"How do I change back from physicality?"

"That I am not one hundred percent sure of right now but if we get there on time Harry will be able to help us. I am going to go on ahead and try to prepare for your arrival. Time really is of the essence."

"Gill, before you go."

"Yes?" I feel that she has something heartfelt to share but is holding back.

"Nothing, it is okay, I will see you there."

My heart sinks as I had hoped for something but got nothing. Maybe she will always think of me as a friend and I have to accept that.

***

I reach the hill where the vortex is located. I was right, it is waning, our time is almost up. I try to make a direct connection with Harry as he will guide me towards helping Arianna. To my surprise there is a new person manning the post.

"Hello, can I help you?" he asks abruptly.

"Yes, thank you. I am Gilbert the Memory Taker, and I am returning from my mission."

"I have been waiting on you; you are cutting it fine, aren't you?"

"Yes, I know and I apologise for that."

"Well come on then, let's get a move on," the operator says briskly. I really don't know if I like his attitude at all.

"I can't go until Arianna reaches here as she will be travelling with me."

"Arianna, let me check. No, I don't have any messenger called Arianna on my list."

"She is not a messenger, but she is from the Zone and she travelled with me here so she must travel back with me. She needs us to help her transcend from physicality."

"Well, she is not on the list so how would I know that you aren't just trying to smuggle a human back with you. I am sorry I can't help you."

Arianna comes dashing up the hill.

"Sorry, what is your name?" I ask, trying to get through to home.

"Mick."

"Well Mick, Arianna is the Boss's daughter and she must come back with me as I promised him that I would take care of her."

"Oh really, okay, wait there and I will connect with the Boss for confirmation."

I wait for him to get back to me. Arianna reaches the top of the hill.

"You made it," I say in delight.

She still doesn't hear me.

"Gill, where are you?" she says, out of breath and beginning to panic.

"I am here, Arianna, right beside you." She still cannot hear me. I move closer and touch her shoulder. To my relief she feels it and places her hand on mine.

"There you are," she says relieved. "What do I need to do?"

As she can't hear me I guide her towards the tree where she found the clothes on our arrival. She opens the hatch and in there is a note detailing what she needs to do.

Hello fellow Zoner. If you are reading this you are ready to return to the Zone. Please follow the guidelines below.

1. You must leave the clothes back in position for the next user and put on this temporary cloak.

2. You must go to the porthole and await instructions from the operator who will assist you in making the transition back to an entity.

3. Please note successful transition is only achieved when you are fully reconnected to the frequency of the Zone and on your allocated time slot.

Good luck and we hope to see you on the other side.

I watch as Arianna follows instructions. She makes her way to the vortex that is shrinking by the minute.

"Sorry, sir, I am unable to reach the Boss, so I am unable to assist you. Are you ready to enter the Vortex? You have only one minute of allocated time left."

"You can't do this. She is here and ready, you must help her."

"You now have fifty seconds of allocated time left."

What am I going to do? Arianna can't hear me to plead her case to him. I cannot leave and abandon her here, this is not where she belongs. If I don't go back now I will not be able to. What am I to do? Okay, pep talk time. *Right, Gill, you need to connect to your heart guide, it will give you the answer you seek.* It is clear, I have no other choice. I look to Arianna who is standing there dismayed. I immediately connect to my heart centre, and I feel it instantly open. A glow shines from me.

"I can see you, Gill." Arianna beams also.

Mick decides to inform me at that point, "Fifteen seconds."

She can see me. The Crystal, I need the crystal. It is a long shot but it is our only hope. I open the crystal's holding vessel and it activates the immense beauty that is this magical gift. It lifts into the air and gets to work straight away, it knows what it is meant to do and it works its sheer magic on Arianna. In no time at all she is the same as me again. It has worked, I am so relieved.

She reaches out and hugs me. "Gill, there you are."

I grab her hand and jump right through the vortex hole just before it closes on us. In the distance I hear Mick call, "Lady, you are not cleared for travel."

But we just laugh as we travel along the vortex, not letting go of each other for even a moment.

We arrive at the gateway just as the Boss rushes through the entry door.

"Arianna," he calls as he comes to meet her. "Look at you. The trip has really taken it out of you, hasn't it? I was afraid you were not going to make it."

"Dad, I am so happy to be home." She hugs him tight. She feels safe again. Home is definitely where the heart is and Arianna's heart is here, just as mine is.

"I am so glad to have you home, now we had better go see your mother, she has not been the same since you left."

"Oh, I can't wait to see her," she beams.

"Before we go, I just need a moment, love."

He walks towards me and my heart skips a beat.

"Gilbert, son, great job." He holds out his hand to shake mine. "I will catch up with you later on, and we can run through everything that has occurred during your mission."

"Righto, Boss, thank you," I say without even thinking. Righto. Where in goodness' name did I pick that up from? He must think I am a complete idiot.

He turns to Mick. "I need to see you later Mick, you nearly actioned a huge error there, and we may have to reconsider your position."

Mick lowers his head and his brazenness disappears.

"But for now I get to spend some time with my daughter who has safely returned to us," Boss says, happily hugging Arianna again.

Boss and Arianna leave together. I exhale and make my way to the chill out zone. I need to readjust before I fully re-enter the zone. It is similar to meditation.

I am back, I reassure myself as I exhale and ease back. That was one mission that will stay with me for some time. A niggle tells me that there is something not fully resolved, although I cannot possibly ponder on that thought right now. I need to get back to my apartment to recuperate and freshen up, so that is what I shall do.

CHAPTER TWENTY-FIVE
When Harry Meets...

The relief of finally being back in the sanctuary of the Waiting Zone is shadowed by the feeling that I have let Angela down. I do not know if she made it across and if she is finally in the longed for warm embrace of her family. I understand the reason why she chose to accelerate the process of moving forward and as her note explained, she felt that she could not wait a moment longer. Unfortunately I cannot be sure if her moment of action didn't hinder the process of transition. I do hope that it hasn't.

As I am once again carried away with my thoughts I am taken aback. Are my eyes deceiving me? Of course it makes sense now. There standing before me is Angela. She is here. I feel like I have been given another chance to make things right for her. Boss and Harry are beside her so I quickly assume that she does not have long to stay here in the Waiting Zone as her time to move forward from life was already close. I am, however, drawn to them; the energy created is not what I expect it to be. There seems to be a lot of emotional energy spiralling around them. I get a flashback, it is Harry!

I am at what feels to be a familiar location. The sun is going down and the warm glow of the dusk sunset surrounds me, it is magical. I see a large farm house that stands dominantly at the top of a long sweeping lane. It is hugged by green fields that wrap tightly around its circumference. I am drawn inside so I make my way through the split door that is open only at the top. I take a seat in the kitchen. It is a working kitchen. There is a general untidiness about the room, nothing seems to have been cleared away after what I judge to have been a busy family day. After a few minutes Harry enters the room, I begin to piece things together in my mind but don't want to believe it. I watch as he pours himself a drink from a decanter that is locked away in a sturdy wooden cabinet. He takes a swig and holds his glass up as if to toast to something. I sit there for a time observing, he seems to have enjoyed most of the decanter.

He eventually rises from the table and makes his way to a room that looks to be virtually untouched. Everything is pristine and in its place, quite a contrast to the kitchen area. This must be the 'good room'. He takes a key from under a vase filled with dried flowers and locks the door behind him, then places the key in his trouser pocket. He makes his way over to an armchair, shuffles about and straightens his back and looks like he feels prestigious sitting there as if this is his throne. He reaches down and stretches his hand under the bottom of the chair and pulls out a wooden box. He smiles when he sees it. It is a very elegant box that must harbour something precious inside, something precious to Harry.

He opens it and inside all lined up like attentive soldiers are ten thick cigars. He pulls one out and runs it along under his nose, smelling it as if it is the most precious thing on earth. After a few moments of savouring every aroma he lights it. He puffs and puffs and then lies back and releases a plume of smoke into the air making little 'o' shapes with his mouth which are in turn mimicked in the thick white smoke that is rising into the air.

This little ritual goes on for a while and then it is as if he falls asleep. I can see what is about to happen and so I try to blow in his face to wake him up but to no avail and I remember that this is a flashback and not an actual occurrence. I watch as the cigar drops onto the shaggy thick luxurious carpet below, it is not long before it ignites and moves onto the table and nearby curtains. Suddenly Harry starts to stir and cough and I feel a sense of relief, all is not lost. Harry has horror in his eyes as he realises what is happening.

He tries to put out the flames with his jumper but he is just fanning them and spreading the fire further. He starts to shout and roar some names, desperately trying to get their attention as he runs to the thick wooden door. He tries to open it but remembers that he locked it. He thrusts his hand in his pocket but the key is not there, he checks again and then under the vase. The fire is taking hold all around the room. He looks towards the window, picks up the large vase, throughs it straight through smashing the glass, and he follows. He is outside and he runs right around to where the kitchen door is.

Flames glow from behind it and his advances are soon pushed back by the fierceness of the fire that has taken hold. He desperately looks up to see if there is any response through the top windows. He is shouting and screaming. He sees a ladder and he props it up against the top window, arms himself with a spade and embarks on the perilous process of trying to make contact. I watch as he climbs speedily up the ladder, I watch as smoke fills the view through the glass, I watch as Harry uses every morsel of strength that he has in his body to smash that window. When it *finally smashes flames billow out and he slips down the ladder but as he catches hold, he strengthens his grip and climbs with conviction to the top. He makes his way heroically through the window, nothing is going to stop this man, not even the prospect of death. I wait and wait. There is a painful cry, it is harrowing to hear a man cry like that. I reckon he chose not to come out of that fire.*

I return my thoughts to the present and am left shell shocked. Harry has been like a dad to me since I came here and I never realised or asked about his circumstances. I am also enlightened about why Angela had to make her way here. Boss is watching me; I think he has been watching me for a while. He has that knowing look. It is as if he knows exactly what I have just encountered in my mind. He makes his way over to me.

After looking directly at me for a few moments he enquires, "Is everything okay, Gill?"

"I think that I understand now, Boss."

"Understand what exactly, Gill?"

"I believe that I understand why I see Angela here."

"And why would that be, Gill?"

"Because Harry is here waiting for her."

"I see," Boss says before a slight pause and then he continues.

"Angela is having difficulty with understanding the same reasoning, and I wondered if you would like to assist me in helping her to comprehend it. It is vital for her enlightenment and I believe that she trusts you."

"How can she trust me when I have been the one who let her down so many times?"

"You didn't let her down, Gill, as you were part of the journey of her coming here. Had she not come here Harry would never have the opportunity to forgive himself before it is his time to ascend."

"So, I have been helping all along and didn't know it."

"Yes exactly, Gill. Now will you help me talk to Angela or not?"

"Yes of course, Boss, if I can be of assistance in any way I would love to."

"That's good, I will arrange for us all to meet in my office, if you could begin to manoeuvre yourself in that direction then I would greatly appreciate it."

He begins to walk away. I quickly make my way to his office and take a seat outside. I have been distracted by my thoughts and didn't see Josie when I arrived.

"Hello, Gill, is everything okay?" she asks and hands me a coffee. It is as if she knew I was coming.

"Oh hi, Josie, yes, everything is fine, it has been an eventful few months is all."

"Is it Arianna? I hear that she had a tough experience of the reality of earth; to be honest she doesn't seem the same since she came back, I met with her last night. What did you do to her?"

I really can't deal with this right now and so I choose to avoid answering that question. It doesn't seem to deter Josie though and she moves one step closer and into my personal space.

Okay, this is quite inappropriate I think, and I should say so but I hold back in a bid to be polite and also partly because I can't deal with this unforeseen complication right now.

She looks seductively into my eyes. I am definitely not prepared for this! Then she hits me with something I have never suspected and hope I never gave her reason to think.

"Gill, you are bound to know that we are made for each other. Arianna is not your type, I am perfect for you, we are kindred spirits and she is different. I see the way that you look at me. It is me that you really want."

"I am sorry, Josie, but I don't know where you got this idea." I am desperate to give her a reality check but it doesn't seem to work and she puts her arms around my neck. Wow, it makes me feel really uncomfortable.

"You and me, we were brought together for a reason, Gill, you just need to realise that. I have been preparing myself for you for some time now, I want to be the best I can be for you." She says it as if she believes this deep down in her inner core.

This is a curve ball that I didn't anticipate. It suddenly dawns on me that all those little things that have been happening around here upsetting my relationship with Arianna were not actually coincidences; it has been Josie all along. The note not making its way to Arianna after the board meeting and, of course, she works for the Boss and pretends to be Arianna's friend so all sorts of scenarios are playing out in my mind. I can't really deal with the intensity of it right now but I do have to make sure the Boss doesn't catch a sniff of this or it may hinder any chance I have of my special connection with Arianna continuing.

I try to push Josie's advances away but she throws herself onto me and as I am a gentleman my immediate reaction is to catch her in case she falls. At that moment there is a *ping* as the elevator door opens and Boss, Angela, and Harry disembark. *Of course, they would have to walk in at this moment!*

Josie quickly composes herself and slaps me in the face as if it were my wrongdoing and dashes back behind her desk to attentively await instruction from the Boss.

How do I explain this one? Do I explain this one? More important matters must precede this issue so it is on the back burner for now.

After an uncomfortable moment bearing the brunt of Boss's disapproving glare, I follow the small group and enter his office. We all sit down, Boss in his chair and Harry and Angela in the remaining two sensible seats. That left me with the fluff chair and I know how awkward I must look sitting in it.

The silence is broken by Boss who takes the lead. He looks to Angela with the sincerest gaze.

"Angela, how do you feel?"

"I don't know what to feel or what to think," she says, sounding depleted.

Harry places his hand on hers and she immediately pulls hers away. The pain cuts too deep for her. I have never seen Harry this vulnerable before. It is clear by his composure that he desperately seeks her forgiveness.

"May I request for Gilbert here to share with us what he knows; if I am correct in my prediction he understands both sides of what you both encountered to end up here."

They both look to me as if I have the magical answer that they both desperately want to hear and their expectation weighs heavily on me.

"Right, me, okay." This is a time that I need to connect and make a difference and I come out with three silly words. Disappointment creeps into their eyes.

All of a sudden it happens. I speak. "Harry and Angela, you have both endured the most horrific experiences imaginable. I have considered this, and you both have endured the same despair, but instead of it happening together where you could both support each other through it with an element of love, you have both harboured the pain of loss separately and with the added element of toxic guilt. I have been gifted with the knowledge of both perspectives. I was told of your experiences, Angela, and I have just had a flashback that showed me what happened from Harry's perspective."

Angela finally breaks her silence. "What happened? For so many years so many reasons swirled around in my head and I need to know the truth."

"Would you like me to tell you, or Harry?"

She looks to Harry who gazes back hopefully. She then looks in my direction. "I would like Harry to explain please, young man". She sits rigid and doesn't look his way.

Harry composes himself as if he is about to take centre stage.

"Angela, I am sorry, I was neglectful and paid the ultimate price. I couldn't face life again without the children and to know that I destroyed the most precious things in our life, well I couldn't go on and so I chose to go with them. They went peacefully, the smoke got to them first, and I never even heard a whimper... The fire, it was so hot...I am so sorry." He breaks down crying.

"Do you mind if I explain what I saw, Harry?"

He shakes his head as he continues to release a waterfall of tears.

I reach for Angela's hand. Thankfully she doesn't pull it away from me. "I receive flashbacks from past events, it is a gift I have been given and possibly the reason I am here and why I have been chosen to do the job I do. When I arrived at your home during the flashback I saw Harry tuck in all of your children, read them a story and kiss them all goodnight. When they were all fast asleep he had a drink and then a cigar; unfortunately he fell asleep and the cigar started a fire. He did all he could to save the children, climbed through a window into the flames but to no avail. When he finally reached them there was no hope. I heard his wails of grief and physical pain coming from the house."

Angela turned to Harry and they looked into each other's eyes, united in grief. At last healing can commence. Harry wraps his arms around Angela and Boss indicates for us to leave, which we do.

When we are outside the door we both stop and peer back into the room. They are sitting in each other's embrace and then there it is, a kiss, a kiss that releases the tightness of their hearts allowing them permission to be free again.

"They will both be able to move forward together soon and reconnect with their cherished angels," I say. "They have awaited their parents coming for almost a lifetime.

"Angela had to come here, Gilbert, if she had not it would never have been fixed. True love never dies and it can conquer all," Boss says as we watch magic happen.

"I never cease to be amazed at the process of advancement, Boss. The Waiting Zone certainly does have its place firmly secured in the spectrum of being. I am proud to be part of it."

"That's good, Gilbert, that's good."

We stand and watch for a time and I feel connected on a deep level to him; this is something I have never experienced before. We worked together to secure this outcome. I feel like I am making headway with him. Then I remember the awkward situation I found myself in earlier. Oh bugger, how am I going to get myself out of this one untarnished? The Boss has a knack of finding me in compromising encounters that need explaining.

CHAPTER TWENTY-SIX
Obsession

Boss turns around to face Josie. "Right you two, I need to know what is happening here," he demands.

I don't know what to say. I feel that anything I do say will come out wrong. How do I explain it when I don't understand it myself?

"I am sorry sir, but Gilbert and I are in love," Josie confidently lies straight to his face; it is as if she truly believes it.

My jaw drops and I am dumbfounded. Anger begins to boil in me. Those few words can do so much damage. I love Arianna and if I am ever going to bring Boss around this cannot be happening. What is wrong with this girl? I have never led her on...have I? Now I am beginning to doubt myself. As I attempt to rationalise it Boss is waiting for my reaction. I am looking like a deceitful Wally right now.

"Boss, I have never ever been out with this woman let alone fallen in love with her."

Josie gets quite upset. "Gilbert, why are you saying these things?" Tears flow from her eyes and she is distressed and in need of comforting. Under normal circumstances I would normally oblige but not in this instance. This, of course, makes me look even more heartless. Boss looks at me expecting me to do something.

"Boss, I am not comforting her, goodness knows what she will make up about me next."

"Something has to have happened for Josie to be so convinced of your love for her."

Boss puts his arm on her shoulder and she grabs it desperately. It is not comfortable to watch as she draws him in and wraps her arms around his waist and wails into his chest. He looks at me to assist him. I have never seen Josie this vulnerable before, she is usually so strong.

"See, look at what you have done to this confident young lady."

"Boss, I really have only ever been nice to her."

She looks up to him with innocent eyes welling with tears.

Boss's composure suddenly changes "Oh really Gilbert, because I am beginning to wonder what your motivation is at the moment."

I do not understand what it is he means by this comment but I choose to treat it with respect. "I am sorry, Boss. I have done nothing wrong."

"Gilbert, you are the only one who can answer that. Is it morally okay for you to take advantage of two young ladies at once? It certainly isn't in my book. You know, I was beginning to actually believe you were sincere about your intentions toward Arianna. Even with everything that Josie has told …"

He stops mid-sentence as if it has slotted something into place.

He straightens Josie up and faces her to him. "Josie, why have you been saying all of those things about Gilbert if you are in love with him?"

"Because he told me to so that you wouldn't get suspicious, I didn't want to lie, sir, honestly, but he made me."

Gee, she is very convincing. I believe she has convinced herself. I do not know how to get my way out of this one.

"To be honest, I really don't have time for this right now, I have a meeting. I will tell you this though, Arianna holds you both dear to her heart and with everything that she has been through lately she doesn't need you two deceiving her. I suggest that you tell her exactly what is going on and if you don't, I will."

Boss walks towards the elevator and the doors open instantly, he steps in and they close.

Josie instantly forces herself onto me again. "Now we can be together, there will be nothing stopping us."

I push her gently away. "Josie, I really don't know what is going on inside your mind but there is no way in the world that we are going to be together. I love Arianna, not you."

"You are only saying that because you are nervous, I know that you want me, I see it in your eyes."

There is no way of getting through to this woman. I try to walk away but she grabs me.

"Josie, let go, I need to go see Arianna."

"I will come with you."

"No, I need to see her myself."

She finally lets go "That's okay, you can be the one to tell her if you want to, Gilbert."

I choose not to reply, she can think anything she wants to. I just need to get out of this situation. I leave and make my way to Arianna. Her glow is beginning to return and my love for her remains strong, she needs me to help her. She was always so pure, full of goodness and belief that everyone has beauty in them. These beautiful thoughts have been given a brutal reality check and she is bruised. Hopefully she will find her balance soon, each day is a step forward. Seeing the good in people is fine and well but when there is none there to find, the challenge to find it is a fruitless mission. It is unfortunate that Arianna's purity of heart had to be tarnished by such malevolence.

She spends a lot of time in her quarters; I suppose it is her safe haven at the moment. I feel her energy as I approach and it fills me with a joyful glow in my heart. Arianna means so much to me, she always will. Maybe she will never be in love with me but that is okay, I know that I should be there for her without expectation. I will be truthful with her and my honesty will be rewarded, I am sure of it.

As I approach I hear muffled voices, she has someone with her. I decide to venture in anyway. I knock on the door and everything goes quiet. I knock again and finally the door opens. It is Arianna, she looks amazing as she again radiates her loveliness.

"Hello, Gilbert, come in."

My heart sinks, she never calls me Gilbert and it is as if she is disconnected from me. As I enter her living area I soon see why. Josie is there. *How does she always do that? What has she been telling Arianna?*

"Have a seat, Gill." Arianna gestures to a short stool-like creation. It is light blue and situated at the other end of the coffee table that separates us all.

I am entranced as Arianna looks at me with those dreamy whirlpool eyes.

"Gill, Josie has told me everything and although I am a bit disappointed that you haven't confided in me, being your best friend and all, I do realise why as I have not been myself lately. I give you both my blessing and I hope that you will be very happy together."

I feel like I am going to explode. "What has she been telling you?"

"Gill hon, there is no need for this, I know that you wanted to tell her yourself, but I just couldn't wait to share our news."

"What news?"

"That we are having a baby, of course."

"What!" I drop to my seat. "That is not possible!"

Josie instantly puts her head in her hands and cries. *I don't feel anything for her, why is she doing this to me?* Arianna puts her arms around Josie and comforts her.

"Gill, what is wrong with you? I would never have expected you to treat anyone like this."

I am so confused. I stand up and walk out of the room. I need to be alone to get my head in order.

I walk for a while and then take a seat beside the lake. Water is always so calming and the serenity that surrounds me has rationalised my racing mind. All of a sudden I remember something that Boss told me a while ago. *'Sometimes even at the strangest of moments things are realigning themselves to create our highest potential and that can only ever be a good thing'.* I am truly hoping that this is one of those moments. I am too confused to take action or respond so I choose to let it run its course and see what manifests.

I sit on for another small while and then I make my way back inside to the lounge.

I enter the large white room; it is surprisingly cosy. There are seats scattered in different positions around the room. I choose a large couch beside a huge window that looks out into the abyss. *Why?* fills my thoughts. *Why is this happening now? Now when I am connecting deeply with Arianna.* I know that everything happens for a reason, that reason always being our greatest good. Maybe through my fears of rejection I have manifested this through the universal law of attraction. It is the power that governs every realm.

What I do know is that the why of it all is not apparent yet. If I keep searching it may get further and further away as I am not focused on the journey of progression towards it which often leads to a detour. I am seeking something that has yet to make itself visible to me. Right, that's it, I must find balance and happiness within and then I will achieve balance and happiness in reality. I need to catch a hold of myself and regain my power!

"Gill, are you listening to me?"

I turn and there is Arianna perched at the side of the couch. *Wow, manifestation sure does work fast.*

"Hmm? Yes, sorry, I was somewhere else."

"Yes, I have gathered that," she says smirking cheekily. Then she shifts into a different mental mode. "Gill, Josie has gone missing; I am worried about her given the vulnerable state she is in. Will you help me find her?"

"Yes, of course I will, did something happen?"

"I think that maybe I said something wrong because she just ran out of my quarters, and I haven't been able to find her."

"Where could she be?"

"I don't know but we need to get moving, sitting here isn't going to find her. She must really love you, Gill."

I choose to say nothing because the truth will make me seem callous right now.

CHAPTER TWENTY-SEVEN
En Masse

We search and search and come up with nothing. She is nowhere to be found. Arianna and I take a seat by the lake.

"Well Gill, I do not know where she is or where else to look."

"Yep, I am all out of ideas too, and breath, if I am to be honest. Do you never tire out?"

"Ah Gill, you are just out of shape. Living too much of the good lifestyle and not taking care of yourself," she says, laughing.

"Oh, it is so good to see you laugh again. I was so worried that I wouldn't see that again, Arianna."

"Yes, I was worried about me too, Gill, but I am coming through it and I know that I am a better person because of my experiences. I think that they have made me grow up."

"Sounds like you have grown."

"Yes, I sure have. You know, it's a pity."

"What's a pity?"

"Well, I don't know if I should say."

"Of course say."

"It's a pity that I didn't realise sooner that I liked you as more than just my best friend."

I am dumbfounded, I have waited such a long time for this glimmer of hope, this moment and it has definitely not presented itself through the circumstances I imagined or desired. *Should I make a move? Declare my undying love?* I am nervous about what will utter from my lips the next time I open my mouth. This could change everything for me.

"Arianna…"

There is a sudden darkness and I am no longer present in the moment. Wow, that was unexpected. I come round to find myself lying sprawled at the edge of the lake; my head is being splashed by a light wave rippling towards me. I look out and see Arianna in a small boat. Someone is with her; I can't make out who it is. I am not sure if that is because I am dazed and harbouring an almighty sore head or if it is because they are so far away. Something tells me all is not right. How can I reach her? They have almost reached the other side of the lake. That territory is unfamiliar to me, I do not know of anyone who has been there. We have always been warned never to cross the lake.

I see Boss's boat moored across the way and so I make my way to it. As I pull away from the zone I notice that I have attracted interest from those inside, including Boss who is not looking happy. I quickly speed off in pursuit of the boat that is now stranded at a dock. It feels like it takes forever to get from one end of the lake to the other.

A muffled sound is coming from inside the boat so I open the door to the cabin. There sits Josie all huddled up in a ball, crying her eyes out. She looks up and when she sees me peering down at her she jumps up and wraps her arms around me.

"I knew that you would come for me, Gilbert, I knew that you didn't mean those things that you said."

I unwrap her arms from around my neck.

"Josie, I didn't mean to hurt your feelings, but I don't know where you got the idea that I love you. You know that my heart belongs to Arianna, it always has. It would be unfair of me to lead you on. I am sure that there is a perfect person for you too but that person is not me. I am sorry."

"But Gill, you are the only one who ever paid me any attention, you are the one who I have connected with."

"I could never give you what you want or what you deserve, Josie."

Her head drops and she takes a step back. "I thought that you were the one, Gill, I really did."

My anger soon turns into sorrow and pity. I recognise the deep impact I have had on her. I put myself in her shoes and I have a sudden realisation that I have been walking in them too. Arianna doesn't love me in the way that I love her, I have been holding out hope when there is no hope. This realisation hits hard but with it comes a sense of relief that I am aware of it now. I look to Josie who has withdrawn into herself. I hold out my hand and she grabs it tight.

"I can never be the one, Josie, because I don't reciprocate the feelings that you so generously have for me, it would never be fair, we would be living a lie. You are closing yourself up to other wonderful sources of potential love that might be perfect for you."

I believe that the same relief and acceptance that I experienced has just washed over her. These moments of realisation can shift us. Experiencing this together has made me more connected to Josie. It is amazing how in such a short time I could go from absolutely despising her to connecting with her on such a deep level. The universe does work in mysterious ways at times.

"I know that you are right, Gill, I am sorry about being so obsessive about it, I so desperately wanted it to be real."

I hug her. "It's okay, Josie, let's move forward. We can still be good friends. Deal?"

"Deal," she says, smiling.

We shake hands on it. Just then we seem to arrive at the other side of the lake.

"Gill, why are we here?" Josie asks, scanning the area.

I look around also. It feels strange. The safe peacefulness of the Waiting Zone is not present here. I don't hear a sound but there is an eerie feeling.

We both disembark the boat.

"Arianna is over here, Josie, I saw her in a boat with someone. I think she may be in trouble."

"I don't like it, Gill, something doesn't feel right."

"It's okay, I am here and you have nothing to be afraid of." She makes me feel strong and masterful and it is a feeling I have not experienced often. I like it.

I shake it off. Something else is more important. Where is Arianna? There is only one path to follow, the one that leads right into the woods. The trees are blanketed with a snow-like substance.

I have an overwhelming feeling that I am being watched, it has filled me with paranoia. I look around to check if Josie is following and I see her looking all around her too, so she must be consumed by the same feeling.

"I don't really like it here, Gill."

"Me neither, but we cannot turn back without finding Arianna."

"You're right, but I have a strange feeling deep down."

"Yes, me too, but I know that we must go forward."

Unsettled yet united, I take hold of her hand, smile to let her know everything will be all right and then we move forward. Shadows catch my peripheral vision. They haunt my thoughts and I try to stop them from invading my focus. As we make our way along the path I can hear a muffled sound in the distance. We get closer and I see a slight twitch in the trees. I hope that we are not too far away.

The next thing I know I am wrestled to the ground. Josie squeals and then she is suddenly quiet. That is the last thing I remember.

CHAPTER TWENTY-EIGHT
Spellbound

I have been remotely aware during my unconscious state. I know that I have been dragged and tied to a log or pole. I can't open my eyes no matter how hard I try, there seems to be something covering them. My sense of conscious hearing is returning and I can hear a distant mumble that quickly becomes recognisable sounds.

"What are you going to do with them?" This voice startles me as I recognise it.

"Send them to complete darkness, the less Enlighteners we have in this realm the better."

"What harm will they do if we release them and banish them from our domain?"

"Young man, you don't understand…we can capture their essence and it will feed many of us for a long time."

"But why would you want to be fed with goodness?"

"To us it is not good, it is ecstasy and it rushes through our system like infused adrenalin."

"So we drain all of the goodness from their souls for our own quick fix and then dispose of their empty vessels to the pits of darkness."

"Yes, now you are thinking along the same lines. You learn fast, my friend. You may be new here but you have produced goods that we have waited many an era to obtain. You have brought us the special one." He has the darkest snigger that makes me shiver to my core.

How are we going to get back to the Waiting Zone? My thoughts are rushing at an accelerated. I feel that we don't have much time. Someone comes over to me and I try to not let them know that I am conscious. The person checks my blindfold and leaves a gap that I can see through. They also check the bonds around my wrists and yet they feel looser somehow. Is someone trying to help me? I can see Arianna, she is acting very strange indeed; it is as if she is under an enchanted spell. She is sitting on a large golden throne with a seductive look in her eyes.

Two men stand on front of her. One wears grand clothes fit for a king and I get the impression that he is a leader of this realm. His clothes and stance demand attention, and I feel that his ego needs to be constantly fed. The other appears familiar to me but I cannot see his face.

The leader holds out his arms straight and begins to chant.

"Hum hum hum hum…hum hum hum hum."

Arianna begins to gravitate before him. Shadows circle around her levitating body, she moans as they pierce her soul. I know that I have to save her. I begin to wriggle my hands and feet gently out of the ropes that bind them. In no time I am free but I hold back on any sudden movements and I keep scanning the surrounding area. The leader lowers his hands and Arianna is seated back in the chair; she looks to be exhausted and delirious. The leader then leaves the area and the shadows follow him.

I try to make out the guy who is standing beside Arianna, and I am horrified to realise that it is Jake. How did he come here? The Waiting Zone is only for enlightened spirits who have journeyed too early. He has done it again; he has hijacked Arianna's purity and put her under his spell. Will she ever be free of this man? My mind begins to rush off on an uncontrollable tangent and so I attempt to rationalise and regain some control of my thoughts. I will not let him take control of her again, she has not fully healed from the repercussions of their last encounter. Goodness knows what will happen when she realises she is not even safe from him in her own domain. To add to the whole scenario, what have they done to Josie? I look around and I cannot see her anywhere.

A woman comes into view. I recognise her...oh my goodness, it is Josie. She has obviously been spellbound also. I am taken aback as she is wearing a seductive black dress, her hair is all tousled, and this is not her usual attire. She walks over towards Arianna. Surely she is going to help her best friend. Jake catches a glimpse of her, a spark of energy emits from him, the same spark emits from Josie. Is this an instant attraction?

They kiss passionately and fervent energy flows all around them, it is attractive even though it stems from darkness. I have to admit that a spark of jealousy is conjured within me. Not only has he had a negative impact on Arianna, he is now tarnishing Josie. Is this man my nemesis?

I now have to save two women from his grasp. Fire burns within me. Fire I imagine superheroes having in their bellies. It fills me to the brim with the confidence I need to defeat the darkness I have feared thus far in Jake. He is the total opposite of me and yet we have crossed paths so often recently, maybe I have a lot to learn about myself from him. I know one thing for certain, I am facing fears that I never believed I would have to encounter while in my earlier mindset. It exhilarates and liberates me to know that I have this power to grow.

I become a shadow of myself and creep into a closer position. To my relief I have not been caught. I find myself behind Arianna, the throne is like a solid barrier between us and yet it serves its purpose by hiding me from any danger.

I overhear Jake and Josie talking.

"Where have you been all of my life?" smooches Jake.

"Right here waiting for you," replies Josie seductively.

She is mesmerised by Jake and he is mesmerised by her. How am I going to rescue her from his grasp?

Arianna begins to stir; I peer around the edge of the throne. I make eye contact with her and smile. I signal for her to remain quiet.

"You are amazing, you know." Jake seems to be enthralled by Josie.

"Yes, I know," replies Josie confidently.

I have never seen Josie act like this before, and she seems to do it effortlessly. They kiss again, and I see this as an opportunity to save Arianna.

"Take my hand," I whisper and pull her towards me. She must still be slightly spellbound as she looks lovingly into my eyes.

"My hero," she says.

Oh, to be her hero, I think as love glows from my heart. To our peril, because the glow of love has attracted the shadows and the leader stands before us.

"So what do we have here?" he demands.

I am still in super confident mode and so I reply, "Us, but not for long."

I grab Arianna's hand and run as fast as I can, calling behind us, "Come on, Josie, quick, run."

She shouts, "I belong here, goodbye."

"It's okay, Gill, just keep running," Arianna assures me.

She stumbles and I quickly pick her up and run as fast as my legs can carry me down the path to the boat. We get on board and I can't get it started. The shadows are gaining, they are coming closer fast.

Arianna shouts, "Hurry, Gill, they are nearly here, hurry."

"I am going as fast as I can."

"Let go of the anxiety and focus," she guides me.

I take a deep breath and clear my mind. I release the anxious fearful energy that is consuming me and after a clear focused moment I try again. The motor starts straight away. Relief consumes me.

"Well done, Gill, now go," Arianna says as she lies down on the bench, her energy levels deflated due to the draining encounters she has endured.

We speed off just as the dark shadows leap for the boat. We bash them off and as they fall into the water, they disintegrate. They cannot survive the purity of the water. So that is why they have never reached us at the Waiting Zone.

I get us on our way and Arianna joins me at the steering wheel. We look back at the figures standing at the edge of the water. We then look ahead and can vaguely see the Waiting Zone. We will reach it. I exhale deeply with a healing breath.

"You were great, Gill," says Arianna.

"But what about Josie? I didn't save her."

"You don't need to worry about Josie, Gill, she will be fine."

"How can you be so sure of that?"

"The leader is Josie's father, she came from the dark domain to spy on us. She was not intercepted because she was born of a bright-sider. The bright-sider fell in love with the leader of the dark side as she used to visit him at the edge of the domains. She was found out and was made to choose where she wanted to reside. If she stayed in the Waiting Zone she could no longer have contact with him. She chose love and went to the dark side. Of course, their love stemmed from goodness and could never be what it once was, so the leader soon fell out of love with her and he banished her from his domain. By this time the bright-sider had a child—Josie—and the leader would not let her take her with her. This broke Josie's mum's heart because she loved her so much and wanted the best for her. So one night she bravely sneaked back and took Josie and put her in a little makeshift boat and set her afloat on the lake. No one knows what happened to her mum, but Josie arrived safe and sound at the Waiting Zone where we grew up together. My dad told me about how she arrived here. I have always seen the good in her but since returning from physicality I recognised that there is also darkness residing inside her heart."

"I would never have known." I am aghast.

"Well, maybe it was her destiny to go back there."

"I think you may be right, she may bring some light to where there is only darkness. It has just occurred to me that she must have loosened the bonds so that I could escape."

"See, there is still goodness within her."

"What about Jake?"

"Jake has been brought here because he left before his time. He is a tarnished soul and so he was brought to the other side of the water—the place for dark souls who have left their physicality early."

"Maybe you were the link between Jake and Josie and they were destined for each other. They certainly did seem besotted, love at first sight kind of magic, in this instance black magic."

"Ha ha, yes, I think you may be right, Gill, it does make sense."

I see that we are approaching landfall. Arianna comes close to me and gazes in my eyes. She is enchantingly dancing with my spirit as a ripple of rhythmic sensation makes its way through my veins.

She lovingly caresses my hair and gently strokes her hand along the side of my face.

"Gill, there is something I need to tell you, I hope that you don't mind."

"No, of course I don't mind." I am enthralled in suspense.

"I think that I am in love with you."

I have waited so long to hear these words and I have imagined them being uttered in so many scenarios but I could never have imagined anything as perfect as this moment. Arianna patiently awaits my response.

"Oh, I love you too," I say quickly so as not to lose the moment.

"Really, Gill? After everything I have done to you, you still love me?"

"Yes, Arianna, I will always love you with all of my heart. I know that we are destined for each other and I was prepared for it only to be friendship but if you are implying that you would like something deeper…"

"Yes, I am implying that I would like something deeper," she says with a magical glowing smile that sets my heart alight.

"I am the happiest man ever," I say in disbelief.

She kisses me; it is the most moving experience of my entire life. I feel like I have been lifted above where I once stood. I will no longer be at the same level, this has enhanced me. I can only hope that it is having the same effect on her. I am happy to say that I think it is as her body language indicates she is enjoying this as much as I am. I feel as if everything has come together and I need never struggle again.

We cease and I savour the memory that I will carry with me forever. A moment that can never be replaced, hopefully only replicated.

"Wait a minute…are you still spellbound?"

"Not unless you want me to be," she says with a cheeky smile. She pulls me down to where she has quickly positioned herself on the deck and we drift off to momentary bliss again. I can see me getting quite used to this… maybe even for eternity.

Epilogue

It took us a while to cross the lake that day much to the dismay of the Boss who was standing awaiting our return unaware of the turn of events that had occurred.

He had initiated a task force to retrieve us from the dark side of the lake but was relieved to discover that he did not have to send them in as that would have completely upset the unspoken agreement between the two sides and caused mayhem.

Of course, when we arrived ashore we were quite flushed and totally enthralled in the loving connection we had committed ourselves to on our return. Fortunately, when Boss learned the full extent of what had happened with Josie he embraced our connection and gave us his blessing.

I am not off the hook yet though as he keeps a close eye on me and ensures that my intentions are pure at all times. I don't mind because it keeps me on my toes, and Arianna deserves the best of me always.

As for Angela and Harry, they both moved on not long ago. Their passing occurred simultaneously which is quite against the odds, but I do feel that the Boss had some influence over that occurrence and they were finally reunited with their little angels.

As for me and Arianna, we spend every possible moment together. Our relationship has been strengthened by what we experienced on that mission. I don't ever see us drifting apart.

I am still *The Memory Taker*, I love my job, and I grow with it each time. I have been on subsequent missions, none of which Arianna had any desire to join me on, which was quite a relief. She now has an important role within the zone that keeps her busy and fulfilled so she is also happy.

Every time I return on a mission I ensure that I spend time with Anna. She has begun to feel my presence and my gift to her is inner wisdom. She is growing beautifully and I enjoy it when the opportunity comes around for me to be a part of her life, even if it is only for pockets of time here and there.

When you reach that place in time that feels as if everything you could ever want is in place, you want to hold on to it forever. Of course that is not always possible. But working hard to keep the foundations of your creation together and building upon that with a plan of how things could come together, then you can't really go wrong. The trick is to work on any issues that arise with a positive problem-solving attitude and the rewards will soon follow.

Your heart is your compass, use it and you will never get lost.

ABOUT THE AUTHOR

Karen McDermott currently resides in Perth, Western Australia, with her husband and six children, after emigrating from Ireland in September 2008. Her children are the most important things in her life. Writing and publishing come a close second.

She came from Ireland—a place of magical beauty—and she now resides in Australia—a place of inspiration and opportunity; these two special, but very different places, together, give her the passion and determination necessary to incorporate positive writing in her life daily.

Karen successfully completed a diploma in humanities, which instilled in her a desire for learning new things; this, combined with the experience of a miscarriage, led her to write this book in order to give hope and a degree of understanding to women who suffer such pain.

Karen has had many successes in life and writing is one she is proud of.